Jared

The Firefighters of Station #8

S. R. Wyatt

LOVE ENDURES

Jared: The Firefighters of Station #8

Published by Love Endures

Paperback ISBN: 978-1-963776-07-2

Cover Design by Erin Dameron-Hill

Published in the United States of America

THE FIREFIGHTERS OF STATION #8

Mike (Book 1)
Shep (Book 2)
Jared (Book 3)

DEDICATION

To all firefighters around the world, true American heroes who put their lives in jeopardy every day. Thank you for your bravery and dedication. Although it may seem you are taken for granted, you are greatly appreciated, valued, respected and this world is blessed to have devoted souls like you. I have first-hand knowledge in a life altering experience. My own home was burned to the ground. While many made comments on the destruction, my thoughts were solely on the safety of the men who came to my aid.

I would also like to thank and give recognition to my inspiration guys who allowed me to interview them for my books. Who willingly answered my questions with enthusiasm and even allowed me into their station, access to their bay, and climb in their big fire trucks. So many wonderful, fun men who were so nice to a stranger. I did not model any character after a certain individual. Since the guys were being respectful, I had to use my imagination for the personal aspects. I combined what I learned with my own ideas and created each firefighter with his own charisma.

ACKNOWLEDGEMENTS

I'd like to thank my granddaughters husband who is a firefighter in Augusta County, Virginia. He shakes his head at the story lines on TV that do not truly show the real encounters firefighters deal with every day. When I think up an idea, he tells me if it is realistic. He's been very patient with me.
For everyone who loves a little romance and a Hot Firefighter.
Keep the Spirit!
Samanthya

Contents

Chapter 1

"911 Dispatch. What is the address of your emergency?"

"Is this the fire man?" a little girls voice came across the line.

"What's your name?"

"Tiffany."

"Hi, Tiffany, my name is Terri. How old are you?"

"Five."

"Is your mom or dad there?"

"Nooo."

"Are you alone?"

"No. My brother is here. He kicked me in the balls."

"Are you hurt?"

The little girl started crying. "It's Charlie. He's stuck in the tree," she said between sobs. "Can you get him down?"

"Tiffany, honey. Don't cry. I'm sure your brother is all right, and we'll get to him as quickly as possible."

"Not him. It's Charlie. He's up in the tree. Aiden chased him up there. When I shoved him, he kicked me in the balls."

"Who's Charlie?"

"My cat. He's scared."

"Sweetheart, he'll be okay."

"You gotta come. I need a fire man to get him down."

"The firefighters are busy putting out fires. When Charlie is ready, he'll come down."

The pitiful voice cried harder. "He's scared. I am too."

"Are you hurt? Did Aiden hurt you?"

"No, but I had to run away. My other brother tried to take the phone from me."

"Tiffany. Don't run away. Where are you now?"

"Hiding in the bush."

"Are you at your house?"

"Yes."

"Where is your mom?"

"She's gone."

"Where is your dad?"

"He's in the miliferry."

"Oh. How old is your brother?"

"Aiden is four. I'm older, and he should listen to me."

"How old is your other brother?"

"Tanner is seven. He thinks he's the boss."

"Tiffany, is there any other adult at the house? Maybe a neighbor or family member?"

"No."

***

There were few days when Jared Collins had a chance to unwind. Today, the hours stretched long into a hot summer afternoon, and the guys were sitting in the fire station bay shooting the breeze. Now and again, dispatch received some entertaining calls, and it looked like it just happened to be one of those times.

"Are you kidding, Cap? Dispatch doesn't send us calls to get a cat out of a tree," Jared responded to Shep's news.

Other than the arsonist who had the crew constantly looking over their shoulders, things around the firehouse had been quiet for the past couple of days—and the captain did not make up stories. As for Jared, he liked taking a breather after the hellish inferno from the other night. Station Eight had received a call at two in the morning, reporting a hotel on fire. The first thing he'd thought of was how big the building was and how many people were asleep inside. Thank God, it had been in the process of renovations and the place was empty. Sounded to him a lot like arson. Different from the firebug currently on everyone's mind. Forensics had come up with an explanation on the training site explosion, but they had no idea who the culprit might be.

Hooley, the fire investigator, had come by last week to give them an update, but with no news as to the identity of the person who'd stolen the equipment from Station Nine. No one recognized the imposter dressed in the firefighter's uniform from the film recorded at the training site.

Jared recalled the incident of that dreadful day and relived the horrific explosion as it blew up on the screen when Hooley had showed them the film. Every gruesome detail.

We have no idea of motive. He could have chosen a firehouse randomly, or he might have beef with a certain individual. We don't know if he is targeting fire departments in general or firefighters, so you need to be on guard.

A cat in a tree was just what Jared needed to get his mind off some nut-job out there targeting firefighters.

"Don't have nothing else to do," Laredo said in a lazy tone while tossing a finger-exercise ball in the air. "Why don't we check it out?"

"If you're bored, go wash the quint," Shep barked.

Jared couldn't imagine why Laredo wasn't already doing that. He kept the thing shined the way a man took care of his muscle car. The paint glimmered. And anyone could see their reflection in the bumper.

"That's not the best part of the call," Shep continued. "The child on the phone was a girl. She said her brother kicked her in the balls."

Jared jerked his head up to see if the captain was yanking them around. Laredo snatched the rubber ball out of the air and jerked upright, dropping his feet to the cement floor.

"Did I hear you right? You did say a girl made the call."

"Yep," Shep answered with a nod. "No lie. She said her brother kicked her in the balls."

Laredo hooted in laughter. "I've got to meet this kid's mother."

"What about the father?" Jared questioned, trying to curb his own amusement.

"What man would tell his daughter she has *cojones*? Got to be the mom."

"Or she got it from her brother," Jared replied with a grin. "Boys will tell girls anything."

"You're about to get your wish," Shep interrupted. "I'm sending you two out to check on this. Dispatch never got a parent on the phone. The kid said she was five years old."

Jared and Laredo sobered immediately, that news grabbing their attention. Children calling 911 could mean a number of things, and if there was no parent, no adult able to come to the phone, that could mean someone was hurt. He now understood why Shep wanted them to check it out. He glanced over to Laredo.

"I'm one step ahead of you, dude." Laredo jumped to his feet. "I'll grab my gear."

"We'll take the engine, just in case we do find an injured person."

"Go ahead and take the truck," the Captain ordered. "Kids love fire trucks. It's not being used at the moment. You'll have a kit if you need medical supplies."

Each vehicle was equipped with a certain amount of medical emergency equipment and bandages. The captain made sure of that years ago when a shaky bridge collapsed after only one rig managed to cross. The quint got separated from the rescue squad and men had been injured on both sides.

"If there is no emergency, you can get the kid's cat out of the tree," Shep added. "If this girl thinks she has balls, she's probably a tomboy. She'll get just as much a kick out of the ladder truck as any boy."

"You got it, Cap." With a big grin, Laredo headed to the truck.

"Wait until the rest of the guys hear about this?" Jared told Laredo. They were headed to a non-working call. No threat of a fire, but a little girl whose cat was stuck up a tree. First time he'd been on this type of rescue. He just hoped they didn't find a real emergency.

When in doubt—send everyone out.

Someone had to respond.

***

Who knew when Jessica agreed to watch her sister's kids that she would regret her decision within twenty-four hours? After dealing with her niece and nephews, she may never have children of her own. She shoved at a strand of hair that had escaped from her ponytail, and exhaled a deep breath.

The kids weren't that bad, but they did keep her in the role of referee. And Tiffany was just as bad as her brothers.

"Rough morning?"

Jessica glanced over to find the neighbor leaning casually against the back gate. Connie had two kids of her own, but they were twelve and fourteen. She looked great. How did she do it?

"Those three will make me old before my time," Jessica said as she strolled over to the backyard fence.

"The boys will be home from basketball practice soon. I'll tell them to take the kids off your hands and give you a break."

"My sister has only been gone two days. I'm ready to call her and beg her to come home."

Connie laughed, the tinkling sound echoing through the back yard.

"Honestly," Jessica grabbed a loose strand of hair and tucked it behind her ear. "I don't know how either one of you do it. Her kids are a handful. I know she needed a break. And look at you. You look so calm, and you're smiling. You survived your kids' hellion years."

"Siblings always bicker. Just don't let them run over you. And do not call your sister. If you need help, call me."

"Thanks." Jessica made a mental note to keep Connie's number handy.

"Come on in. I've got plenty of coffee. You look like you could use the extra caffeine." Connie opened the gate and motioned for Jessica to follow her. Coffee sounded perfect. She needed the caffeine to keep up with the rugrats.

As soon as Jessica stepped into Connie's kitchen, she smelled the coffee bean aroma. She plopped down onto a chair at the kitchen counter and propped her head on her hand, her mouth already salivating.

"Do you take vitamins, or do you have an energy drink stashed in the cupboard?"

"I make sure I get thirty minutes of uninterrupted me time every day. Rick helps."

Connie and her husband seemed like the perfect couple. Rick was handsome, and the boys looked just like him. Jessica had noticed he had a good rapport with his kids. She'd seen him playing basketball in their driveway. Bet that was when Connie got her *thirty minutes* of uninterrupted time.

"Cream or sugar?"

"Just some milk, please."

As Connie opened the refrigerator, Jessica pulled her cup closer. Steam swirled in the air, and again she inhaled the pleasing scent. She could already feel the tension ease from her shoulders.

Connie's laugh had Jessica snapping her eyes open. "If the smell of coffee puts that look on your face, I can't wait until you taste it."

"Coffee is the brew of the gods," Jessica said, shrugging her shoulders. "I love my java." She poured a generous blob of milk, then blew across the top as if that would cool the hot liquid.

Connie sat on the stool beside her. "So. Are you doing okay?"

"Oh, it's not as bad as I make it sound," Jessica said with a wave of her hand. "It's great, actually. I love those kids. They're just a handful. I know why my sister needed to get away."

Connie lifted her cup and blew across the top. "Your sister loves them fiercely. She fretted over the decision to go, but this was her chance to be with Chad."

"I guess you all are pretty much in the same boat." After all, her sister and Connie, both, were married to army men. "At least you're neighbors. You two can support each other."

"Military life isn't for everyone. The wife sacrifices a lot too, but she needs to be there for her man when he does come home.

"I don't know how she does that either. With Chad being in the military."

Connie set down her cup. "What do you mean?"

Jessica stared at her coffee as she thought about everything Ravin had to deal with. "Holding a marriage together and raising three children by herself. Chad's gone so much. I can't even begin to imagine the worry my sister will have to deal with when he goes to Afghanistan."

"That's why it was important for her to go meet him. They need this time together."

"They'll only have a week before he leaves."

Connie stared at Jessica a moment before she spoke. "Did you know Raven talked it over with me? She wanted to go, but felt guilty leaving the children. She was pretty torn up about it."

"That's my sister. She thinks of everyone else before doing what she wants."

"I'm glad you could help her out."

"Are you kidding?" Jessica's eyes widened in surprise, and she spun toward Connie. "I'm happy to help. Raven is a great mom. She certainly has no reason to feel guilty. Good grief. Who knows when she would get another chance. As for me, I'd help out more often if she'd let me know what's going on. Raven is so independent."

"She's a military wife. She's learned to take care of herself."

Jessica rolled that over in her mind. Raven was two years older, and already had three children. Even growing up, Jessica remembered her sister being strong and self-sufficient.

Raven and Chad had met when Raven was twenty-one and they'd been together ever since. Jessica couldn't help but wonder if she would find a love like her sister had with Chad. And like the devotion she saw between Connie and Rick. Seeing them, Jessica knew it was possible.

A wailing sound drifted in from outside.

Connie turned her attention to the window. "Do you hear sirens? They seem awfully close."

Jessica tilted her head and listened. "Yes, they do." The piercing sound and a sharp horn grew louder.

"It sounds like it is coming down our street," Connie said as she rose and headed to the living room. She stepped to the big picture window and drew back a curtain. "I see a red fire truck. Oh my God."

"What?" Jessica asked coming up behind her.

"They're stopping in front of Raven's house."

CHAPTER 2

Jared climbed from the passenger side of the quint, keeping his focus on the three children standing at the curb. Bouncing more like it. One boy with a big grin, and a smaller one with big eyes, hopped around like jack rabbits. A little girl clapped her hands, and Jared wondered if she was the one who had made the call.

Before he stepped on the lawn, the three rushed him at once, all talking at the same time. He heard Laredo laugh from behind him.

"Woah, slow down," Jared said trying to get them to stop.

A shrill whistle echoed in his ear and all eyes flashed to the firefighter beside him.

"How'd you do that?" the oldest boy asked.

"Easy, *chaval*," Laredo answered. "Just put your fingers in your mouth like this and blow." Laredo did as he explained and another whistle shot from his mouth. The kids stood in awe.

"You came!" the little girl cried, then pointed up into a tree. "Charlie is scared."

Charlie, huh. Jared glanced up, and sure enough, he spotted a black and white cat clinging to a branch above them.

"Well, would you look at that," Laredo said. "Charlie looks like he's *contento*. Is anyone else hurt?"

She said her brother kicked her in the balls.

Jared placed his hands on his knees and hunkered down to the little girl. "Are you the one who called the fire department?" She nodded her head. Her big eyes grabbed his gut. "My name is Jared. What's yours?"

"I'm Tiffany. This is my brother, Aiden. And that's—" Her voice turned angry. "—Tanner."

"I told her not to call," the older boy spoke up. "I tried to take the phone, but Tiffany ran off." He glared at the little girl. "Now you're gonna get it."

"You shut up, Tanner."

"You shut up," the youngest of the bunch spouted.

"You too, Aiden."

"You shut up," the little fella said again.

Before the kids could get into a tug of war, Jared figured he better jump in. Just then, a blur from the side of his vision came tearing across the lawn.

Tall, wispy blonde hair, and great cheekbones. Slender with some pretty impressive curves and long, long legs. She wore a strappy tank top and cut-off denim jeans that barely covered her essentials. Her short shorts showed off smooth thighs and a shapely backside.

He forced his gaze back to her face and those velvety brown, almond shaped eyes.

"What are you doing here?" the woman asked, as she panted. Her eyes darted from him to the kids and back again.

Jared grinned like a fool. But, being in uniform, he reined in his playful seduction mode and remembered to be polite.

"We're responding to a 911 call, ma'am. Do you live here?"

She tucked a stray curl behind her ear. "Are you sure you have the right house? I didn't call anyone—"

"I did. Tanner chased Charlie up the tree."

The stunning woman gasped as a look of pure shock covered her beautiful face, just before she turned to the little girl.

"You—"

"I told you. You're gonna get it." Tanner taunted. Jared supposed he was the girl's older brother.

"Gonna get it," the smallest of the group repeated.

"Tanner scared Charlie. Look at him." The little girl started to cry. The bigger boy crossed his arms over his chest and glared at the little girl. Then, the little fella looked up to—what appeared to be—his idol, and imitating the older boy, did the same thing.

Jared wanted to snort. This woman had her hands full. Now if he could just keep his eyes where they belonged. Damn, the woman looked fine.

"Tiffany, stop. Charlie is fine. And you two. Don't move. I'll speak to you inside." The woman looked at Jared, and he nearly swallowed his damn tongue.

"I'm so sorry. I had no idea Tiffany knew how to use the phone. I can't believe she called 911." The woman was clearly nervous. Upset that her children had called in an emergency without her knowing. She twisted her hands, while balancing her weight from one foot to the other. As he studied her, she swiped a few tendrils that hung in her face, showing the curve of her cheekbone. He'd seen plenty of beautiful women. She wasn't exquisite, but there was something that drew him.

"That's all right, *señora*." Laredo's voice jerked Jared back to sanity. By his leering grin, he knew what Jared had been thinking.

Why was he reacting like this? She was married, for God's sake. A line he did not cross. She bit on her bottom lip. A bolt of adrenaline shot to his groin.

"Can you get my cat down?" The little girl looked so pitiful, and her sniffles were piercing his heart. This kid would be dangerous when she grew up. Laredo beat him to the punch.

"Sure thing, Princess. Now you dry up those tears and watch this. You boys watch out now." Laredo swaggered to the side of the truck where the controls were.

Cocky bastard. He was showing off.

The kids started jumping up and down in their excitement. It was obvious this woman did not have control of her kids.

Jared gestured for the kids to move back, and for the first time, spotted another woman he hadn't noticed before. Almost as tall as the blonde, the sun brought out red highlights in her brown hair. Unlike the blonde, the second woman was completely at ease with the situation. He figured she must be a neighbor. The blonde gave him a nervous smile. *Dammit.* He motioned for her to follow him.

"Can I speak with you over here?"

Her big brown eyes widened, and he felt the pull in his gut. Chocolate, dark and deep as syrup. Warm and—

He shook himself.

"Calling 911 is pretty serious, ma'am. Usually, it means someone is hurt." His voice came out gruff from the anger he was directing at himself. Feeling lust for a woman he'd just met wasn't the problem. Her being married definitely was.

"I really am sorry. I'm afraid these guys have a mind of their own," she said indicating the children.

He'd already realized that. "That may be true, but it's your job to keep them in line."

Air rushed out of her lungs as if he'd punched her. He hadn't meant to be so direct. Or harsh.

Her shoulders reared back, and Jared's eyes zeroed in on her hard nipples, poking through the thin tank top.

Jesus Christ.

He swallowed, willing his budding erection down.

There was no excuse for his actions. He glanced about, looking for a distraction. No sign of an injured person or other emergency. Still, he needed to make sure.

"This is an emergency vehicle, ma'am. For emergencies. Your little girl called 911. Is there an injured victim here?"

"No. I don't think so." She glanced to the woman with her.

"You don't think?" Jared held on to his temper by a thread. Anything to keep from sliding into his customary habit of flirting. His reaction to this woman puzzled him. He'd lost all control.

"Woman, you need to be more aware of what's going on around you. And you *need* to pay more attention to those children."

He flung out his arm as he pointed directly at the little heathens hooting on the sidelines as they watched the bucket of the quint flow smoothly to the exact branch of the cat. He hoped the damned critter scratched the grin right off Laredo's face. As if knowing Jared and the woman watched, Laredo glanced down. He winked.

Jared blinked. A wave of jealously stabbed his gut. He went to shove his hand though his hair and smacked up against his helmet. *Damn*. He was losing it.

"Look, *Ma'am*," he said the title with some disgust. "We have better things to do than rescue cats that don't need rescuing. Do you think you can make that clear to your kids? Make sure this doesn't happen again."

The stunning woman put her hands on her hips, and skewered him with her eyes. "Well, aren't you just the big fireman? So full of wisdom on child rearing."

If looks could burn, he'd be cindered to a crisp.

"Do you have children, Mr. Fireman?"

"Name's Jared, ma'am. I'm a firefighter."

"Well, *Jared*," she hissed the name scathingly. "You are in no position to lecture me on raising children." The woman was mad as a hornet. He'd bet her sting was just as chafing. Her glowing face only made her more desirable.

Great.

"Ma'am, I'm a first responder. To emergencies. This is not an emergency."

"Your partner doesn't seem to have a problem."

Sure enough, Laredo was in flirting mode and putting on quite a display. He talked to the children as he showed them the blasted cat was okay. With the creature on his shoulder, he looked too damn smug as he played the hero, showing every tooth in his big grin.

"Are you the only member of the fire department with such a *warm attitude,* or do you only use your charm on people like me?" Jared's eyes narrowed as he listened to the woman's reproach. "Because I can assure you, you are sadly lacking."

This woman had turned the table on him quite effectively. He felt like an ass.

"How dare you criticize me," she continued, her voice dripping acid. "I don't know who you report to, but I will find out. And I will gladly make a statement to your boss about your ill-mannered behavior."

She spun on her heel and stomped over to where the children were. The little girl was deliriously happy, squishing the cat in her arms. The woman rounded up her kids and herded them across the lawn, never once looking back in his direction. Words like *arrogant* and *know-it-all* drifted back to him.

Laredo stepped beside him. "What was that all about?" The asshole was actually smiling. The men at the station referred to Laredo as Casanova. Bet he never had a woman rant at him. Damn his Spanish hide.

"Women," Jared grunted. "Give them an inch and they take a mile. Trying to control the world and every man in it."

Laredo laughed. "That's a first. Wouldn't have believed it if I hadn't seen it. Wait until I get back to the station."

Jared knew he was in for a lot of ribbing. Once Laredo told the guys what happened, he'd never be able to live it down.

What had gotten into him anyway? He never pissed women off. He loved women. All women. So what if she was married? It wasn't like he was going to pounce on her or anything. *Shit.* Even married women liked to flirt sometimes.

But his attraction had been more than that. The woman had knocked him on his ass like a bolt of lightning.

And he had no idea how to handle it.

***

Jessica stomped across the lawn in a temper tantrum, just like one of the kids when they were in a snit. She'd never had such a volatile reaction to a man. A man sexy enough to have her melt at his feet.

The flurries in her stomach buzzed in anger and excitement. Well, he'd started it. He'd pissed her off with his superior attitude. It'd taken a while, though. She'd been too busy drooling over his gorgeous face and impressive body. She couldn't see his eyes through his sunglasses, but they had to be blue.

She wondered if they were blue like the sky, or blue like the water in the Bahamas, or more of a clear blue. She caught herself and sighed in frustration.

Who did he think he was, anyway? The man was rude and condescending, and here she was drooling. She glared at the three pairs of eyes watching her.

"Go to your room. All of you."

"But Jessie—" whined Tanner.

"No buts."

"Why do I have to go to my room? I didn't call the fire man." Sweet Aiden. He didn't deserve her scowl.

"You chased Charlie and made him scared."

"Enough, Tiffany," Jessica said, much calmer now. "No more arguing. Tanner. Go to your room and take Aiden with you." The boy turned and marched down the hall. Aiden followed, his steps wide and loud, trying to imitate the stomping of his brother. He needed watching. Aiden was becoming more like Tanner every day.

She turned back to Tiffany. The little girl stood cooing to her kitty and rubbing his back. Jessica didn't have the heart to scold her.

"Go to your room and I'll deal with you later."

"Okay." Tiffany skipped off, more than happy to have Charlie in her arms.

"He's the sexiest thing I've seen in a long time."

Jessica whirled around to find Connie standing in the doorway with her arms crossed. Jessica said the first thing that came to her mind. "You're married."

"I'm not dead." Connie shrugged and then plopped down on a chair at the kitchen table. Jessica released a sigh and waited for her limbs to unwind. *What a morning?*

"Want some coffee?"

"No, I think I've had enough. But I will take some iced tea. I suddenly feel hot." She fanned her face with a teasing glint in her eye.

"He was condescending," Jessica said as she opened the refrigerator. "He had the nerve to lecture *me*."

"He thought you were their mother."

"So what?" Jessica said, getting the ice. "Even if I was, he had no right to criticize me or tell me how to raise my children." When she turned with the tea pitcher, Connie raised an inquisitive eyebrow.

"Well, you know what I mean."

Jessica didn't believe in love at first sight. Although, she had to admit the air had buzzed between them from the moment they laid eyes on each other.

"The other one seems quite nice. And Latino. Hot. Hot. Hot."

"I don't care about either one of them. Their egos are probably bigger than their bodies."

"Their strong, sculpted bodies."

Jessica smacked a glass onto the counter, the *whack* ringing loud. She picked it back up and examined it to see if it cracked. It seemed okay. "Will you stop?"

Connie laughed. "Come on, Jessica. You're single. You can look. And drool."

The image of the firefighter was clear in her mind. Yep. She had done just that—before the guy opened his mouth. At a glance, she'd noticed his good looks and had expected him to flirt outrageously. Under that heavy coat that hung open, a navy-blue shirt stretched over some pretty impressive abs. She could imagine her tongue hanging out, but then she nearly bit it at the surprise of his reprimand. Which she had in no way deserved.

She'd been so embarrassed and ready to wallop the kids, but he'd jumped right in with a dressing-down and ticked her off.

"I expect smoke to come out of your ears any minute."

"Hmm?" Deep in thought, she forgot Connie was there.

"You're frowning. You're concentrating so hard I thought you'd start a fire of your own."

"Pun much?" Jessica shook her head and carried the glasses to the table. If you want me to admit it, then yes, his body was fine. Blond hair, blue eyes, drop dead gorgeous."

Connie smiled. "Blue eyes? How could you tell?" She sipped her tea.

Jessica shrugged. "Blue or not, he should have kept his mouth shut."

***

That woman had the bedside manner of an alley cat. Jared recalled the stubborn set of her chin, while her eyes had challenged him to grab her and kiss that sassy mouth.

The woman was too pretty, and she looked too young to have three kids. Add her abrasive attitude, and he couldn't understand why he found her so damn appealing.

She sure was pretty, standing there spiting sparks at him.

She was married for Christ's sake.

His attraction for her had fueled his anger at himself. Why had he felt threatened? His reasoning vanished. He had planned on offering her some much-needed advice on keeping an eye on her children.

He'd known she wouldn't appreciate it before he opened his mouth. But damn, he couldn't stop himself. And his damn body would not listen to reason. So, he'd snapped at her, thinking anger was the answer to smother his desire.

Wrong.

Her own temper had spiked his awareness and fed his interest. He had a moment of madness where he wondered if she'd be that feisty in bed. *Hell.* Thinking of the woman was slowly driving him insane.

Guilt plagued him. She had not deserved his anger. His reaction to her alluring appeal wasn't her fault. He'd had no right to tell her how to raise her children. It was her business. Not his.

So what if her children ran wild? It was no skin off his nose.

"Feel better?" Laredo's words sounded loud in the quiet of the engine's cab.

Jared glared, immediately realizing he had no reason to be mad at Laredo either. Hell, Laredo was just being himself. Jared should not have reacted when Laredo had winked at the woman.

Shit. Jealously was new to him. Even worse, the woman was off limits. He was known for being free and easy with the ladies, a reputation he lived up to with pleasure. No woman had ever snared him, and none would. So why was he being such a dick?

"Too bad the señora is married."

Yeah. Jared silently agreed.

***

Look at her, all stiff and snotty.

Seth bet he could bang the starch out of her backside. She'd like it, too. Just what the nosy bitch deserved.

He followed her to the third floor. When she took the elevator, he took the stairs. It wouldn't do for her to recognize him.

He wished he knew how much she'd overheard. Damn, that's what he got for using his phone in the hospital hallway. Who knew a nosy nurse would be listening? How could he know if she'd said anything to anyone? There was only one way to make sure she wouldn't tell a soul.

He slid through a door and peaked around a corner, watching the movement behind the counter at the nurses' station. One woman stared at a computer; another was on the phone. A doctor smacked a folder that resembled a patient's chart on the counter and leaned on his elbow, flirting with the woman.

Prick. Seth bet, before the night was over, the fancy doctor would have her knees up around his ears. Seth didn't give a shit. The only one he cared about was the bitch he followed to this floor.

No one suspected him for the explosion. Hell, no one even knew about him. The fire department was chasing its tail trying to figure out who had entered their precious sanctuary and messed with their equipment. Patience was a virtue. Isn't that what he'd been told? All he had to do was wait.

The staff on duty went about their business. Their routine hadn't changed for the past three weeks. Even the snotty nurse. She drove to work every day at the same time, taking the same route, and every night she went home the same way. Even the gas station and Super Mart she'd stopped at was on her consistent route.

Predictable as the sun setting each evening.

She strode down the hall and went into a patient's room. Just like clockwork.

Perfect.

Seth hurried down the stairwell and marched outside. He double-checked to make sure she had parked her car in the same space she always did.

Carl stood at the back of his pickup, smoking a cigarette. When he saw Seth, he tossed it on the pavement and ground it with his boot.

"She there?"

"Yeah," Seth replied. "All clear. She'll be coming out right on time."

Carl took what he needed from the back of the truck and slipped behind the row of cars. The guy was so smooth, even Seth had trouble seeing him.

You're responsible for this, you bastard. I was only after your brother. It's your fault the stupid bitch got in the way.

The big business man. My brother's partner. The one who set up a major deal then stabbed Shawn in the back. Shawn went to prison while that asshole kept living his important life, with his big deal corporation. My brother was a part of that corporation. You were partners. Then you stabbed him in the back.

The company owed Shawn.

Now owes me.

Shawn survived for two years before those bastards finally killed him.

His brother.

His blood.

The saying goes "revenge is best served cold." But Seth liked things hot.

The bastard had a brother in the Staunton Fire Department. Another fucking hero. Lucky bastard escaped the explosion at the training site, but Seth wasn't done.

His own brother had suffered. It seemed reasonable that he should target the brother of his enemy. Soon, his nemesis would know what it feels like to have a brother in danger. He would feel the sting of revenge from *his* brother's suffering.

Too bad the blonde nurse couldn't keep her nose where it belonged.

Carl opened the passenger door and hopped in. He gave a nod the job was done. Won't be long now. Seth cranked the engine.

Goodnight, bitch.

CHAPTER 3

Jessica rolled her shoulders, hoping to relieve some of the tension in her neck. Aching muscles tightened at the intrusion. Her eyes were tired after a long shift at University General.

A new resident was on call for Dr. Armstrong. He had the smarts and made sure everyone knew it. His bedside manner was decent, but he could use some work in the humility department.

Waynesboro had its share of gang violence, drug-related shootings and domestic disturbances that usually ended with a wife in the trauma unit. Car and motorcycle accidents were pretty much a daily occurrence. Since the Parkway was only a few miles away, most of the accidents came from people driving too fast on the mountain.

People would think she'd get used to the upheaval or sick of the strain and suffering. But she tried her best and received a measure of comfort knowing she was helping someone, or maybe even saving a life.

In the midst of confusion, a clear head was needed. When a patient came in, her training kicked into gear and her instincts took care of the rest. Now and again, she took a shift on the ward away from the trauma unit to maintain her sanity. And she got to check up on the patients recovering from their ordeal in the ER. No matter a person's skin color, bank balance, or whether they were gay or straight, everyone bled the same color.

An act of kindness meant a lot to a patient, or a family member. Something the resident doctor needed to learn. Not everyone was impressed with his PhD, or cared if he was the best surgeon in the city. Perhaps a wife or mom just needed someone to hold their hand.

Like the patient in room 405. A motorcycle accident. Jessica had been in the ER when the rescue squad brought in the teenager, unconscious, with a possibility of losing his left leg. The surgeon had put the young man back together, but the boy remained unconscious. His mother still sat by his side. No other family members were there. No one to hold her hand. No one to give her comfort.

Jessica knew not to get emotionally involved with a patient, but her heart went out to each and every one. She took a breath and slipped inside. The mom was asleep, her head tilted to the corner of the high-back hospital chair. Stephanie, a nurse, looked up from checking the patient's IV.

"Before you ask, he's stable. Hasn't woken up yet." She glanced at the mom. "Poor woman. She's exhausted. Won't leave his side."

"Have a tray brought up from the cafeteria. When she wakes up, she should eat something."

"I will. And I'll try to get her to eat."

Jessica stepped into the hall, and Stephanie closed the door softly behind them.

Jessica entered her notes on the last file and rubbed her eyes. After a few quick blinks, she glanced at the clock above the nurse's station. Ten minutes before her shift ended and the next group of nurses arrived.

She'd been putting in more hours than she should. Mainly to help those who needed time off with their families. Jessica had no family waiting at home. Just her and her cat. She'd rather have a dog, but a small apartment was no place for a big dog. What she would give for a house of her own. Raven's house was not only spoiling her, but making her crave a place of her own. A big farm would be perfect, but she would settle for a small house, as long as it had some land. Maybe she'd get more than one dog. The kids would love that. Acres where they could run wild, a floppy-eared dog bounding at their sides.

Her sister said she didn't have the energy to take care of a dog, and the kids were not responsible enough to care for one. With Raven's husband being in the military, she never knew when they might have to move, and a dog would complicate things. But the kids would love one. Maybe a dog would help them discharge some of that energy and curb their getting into mischief.

Anyway, Jessica needed to budget her money. A house took funds she didn't have, so she worked extra shifts and saved for her dream house. She didn't need a man to get a house for her.

In college, her boyfriend had been a football star. Jessica had done his laundry, bought his supplies, and when he wasn't at practice, he'd spent his time in her dorm eating her food and drinking her drinks. Even her roommate hadn't like him hanging around and had tried to tell Jessica he was using her. This went on for three years, until she saw him go into another girl's room. That could have been explained away, but their hands all over each other told Jessica what she'd been unable to face.

The fight that followed had left her to endure the consequence. *Memories best left buried.* Anyway, she'd kept her distance from good looking, popular boys ever since. A pretty face, a handsome smile, was not to be trusted.

"Think I'll make one more round," she said to her co-worker.

Sylvia had two more years before retirement. Reading one of the patient's charts, she nodded without looking up.

Quiet as usual this time of night, Jessica thought as she silently made her way to the first patient's room. Glancing inside, she noted a form in the hospital bed. Sound asleep. She continued on to the next room. Seeing the bed empty, she stepped into the room. Allowing her eyes to adjust to the darkness, she glanced around, looking for her patient.

A hand landed on her shoulder.

With a scream in her throat, she whirled around, nearly knocking the poor man over. "Mr. Rodgers. What are you doing out of bed?"

"I had to take a piss." Eighty, and with a mind of a twenty-one-year-old, he said exactly what he thought.

"You should have called a nurse to help you."

"I don't need no nurse watching me pee."

Jessica smiled at his direct language. The old guy knew she wouldn't take offense. "You shouldn't get out of bed by yourself. Now come. Let's get you back to bed." She reached out to steady him.

"Now that I don't mind. A pretty little thing like you can tuck me in anytime. Just don't let the draft in my backside."

A chuckle escaped as she helped him into bed.

He pulled the covers to his chin. "Ain't you gonna kiss me good night?"

"If it will make you go to sleep any quicker, all right." She leaned over, puckered her lips, and gave a loud smack against his cheek. He gave a wolfish smile and closed his eyes. A triple bypass hadn't slowed the sweet old man down one bit.

By the time she checked the other rooms and returned to the nurse's station, Sylvia had gone. Two replacements were at the desk.

"Hey, Jess. All quiet on the home front?" Abby asked.

"Yes. Mr. Rogers was up, but he's back in bed now."

"He's a character. Bet he was a smooth operator back in his day," she said, smacking her gum.

"He's a smooth operator now," Casey added.

"Jessica checked her watch. Eleven fifteen. "I'm beat."

"Dark as death outside. The clouds are hiding the moon. Quiet too. Nothing happening."

Abby wrinkled her brow and gave Casey a withering look. "I like it quiet. It's a good sign the patients are content, and there are no alarms or emergencies."

"I just meant it would be nice if we had some action."

Abby's gaze narrowed. "What kind of action?"

"Well, evidently not what you're thinking," Casey said aghast. "We're surrounded by patients."

Jessica's laugh brought both faces around to her. "I'm going home and getting some sleep. You two let me know if anything interesting happens."

Sirens rent the air.

"Emergencies coming in," Abby said.

"That sounds like several sirens," Casey jumped up and hurried down the hall to a visiting room, Abby and Jessica on her tail. The three stood before the floor to ceiling glass window.

"Oh my God. Look."

Jessica stared in shock. In the hospital parking lot, a staff member's car blazed in flames. More sirens, fire trucks and other emergency vehicles sped onto the scene. Men bounded from their trucks, grabbing hoses and scurrying about in an effort to contain the fire.

"Whose car is that?" Casey said.

"God, I hope no one was in it," Abby breathed.

"I'm going to find out." Jessica ran back down the hallway, gathered her purse from the nurse's station, and vaulted to the elevators.

If she'd been fifteen minutes earlier ... she could have been in the staff parking lot. What in the world? She hadn't heard an explosion. How had the fire started? She prayed that the owner was not in the car.

When the elevator dinged, she burst through the opening. Several people stood at the exit and more watched outside. Flames engulfed what was once a white car. Hurls of black smoke swirled in the air and swept up into the night sky.

While the spectators stood silent, shouts from firefighters ravished the air. Men scurried, pulling and tugging equipment. Water gushed in arcs on the consuming flames. Flashing lights lit the night, announcing the urgency of the situation.

Burnt metal assaulted her nostrils. She knew what burning flesh smelled like. Closing her eyes, she willed bile not to clog her throat.

Please, please, she prayed. No one was in the car. No one was in the car. Maybe if she repeated the chant, that would make it so.

"Alicia!"

Suddenly, a strong arm grabbed her and whirled her around.

"Oh. Sorry. I thought you were Alicia. Oh God. Where is she?" Fear etched with panic covered Nash's face.

"Nash. What's wrong?"

"That's Alicia's car, and I can't find her."

"Oh, no!" Jessica's breath caught in her throat. Not Alicia. She worked the same shift as Jessica. Nash and Alicia weren't dating, but every one pretty much knew Nash had a thing for her.

Terror etched Nash's features. He bolted forward and a fireman blocked his path. Heated words were exchanged. She couldn't hear exactly what was said, but Nash was arguing and gesturing wildly. The fireman, taking no nonsense, blocked Nash and ordered him to remain with the other bystanders.

Then the fireman glared at her and yelled, "Keep your boyfriend back."

Shocked, Jessica's mouth fell open. Before she could yell 'he's not my boyfriend', the man turned and stalked away.

Something about his tone and the way he strode toward the others seemed familiar.

"Hey, Nash." A tall brunette rushed to his side. "Someone saw Alicia get into a car with a guy. She's not in there." The woman pointed to the burning automobile.

Nash stilled; his body deflated like a balloon. His eyes went blank, and he stared as if he was afraid to believe her. Jessica understood his actions. She put a hand on Nash's back.

"Are you sure?" she asked the brunette.

"Yes. The security guard saw her."

"Thank God." Nash said on a harsh breath as he threw his arms around Jess. "When I saw her car ..."

Jessica didn't know what to do other than hug him back. She could only imagine the shock and anguish he'd just gone through.

She didn't think she could stomach the thought of Alicia being in the charred black rubble, either.

***

Jared turned his back on the woman, trying to get his head back on the burning car and the crowd getting in his way. He recognized the woman as the mother of the children who had made that 911 call, wanting the fire department to get their cat out of a tree. As if he hadn't had her on his mind the last few days. He sure as hell didn't need her distraction on the scene. He needed his head squarely on his shoulders.

A vehicle engulfed in flames, black smoke swirled in a cloud like a tornado. His concentration needed to be on keeping these people back. They should have more sense than rushing to a burning car. The damn thing could explode. Then he'd really have his hands full. He didn't need to deal with scorched people as well as a burning car.

Laredo and Cooper aimed the hoses, and in a matter of minutes, the threat was contained. Jared glanced over his shoulder to the gaping crowd. A man had the blonde in his arms. Before Jared had recognized her, he'd thought the guy was her boyfriend. Now he wondered if the guy might be her husband.

Twenty minutes later, the fire out, only steam rose from the charred heap.

"Okay, let's pack it up." Shep's voice came across the radio. As Jared turned, the woman rushed up to him.

"Was anyone in the car?"

Jared flipped up the shield of his helmet. Big brown eyes stared at him, and worry lines creased her brow. He wasn't sure if she recognized him. She'd been feisty when they'd argued under the tree. Now she looked devastated. His heart turned over.

"No, ma'am. No one was in the car."

"Thank God." Her breath rushed out and her hand latched onto his arm. He doubted she even realized it. Then he noticed her tremble.

"Are you all right?" He held his arm steady, when what he really wanted was to take her in his arms and hold her. Comfort her, of course. Nothing sexual. Just make sure she didn't faint. At least that's what he told himself.

Where was her damn husband anyway?

"Me? Yes, I'm ... fine. I just thought ..." When she looked at the car again, he knew exactly what she'd thought.

"Do you know the owner of that car?"

"Yes. She's a co-worker. We couldn't find her. I was afraid—"

This time he did put his hands on her arms. "She wasn't in there. No one was in there. The car is empty. Do you understand?" God, he didn't know what else to say to her. To get through to her. He'd never dealt with a hysterical woman before.

She shoved a loose strand of hair from her face, and the look she gave him could have melted ice.

"I am not an imbecile. I heard you and I understood you." She shrugged off his hands as if she couldn't bear his touch, and stood as straight as if there was a rod in her backbone. Jared knew right then and there she remembered him.

He jerked his arms back, fisting his hands at his sides. He should have remembered her viper tongue. *Try to help someone, and this is what you got.* She turned on him like a bad-tempered dog. What was it with this woman?

"Look, Lady. I've got work to do, and you're standing in the middle of a fire rescue scene."

"I see, *Mr. Fireman*, your manners have not improved."

Damn, she looked good standing there with her hands on her hips, all feisty and breathing fire. Jared summoned his anger to smother his attraction.

"Lady, you wouldn't know what manners were if someone showed you in a dictionary. Now, if you'll excuse me ..." He stepped around her, hearing her gasp and ignoring anything else that might come out of her mouth. He didn't need a crazy woman interfering with his job.

"What was that all about?" Mike asked when Jared tossed his tank in the back of the truck.

"That, *mi amigo*, is the mother of the kids who blessed Jared out."

Damn Laredo and his big mouth.

"The cat in the tree? The little girl who—"

"Her brother kicked her in the *cajonas*," Laredo finished for Mike. "Yep. The same one."

"Dude." Mike chuckled as he turned to Jared. "What did you do to her?" Mike took off his helmet and watched the woman stalk back into the hospital. "Looks like she is the one woman resistant to your charm."

"Don't know how that woman got a husband, let alone had three kids. She's about as warm as an ice block." Her image flashed in his mind. All fire and brimstone.

Then he recalled her expression, just before her eyes filled with resentment. He'd seen concern. Apprehension. Anxiety.

The devil woman wouldn't admit it, but she'd felt a moment of compassion. For him.

Jared wanted to laugh. Even more, he wanted to point that out to her. The *Ice Queen*. Looking all sympathetic, and worried.

Damn. She looked pretty hot in her cute little scrubs. Pink with a bunch of little things flying about. She looked good enough to eat.

Whoa. Where the hell? The woman was married. He felt sorry for her poor husband.

"I thought all women like you," Mike clapped a hand on Jared's back. "That one's out for blood."

Laredo laughed. "I think she likes to spit fire."

"Or ice chips."

"Either one, my man. For some reason she has turned her anger on you."

"Dude. My idol," Cooper said, as he came within earshot. He'd been rolling up the hose and now tossed it in the back.

"Shut up, Cooper."

"You cannot be losing your touch. You are my main man." He smacked his hand against his heart.

"I'm not losing anything. That woman is a—"

"Can it with the name calling, Jared." Mike gave him a dark look. "That isn't like you."

Jared gritted his teeth. "She just gets on my last nerve."

"But you are Hollywood. Suave, debonaire, laid-back ..." Cooper demonstrated slow movements with his hands. "I learn my skills from you. If you are pissing the women off, I cannot shadow you anymore."

"That woman was born mad at the world."

"She's married," Laredo told Cooper.

"Married? What'd you do, Jared?"

"That's what I asked him," Mike said. "I'm still waiting for an answer."

"All right, guys. Let's break up the slumber party. Stow that gear."

When Shep spoke, you got your ass moving. "Right Cap."

As Jared unsnapped his bulky coat, he glanced at the crew. Asshats. Shit-eating grins on all their faces.

That's all right. He could take it. This was just one woman. One he didn't even want.

He'd be back on his game tomorrow. And to prove it, he'd take Cooper to Roanoke. The big city with lots of pretty girls."

CHAPTER 4

The way the week was going, Jared needed action. He spent entirely too much time thinking about a certain blonde and her three kids. Frustration ran high at the station, with still no answers as to what happened at the training site, other than the explosion had been arson. Jared found, to his exasperation, trying to free his mind and make sense out of both situations had him chasing his tail. Thanks to the Cap, the firehouse had a pool table the guys put to good use.

"You're on," Laredo said, watching Jared take the break.

With a loud *crack*, balls shot across the table with two landing in corner pockets.

"You want to pay me now?" Jared chalked his cue and studied the break.

"I think I'll wait for my turn."

"Six in the corner." He leaned down and lined up his shot. "You may not get a turn. I plan to sink all my balls first."

"Who's sinking his balls?" Cooper caught the tail end of the conversation, and of course, he had to jump right in.

"Leave it to you, pup, to assume we're talking about sex."

"You're always talking about sex."

Jared shot again, sending the orange ball into a side pocket. "Not this time, pup."

Cooper stepped face to face with Jared. The boy stretched to his full height and reared back his shoulders.

"Who said you could call me pup?"

Jared had to hand it to the kid. He had balls. "Are you priming to get a smack down with them shoulders fixed back like that?"

"I'm an inch taller than you."

He was no kid, either, but Cooper was the newest member of their team. "It's going to take that and more, *pup*."

Cooper slumped. "Come on, Jared. Only Mike calls me that. Besides, you said you were sinking your balls."

Mike laughed. That big boom of a laugh that got everyone's attention. With shoulders as wide as a cement truck, he had a powerful set of lungs.

As for Cooper, he might be the youngest, but he was far from puny. His lean frame would fool the non-observer, but every inch of his trim body was pure muscle. He ran every morning at dawn and worked out in the weight room right alongside Mike.

Jared sank the eight ball and handed his stick to Cooper. "Here. I'm done."

Cooper gave a snort. "Who wants—?"

Barry, one of the new recruits stepped forward. "I'll take you on."

Cooper passed the pool stick on to his new partner. "I'll break."

Jared grabbed a jug of tea from the fridge, ignoring the image pricking his brain—as much as he could, anyway. The game had occupied his mind for a while. Now it was right back to the very thing he'd been trying to ignore. He glanced at his watch. Two hours and his shift would be over. Restless energy pumped his blood making him edgy. There had to be something to divert his thoughts. Anything. Even an alarm—

Christ. He must really be in bad shape if he wished for a 911 call. He might be restless, but an alarm meant somebody else was in trouble. And he wouldn't wish that on anyone. He couldn't understand his crazy thinking. Why the blasted woman hung in his mind like a leech. Sucking the common sense right out of his head.

He filled a glass, then tossed back a healthy gulp and relished the coolness on his throat. The crack of pool balls jerked him from his musing. Coop strutted around the pool table like a peacock. His game was every bit as good as Jared's.

"What are you staring at?" Mike stood about three inches taller, but his size is what daunted. One look at his massive arms and men got the hell out of his way.

"Pup," Jared answered using the nickname Mike had labeled on Cooper.

"Cocky little bastard. Reminds me of you."

Jared had heard it before. Many times. He liked to think of himself as confident instead of arrogant. When he hit town nine years ago, he'd been in short supply of it. Station Eight had given him back his self-esteem. The men had, anyway. He'd come to love his teammates. His brothers. They'd given him support, had faith in him, and he would lay his life down for each and every one.

"No comeback?"

Jared shrugged.

"Cassie is with her mom and sister tonight. Want to head over to The Pitt Stop and get a cold one?"

Jared glanced at the glass in his hand before he spoke. "You're reading my mind."

***

Jessica would normally go to bed, but she was keyed up after the fiasco at the hospital. Besides, she wanted to thank Connie for keeping the kids at her house last night. She walked around to the back door and knocked. When the door opened, Connie looked her up and down.

"Looks like you could use some coffee."

"Hi, Connie. You're right."

"Come on in. I'll fix you some breakfast." Connie turned and walked to the stove.

"Oh no. You don't have to go to that trouble."

"No trouble at all," she said, lifting a dish from the corner of the granite counter. "I made pancakes this morning. I have extra. I'll just nuke them."

"Kids get off to school without any problems?" Jessica slung her purse over the back of a chair and dropped onto the wooden surface.

"Yes. Tiffany wanted to take Charlie, but I told her she needed to ask the teacher for a show and tell day."

"Thanks for letting the cat come with her. She won't let that cat out of her sight since the tree incident."

"She keeps an eye on Aiden, too."

"Thanks for taking care of Tiff and the boys."

Connie placed a steaming mug in front of Jess.

"Ummm," she murmured as she inhaled the rich aroma. "Just what I need. Thanks."

"My boys loved having them over. For teenagers, they're really good with the kids."

"I was a little worried about Aiden. He's so young."

"I think pre-school is good for him. With Tanner and Tiffany for siblings, I don't think you need to worry about him being bashful or hesitant."

"I've noticed he imitates Tanner a lot."

"Little people pick up things quick. Aiden watches his brother, but he followed my boys around last night."

"That's Aiden. I hope it wasn't a problem."

"Of course not. Kenny and Sonny actually had a good time."

"Your boys didn't complain about having to watch little kids?"

"Nope. As for Aiden, he left with a smile on his face this morning. He wanted to know if Kenny would be here when he got off the bus."

"I really appreciate it. With Jillian going into labor, the hospital needed to replace her quick. If not for that, I wouldn't have filled in last night. Thanks for helping out. It was just the one night. The hospital has a replacement for the next six weeks."

Connie waved a hand. "Glad to do it."

"I'm looking forward to being off the next two weeks. Once Raven comes back, I'll be on night rotation to cover vacations."

"Yep. It's that time of the year. School will be out then."

"Thank goodness Raven's visit with Chad is now while the kids are in school. If I had them all day, every day, I'd be worn down to a frazzle."

Connie laughed. Jessica reached up and removed the clip from her hair, letting the mop fall down around her face and shoulders. She ran her hands through the tangles, smoothing the strands from her scalp to the ends.

"So, tell me why you're late."

Jessica swallowed and placed her coffee back on the table, still cupped within both hands.

"A nurse's car caught on fire."

"Oh my God." Connie slapped her hand over her chest. "Did anyone get hurt?"

Jessica remembered her encounter with the firefighter. She'd basically asked him the same thing when she wanted to know if anyone was in the car.

"No, thank goodness. No one could find Alicia, that's who the car belonged to. We were afraid she was in the car. Pandemonium broke out for a while. One of the male nurses went crazy looking for her. He even mistook me for her. When he saw my face instead of Alicia, I thought he was going to lose it. Thankfully, another nurse said she'd seen Alicia leave with someone else."

"Thank goodness. I can imagine his relief."

"Yes. When he heard the news, he hugged me. Nearly squished the breath out of me. I don't think he even cared who he was holding, as long as it was a live body."

"Hmmm," The microwave beeped. Connie got the pancakes and placed them on the table. "Sounds like an excuse to get his hands on you."

"Nope. He's got a thing for Alicia."

"Oh." Connie shrugged. "At least Alicia is okay."

"We hope. No one's seen her." Jessica spread butter over her pancakes. "I saw that fire guy this morning."

"You mean those hot firefighters with that big ladder truck who helped the kids?"

"One of them. He was just as arrogant and bossy as the day he was here."

"Oh, you mean the one who took you to the side for a private conversation?"

Jess paused and glared at Connie. "I mean the nasty man who had the nerve to instruct me on Raven's children."

Connie grinned. "You've got to admit he's damned good looking."

"The man might be damned good looking, but he was damned arrogant too."

Connie lifted her cup. "Oh, I don't know. Sometimes a guy will act all mad when he's really shy."

"Shy? He's an asshole."

"A cute asshole. Built too."

With his pretty face and cavalier attitude, he had to be a player. Even though Jessica didn't want to be interested, God help her, she was. Very. Who would not be over a sexy hunk who looked like Hollywood, California sin? The way his T-shirt clung to him, showing off those muscles …

Oh, yeah, he had that blond, pretty-boy thing going for him that was so popular with women. And baby blue eyes that sizzled, making every woman know exactly what he had on his mind.

Being a firefighter, she supposed he had to stay in shape. She couldn't help but wonder what he looked like without that shirt.

She shook her head at her foolish thoughts. His personality didn't match his looks. She'd expected flirting and showing off his physique. Not a bad tempered, ill-mannered dictator. She shivered in mock horror for Connie's benefit.

Connie laughed.

"Okay, he's built. Good looking. And mean."

"He thought you were married. What are you going to do about that?"

Jessica glared at Connie as though she'd lost her mind. "Are you kidding? I hope I never see that guy again."

Connie just stared over the rim of her coffee cup. She didn't believe one word.

Jessica wasn't doing a very good job of convincing herself, either.

***

Several hours later, the crew met up at The Pitt Stop. A great place to unwind. The place had good food, a variety of drinks, and lots of cold beer. Jared leaned one elbow on the bar as he took a swig from the long-neck.

"What's on the menu this evening? Blonde? Red head?"

Mike was right. Cooper was behaving more like Jared every day. He sort of took the boy under his wing when he'd showed up at Station Eight. Cooper had practically begged Shep for a chance at the job. The guys didn't know what to expect, and some had made bets on how long the kid would last. Cooper had proved them all wrong. He'd turned out to be a hard worker. Jared had never seen anyone so eager to prove himself. Something drove that kid. Maybe someday he would share his story. Until then, Jared would mid his own business.

"Young crowd in here tonight. Most of 'em your age, Coop."

"We're all over twenty-one."

"A lot of them don't act like it."

Cooper raised a brow, then shrugged as if what Jared had said didn't matter. "Check out that group over there." Cooper pointed the neck of his beer bottle to the center of the room where a group of females looked like they were having a party. Nice to look at. They wore skimpy short-skirts, and showed so much skin it didn't leave much to the imagination.

His throat was suddenly dry, so he turned up his beer and took a long pull.

"I'm not complaining, mind you," Cooper paused, then continued, "but those gals look like they're dressed for a strip club."

"Less clothes to remove," Laredo piped up. The guys at the station called him Casanova. Latino, with his dark looks and air of magnetism, he fit the bill. He lived other guys' fantasies. The guy looked tight tonight—black open-collar shirt, exposing a silver cross on a heavy chain. His hair might have been a tad longer than the other firefighters, but he kept it slicked back. He put goo on it—he said—to control the natural curls. And he was getting a lot of attention from the ladies.

Jared wasn't worried. He had his share of babes looking at him. Women just seemed to like blond hair and blue eyes. But he would admit he got a few grooming ideas from Laredo. Personally, Jared liked the Hollywood style—playboy look. He never went without his sunglasses.

"Ponytail must have borrowed her daddy's handkerchief for her top," he said out loud.

"Good thing she's skinny. If she had big boobs, they'd fall out."

"Again, not complaining." Jared clinked bottles with Cooper.

"Cassie will have my balls if I even look at another woman." Then there was Mike. Big as a moose and built like a dump truck. Since he'd hooked up with Cassie, he was out of the game, but he still went with the guys for a beer now and then.

"You don't have any left, man." Laredo ignored the glare from Mike.

"She's not here. None of us will tell her." Cooper might be younger than the rest of them, but he wasn't stupid. He had learned quick, being the brunt of their jokes. Now he jumped right in, egging things on.

"Doesn't matter. She's the only one I'm interested in."

"Once you get hooked, all the fun gets sucked right out of you," Laredo mumbled as he lifted his bottle to his mouth.

Jared grinned. "Next thing you know, he'll be talking marriage."

Cooper cringed. "I'm too young to recognize the word."

"I refuse to give up on being single." Laredo punctuated each word like a true Latino.

"I'll give pup some slack, but you, Laredo, I can't wait to see you fall."

"I told you not to call me pup."

Laredo ignored Cooper's outburst, focusing on Jared. "Not going to happen, Jared. I like my life just the way it is."

Jared followed Laredo's gaze to a hot number in a short skirt and plunging neckline. The sexy brunette eyeballed Laredo with a gleam in her eye and a come-hither smile. The two blondes with her analyzed the group as if they were sizing up their options.

"What you lookin' at, pup?"

Cooper glared at Laredo. "The same thing you are."

"You think she's into you?" Laredo said with a snort.

"Sure. Look at her friends, pointing and shoulder bumping."

Laredo narrowed his eyes. "The one in front is mine."

"I don't know, dude. She's looking at me." Cooper stepped in front of Laredo. "I'm going to make my move."

"Woah, *amigo*."

Mike tapped Cooper's arm. "You're either brave, or very, very stupid."

Jared understood Mike's comment. The kid was about to step on Laredo's toes.

"Come on, guys. Just because Laredo has that Italian/Spanish thing going for him, he thinks women automatically fall at his feet. Maybe this gal likes the blonde, pretty-boy type."

"You just described Jared," Mike said.

"Dude. I was speaking about myself. But I'm willing to share."

"Share?"

"I only have one set of hands, and there are three of them."

"Cooper," Laredo said, "if you cannot take care of three women, you have not been paying attention."

Mike laughed. "You sure you've been shadowing Jared?"

"Perhaps I should show you how it is done." Laredo never took his gaze from the women as he counseled Cooper.

"I'll take the brunette," Jared heard himself say. He couldn't be sure if he made the choice by the woman's obvious interest, or to deny a certain blonde any claim in influencing his decision. Why in the hell was he thinking of her at a time like this? He had to get the little housewife out of his head. What better way to forget one woman than to replace her with another.

"There's my guy." Cooper's grin stretched from one side of his face to the other.

Why'd the kid select *him* to be his idol?

"You look like the tomcat that got the cream." Mike said.

"How about a little puss on the side?" Laredo stood, keeping his gaze on the women. "Come on, pup."

CHAPTER 5

Even though you went to bed, that did not mean you would automatically go to sleep.

Jessica tossed and turned. Twice, she'd seen the snarly firefighter. If fate had brought them together, she couldn't imagine why. He might be the image of any girl's dreams, but his detestable personality shot those illusions to hell. So why couldn't she get the man out of her mind?

When she'd first seen him, he'd taken her breath, what was left of it after seeing the fire truck. Her sister's children kept her in a state of hyperventilation. One catastrophe after another. As if her heart hadn't already been pumping in overtime, the darn thing nearly stopped when he opened his mouth.

She'd known a moment of vulnerability. Then her senses had kicked in and she took charge of the situation. The children were okay, she hadn't seen a fire, so she had forced her erratic beating heart to slow. Then the devil set it to palpitating again with his patronizing remarks.

Jessica threw back the covers, groaning in frustration. A trickle of light filtered through the top of the bedroom window, giving enough luminosity for her to see the ceiling. Great. She was wide awake. How long would she lay here thinking of a man she had no desire to give space in her head?

Counting sheep never worked for her when she couldn't sleep. Coffee sounded good, but caffeine would not fix the problem. She rolled to her side and stared at the small beam filtering into her bedroom. The street lights were nice to have in the neighborhood, and normally didn't bother her. And the coverings on the window kept out most of the glare.

Even though she knew not to, she glanced at the clock. Four a.m. She undoubtedly would look at it every five minutes from here on. It would be a long night. She closed her eyes and tried to—

What was that?

Shit. Now she was imagining things.

She heard it again. A voice? Someone was talking.

Raising her head from the pillow, she listened in earnest. The sound was faint, but definite.

Tiffany?

Jessica threw her legs over the side of the bed and quietly rushed down the hall. She stopped in the doorway and stared at the tiny figure on the bed. When Tiffany moaned again, Jessica crossed to the bed and placed a calming hand on the little girl's shoulder.

"I'm here, sweetheart. It's me. Jessie."

Tiffany mumbled in her sleep. Jessica couldn't make out the words. Was Tiffany having a bad dream?

"Tiffany. It's Jessie," she repeated in a soothing voice. "I'm right here. Everything is all right, sweetheart."

Tiffany's eyelids opened. Even with the dim night-light, Jessica could see something was wrong. She turned on the lamp. Normally bright and focused, Tiffany's eyes looked dim and hazed. An eerie feeling raced down Jess's back. More words mumbled from Tiffany's lips. Unrecognizable. Mutterings Jessica couldn't make out. She tried turning her niece's head, tried getting her attention. Even though her eyes were open, Jessica feared the little girl could not see.

Oh my God. What should I do?

Being a nurse, Jessica knew when a patient was unresponsive. But this was her niece. Tiffany's limp body and sightless eyes scared the bejesus out of her.

"Tiffany, look at me. It's Jessie. Can you hear me?"

"Have to beb ow."

"Tiffany. Wake up," Jessica said in a louder voice. "Tiffany. It's Jessie. I'm right here. Come on, Honey. Wake up." Fear squeezed her chest. Jessica knew not to panic, but it was damn hard when the little girl she loved as her own didn't recognize her.

Tiffany gasped for air. Her little arms grabbed Jess's pajama shirt. Then she started to struggle, pushing Jessica away.

"Honey. Where are you going?"

"Go now. Beb go ow."

"Tiffany. Oh God, you're scaring me." She searched her mind furiously for anything her sister might have said regarding Tiffany. Didn't she mention Tiffany had gone downstairs once. Raven found her sleepwalking? Could Tiffany still be asleep now?

From everything she'd read, Jessica knew she had to handle this carefully. Not to shock or scare Tiffany awake. She hugged the little girl to her chest. When Tiffany continued to struggle, Jessica let her go and watched.

Tiffany got out of bed and walked to the door. "Tanner. Come here."

Now *that*, Jessica understood. Tiffany stepped into the hall and Jessica followed. When Tiffany collapsed, Jessica nearly had a heart attack.

"Tiffany," she called in a shaky voice. "Tiffany."

As the child gasped for air, Jessica made sure her airway was clear. Dear God, she could not do this alone. She cuddled her niece and ran to her phone, and called 911.

***

Jared recognized the address and silently swore. A ton of mixed feelings rushed him all at once. A child. Damn, he hated those the worst. Calls that involved children. This one couldn't breathe. The address was the same one he'd responded to when the little girl called in about her cat. The little girl who'd been kicked in the balls by her brother. He hoped this call would turn out to be as non-threatening.

Then he recollected the mother. The sexy, hot, delicious blonde who, for whatever reason, kept popping into his head. The more he tried not to think of her, the more her image appeared. What was that saying about forbidden things being more tempting?

As Mike pulled the squad to the curb, Jared identified the house. He pushed his thoughts aside and went into operation response mode. Since this was a medical distress call that did not require helmet and full gear, he wore the same clothes he'd been wearing at the station.

Before he could ring the doorbell, he saw the woman through the glass door. The caller had identified herself as Jessica. Her eyes wide with anxiety, she motioned for him to enter.

"I didn't know what else to do," she sputtered. Jessica held the little girl on her lap, snug against her chest.

Mike placed the med kit on the floor and stepped forward. "What's her name?"

"Tiffany. She's awake now. I think she was in some sort of trance, like sleepwalking."

The wide-eyed little girl stared at them, but remained quiet.

"Hi there, Tiffany. My name is Mike." Even braced on one knee, Mike's size took up half the length of the sofa.

"Hi." Her voice was so weak it grabbed Jared's heart.

"That's my buddy, Jared." Mike tossed a thumb over his shoulder.

"I know you. You got Charlie out of the tree."

Jared would never live that one down. Tiffany didn't look anything like the rambunctious little tomboy giving her brother hell. His heart ripped at the fragile rag doll curled up in Jessica's arms.

Mike drew her attention back to him. "Is Charlie your cat?"

Tiffany nodded her head while clutching a stuffed animal in her hands.

"Who's this?" Mike pointed to her furry toy.

"This is Billy. He's a ga-raffe." At least she was speaking. Her quiet voice grew a little stronger with each word.

"Hello there, Billy. Is it okay if I take a look at Tiffany?"

"He doesn't talk. Sometimes I pretend he does."

"That's okay, Tiffany. I have a bear at my house. Sometimes I talk to him, too."

Her little eyes opened wide. "A real bear?"

"Well, he seems real to me," Mike answered. "He's just like your giraffe. And I talk to him."

"You do?"

Jared knew Mike examined Tiffany's movements and her speech, judging her reaction while he calmed her with chit chat. The best way to assess a situation and not frighten children was to make them comfortable. Mike was the best EMT in the fire department. If anything was going on with the little girl, he would catch it.

"Are you thirsty, Tiffany?"

"I don't think so."

"Well, I sure could use a glass of water. Is it okay if I sit with you while your mom gets me a glass of water?"

This was Mike's opportunity of assessing Tiffany, giving Jared the chance to speak with Jessica in detail and find out what happened.

"Jessie's not my mom, silly. She's Jessie."

Jared's breath lodged in his chest.

"Tiffany's mom is my sister," Jessica clarified. "I'm her aunt."

Jared's ears rang with the news.

Aunt.

"Tiffany's dad is in the military. For the past two months, he's been secluded in Arizona for special training. He received some free time, but for security reasons, cannot leave the area. He's being shipped to Kuwait. I'm watching the kids so Raven can see him before he leaves."

The rest of the conversation dulled. *Jessie's not my mom, silly. She's Jessie.*

Jessica turned, snapping him from his trance.

"I'll get your water."

Jared followed Jessica to the kitchen.

"Mike doesn't need the water. It's a way for him to examine Tiffany, and me to get the facts from you."

When Jessica dropped her head and braced her arms on the counter, Jared's training took over.

"Deep breaths," he said stepping closer. He wanted to take her in his arms and suddenly realized it would be okay if he did. The barrier of her marriage was gone. Jessica was the aunt. Even so, his personal feelings did not matter. The rubrics of his position demanded he behave in a professional manner.

Still.

Jared placed a hand on her back. "Jessica. Mike is with her. From what I've seen, she'll be fine."

Suddenly, she was in his arms.

"I got so scared. I'm a nurse, and I didn't know what to do." Jessica was sobbing and needed his reassurance. Jared did the only thing he could. He put his arms around her, and hugged her back.

"It's okay, now. Tiffany will be all right."

"Oh my God. I ..." She shifted and raised her head. "I'm sorry."

He brushed her silky hair back from her face. "Don't be. She's a little girl, and you were worried."

"I'm trained—"

"She's your niece." Man, he loved the sound of that.

Jessica scrubbed at her eyes then turned from him. He felt the loss of her heat immediately. He watched her grab a paper towel and dry her eyes.

"I can't let Tiffany see me like this."

He stepped closer, reaching around her and turned on the water. "Splash some water on your face, and you'll be good as new."

Her gaze locked with his, causing a jolt to his gut. Fear, gratitude, and yep—awareness. She smelled good too. Her scent was all over him. If this wasn't an emergency call, he could take her into his arms and kiss her until they both lost their breath.

He cleared his throat. "Um, the water."

"Oh." Jessica quickly washed her face and grabbed another paper towel. She dried her face, then threw the towel in the trash can. "Okay. I'm ready."

"Why don't we get a glass of water for Mike, anyway?"

And some ice for me.

CHAPTER 6

Like a lighthouse beacon, Jessica's sister drew people to her with her welcoming smile. With three kids, and a husband gone most of the time, Jessica didn't know how Raven managed to keep her sanity, let alone her positive attitude. The week flew by fast, and now Raven was home.

"Hi, Jess, Come on in."

"Kids already gone to school?"

"Yeah. You know, when Tanner and Tiffany started school, and I had to put them on the school bus, I cried. This morning, I cried again. I missed them so much. And Chad didn't even get to see them."

Jessica swallowed. "They missed you, too."

"Thanks again for watching them so I could be with Chad."

"I was glad to do it. And, I'm sure you showed your man how much you missed him."

A warm, happy glow lit up Raven's face. "We stayed in bed the whole week."

"TMI, sister," Jess said, quickly shaping her hands in the known gesture, representing the phrase.

Raven and Chad deserved time together. They were the rare couple, married ten years and still loved each other to distraction.

Jessica wondered if she'd ever find a man like Chad to love her. An honest man.

Letting her thoughts drift, she conjured up the handsome firefighter. Hot? Droolworthy. The last time she saw him, he'd seemed like a different person. Caring. Considerate. Had she really thrown herself in his arms? Well, in her own defense, she'd been distraught. And he'd held her.

Maybe she didn't notice at the time, but looking back she remembered how good it felt.

How good he felt.

Jared was most likely a ladies' man; he looked good enough to eat. How could she expect him to be faithful to one woman? Hadn't she sworn off good-looking men? The preppy types she'd romanticized about in college? The one's who used charm to get a girl into bed and then— *No.*

The man of her dreams would want only one woman. He would be completely devoted to her. Was she asking too much? She longed for a strong pair of arms to hold her at night. Every night. Until they were both ready for a nursing home.

The only problem—trust.

She had given her body and her trust once, only to have her heart broken and her trust shattered. It was her sister who'd saved her from despair when she'd found out Jessica was pregnant, and it was her sister who'd stayed by her side and given her strength to go on when she lost the baby. It was a long time before she'd even considered dating again.

She'd be better off living in the here and now. Not in some fantasy that involved a man who clearly loved women. Plural.

Jessica had made a plan and stuck to it. She graduated top of her nursing class, and steered clear of pretty boys ever since. For the last five years, she'd kept her promise and now the hot firefighter was the first one who tempted her to break it.

"Connie told me some hot firefighter has caught your eye."

"I'm not looking to hook up with a firefighter who knows he's hot."

"He's got eyes for you. So, he must like what he sees." Bless Raven for trying to build up Jessica's confidence, but Jess couldn't help but question the guy's motives. After all, she'd learned the hard way that guys were not to be trusted.

"I'm sure he flirts with all women. Probably uses his charm like a preamble to sex. No doubt he has women falling at his feet."

Raven placed two steaming cups on the counter, then came around to sit on the stool beside Jessica. "Don't you think you're pouring it on a bit thick?"

Jessica thought about that for a moment. If she had to admit it, then yes. Maybe she tried to convince herself the hot firefighter was a bad egg. While she was admitting things, she might as well acknowledge her feelings. Yes, he was appealing. Yes, he was hot. But, when Jared looked at her, his eyes smiled, yet she'd also seen a hidden longing that rocked her. There was much more to him than her first impression.

Raven sipped her coffee. "I just want you to be happy."

"I am happy."

Raven raised a brow. "You need to live a little. Have some excitement."

"I have enough excitement at the hospital. Yesterday, the ER admitted five kids from a party. Overdose. Mr. Simpson faked a heart attack so he could ride in an ambulance. A man from a construction site accident came in with a steel pole through his leg."

"Anyone else interesting show up at the ER? Like your fire guy?" Raven asked with a sneaky grin.

"He's not my guy. And he's a *firefighter*. With the *fire* department."

"They take people to the ER, too. Don't they?"

Jessica tried to steer her sister in another direction. "You should explain calling 911 to your children."

"Look, Jess, I know they can be challenging."

"Chasing after those three was like trying to lasso the wind."

Raven laughed. "Good likeness." Then her tone grew firm. "I can't believe Tiffany called 911."

"Well, she did. At least you know she can do it."

"We've had a conversation with all three kids. But I guess I need to stress the importance of what is considered an emergency."

Jessica silently agreed.

"So. Connie said there were two hot guys here from the fire department." Raven sipped her coffee but kept her gaze on Jessica.

Of course Connie did.

"Yes. And they brought the long truck with the tall ladder. The kids were ecstatic."

"Hmmm. I was only gone a short while and Connie found a man for you."

Jessica rolled her eyes. "I told you he is not my man."

"I know. I know," Raven said, waving a hand. She sipped her coffee and stared at Jessica over the rim. "Hot. Fire. Guy."

"You know why I cannot jump into a relationship."

Raven sat her cup on the counter. "Oh, honey. That was a long time ago."

Jessica stared at her coffee cup, not wanting to relive her memories.

"Jess, you don't have to get serious. Just have some fun."

Bitterness hit her right along with the harsh memory. How stupid she had been. "I had fun—never mind."

"Oh, Jess." Raven placed her hand over hers. "Please, talk to me."

"No. Not now."

"You can date a guy and take things slow. Get to know him."

"Let it be, Raven."

"Tell you what. Connie can watch the kids. I'm taking my sister out on the town."

***

The hospital kept Jessica so busy she hardly ever took time to go out with friends. Tonight, she was glad Raven had insisted. Connie's husband said the kids could spend the evening with him and their boys, so she came as the designated driver. Raven called Keri, another friend whose husband was also in the military, so Jessica called Casey, a co-worker. Five women out on the town, what could go wrong?

Pargo's was a restaurant, and the bar side a favorite hangout for singles. They were there to have fun, so they sat on the bar side. Not necessarily to pick up guys, or be picked up. Just to drink and have a good time. The waiter was cute. Very young, still in college. Most of the waiters and waitress were college students, for JMU was a mile up the road.

"Hello, ladies. You out by yourselves tonight? Leave the men at home?" Not only was the waiter cute, but he had the lively personality of a flirt.

"You don't take candy to the candy store," Connie told him with a wink.

"I have a lively bunch tonight. I'm Travis. What'll you have, ladies?"

Raven went first. "I want sex on the beach."

"On my bucket list. Can't wait." The waiter froze in mock confusion, and pasted a dramatically fake look of surprise on his face. "Ohhhh. You mean the drink."

Raven looked at Connie. "I like him."

"And for you, my lovely candy lady?"

"How did you know I have a sweet tooth? It will have to be eye-candy for me." She held up her left hand and flashed her ring."

"Nice rock. Better hold on to that one."

"Piña colada."

"Make that two," Keri added.

Jessica couldn't find what she wanted on the menu. "I want something blue. I forget the name. Blue Hawaiian or something."

Travis cocked his hip, and pointed his pen. "For you, doll, I'll add a dash of food color to any drink you want."

For fun, she batted her eyelashes at him.

"One big Kablue-na." He scribbled on his order pad.

"That's the one."

"Never heard of it," Casey said. "Give me one, too."

"You got it. Two for you." He held up two fingers.

"No, I meant also."

Travis gave her a sassy wink. "Be right back ladies. Don't do anything I wouldn't do." And he walked off.

"He's adorable," Connie said.

"What's in that blue kahoona?"

"Big Kablue-na." Jessica narrowed her eyes as she thought. "It has rum, coconut, and a shot of Petron."

Casey's eyes widened. "Holy shit. Tequila?"

"That's the one."

"Hey, if we're doing Tequila shots, I want in," Keri added.

"Not me. I have to drive you drunks home, and I'd rather you guys not puke in my car."

Casey picked up a menu. "Are we getting anything to eat?"

"For sure. Later," Raven replied. "We'll need something to soak up all the liquor I plan on drinking."

Keri leaned over the table, getting the girls' attention. She gave a nod to Connie. "Don't look now, but that guy at ten o'clock is checking you out."

Connie brazenly spun around on her chair. "You mean that one, over there?"

"Good grief, Connie. Be obvious, why don't you?"

"She doesn't know what *don't* means," Raven said.

Connie waved at the guy, then flashed her ring finger. The man raised his glass, and gave a nod. She spun back around. "Damn. Where's my drink?"

"Impatient, are we? Here you go, ladies." Travis lifted the glasses, one at a time, and placed them exactly where they belonged. "This one for the lady who wants sex ..." he hesitated theatrically, "...on the beach. This one for my candy lady," he said, meeting Connie's eyes. "This one for the lady who looks thirsty." He sat Keri's drink down. "This one for the lady who ordered T W O. One at a time, dear heart." Then he met Jessica's gaze. "And, ahh, this one for the pretty blonde who will not be leaving alone tonight."

"Not leaving alone? Of course not," Raven said. "We came together, we leave together."

"You know that's not what I meant. If you play your cards right, each of you could leave with a handsome man on your arm."

"I'm married."

Travis leaned close to Keri. "Then you can be the designated driver."

"That's me," Connie said holding up her hand.

Travis glanced at Casey. "And how about you?"

"I'm available."

"Then perhaps *I* should take you home," he said leering at her.

"You're too darn cute, you know that?"

"You ladies are fun."

Connie propped her elbow on the high table and cupped her chin in her hand. "Just how old are you?"

"Old enough to know better, and too young to resist."

Every one of them hooted.

"That boy is going to be a heartbreaker," Raven said.

"I call dibs," Keri said.

"What do you mean you call dibs? He's too young for you."

"I'm going to freeze my body and wait a few years."

"Toast." Raven held up her drink.

"Over the lips and across the gums?" Casey asked.

"Hell no," Connie protested. "We can think up something better than that."

"Oh. Me. Me. Me." Keri patted her hands on the table like a drummer. "I got one. Everyone pick up your glass." When each person had their drink raised in a toast, Keri spoke. "Here's to you." She raised her glass while glancing at each one of them. "Here's to me. Friends we shall always be."

"Here, here." Connie went to take a sip of her drink, and Keri stopped her.

"Wait! I'm not finished. But if we should ever disagree ..." Keri looked each girl in the eye, then offhandedly twirled her glass. "... Fuck you. Here's to me." She had her glass at her mouth before what she'd said sunk in. Everyone cracked up.

"That's hilarious."

"I've got to remember that one."

"I can't help but notice you ladies seem to be having a good time."

Jessica glanced up to see a nice-looking man standing next to her. He held a drink in his hand.

"We were before you got here," Keri mumbled.

"Keri!"

"What? He didn't hear me. He's all goo-goo for Jessica."

"Jealous?"

"Not even. I got a hot man at home, waiting for me. Or rather, me waiting for him. It's always hot when he gets home from deployment." Keri giggled.

"TMI, girlfriend."

Jessica couldn't help but hear Keri and Casey's back and forth. She tried smiling, distracting the man, to cover their chatter.

"Can I buy you a drink?"

"All of us?" Casey asked.

The guy had been looking at Jessica. He tried to cover his surprise, but he graciously smiled and said, "Of course."

"Good, I'll have another one of these." Casey turned to Jessica. "This is really good."

"Remember what's in it."

Keri signaled their waiter. Travis came over right away.

"This kind man has offered to buy us ladies a drink. Another round, please."

Travis glanced to the man and back to Keri. "Back in a flash."

"Tell me," the guy said. "You ladies come here often?"

Oh puh-lease.

Keri opened her mouth. Since she would more than likely crack an insult, Jessica quickly drew the man's attention. "You are very kind. Thank you." Then she realized he never gave his name. "I don't want to be rude, but this is ladies' night out."

"I thought the idea of a ladies' night was the ladies go out, and meet gentlemen."

"Gentlemen— Ooff."

Jessica wasn't sure if anyone else saw it, but she had seen Connie elbow Keri. Again, Jessica diverted the man's attention. "Yes, well, actually we're—"

"Celebrating!" Connie said, enthusiastically. "We're celebrating my anniversary. My wedding anniversary." She flashed her ring finger, which seemed to be the thing to do this evening.

The man took a step back. He quickly scanned the ladies' fingers, to see who else was wearing a wedding ring. Jessica wanted to laugh.

Right then, Travis showed up with the drinks. He set each one down, but not with the narrative he'd given them the last time. Then he turned to the man. "May I have your card, sir?"

Jessica busied herself sipping her drink, avoiding the guy's response. She half expected him to stomp off in anger, but she did see him hand over a card.

"Thank you so much," Casey said after taking a large gulp. "This is really good."

"You are welcome. I hope you ladies enjoy your evening." And off he went. No smart remark. Not even a scowl.

"Thank God." Keri sniggered, and soon everyone was laughing.

Travis came back to the table. "You ladies crack me up."

"You cracked me up when you asked that guy for his card."

"You know him?" Travis asked.

"No!" Keri smacked her hand down on the table. "Do you?"

"Nope. He comes in here now and again. If you ladies need anything else, just whistle."

Casey puckered up and made a funny sound. "Oh God. I've lost my whiffle."

Travis gave her a wink. "I'll hear you."

"I hope no one else comes over here," Keri said as she lifted her glass.

"You know, Jessica and Casey are single. Maybe they—"

"No!"

"No!" They both shrieked at the same time. Then laughed.

"I'm perfectly content with my newfound boyfriend," Casey said.

Keri stared at her. "New boyfriend?"

"Yes." Casey tossed her hair over her shoulder with flair. "I know you like him, but he belongs to me."

Keri looked at Casey like she'd grown two heads. "Excuse me?"

Casey pointed to Travis. "I won't even freeze my body. I happen to like younger men."

Jessica nearly spit out her drink. Everyone else laughed.

Travis rushed to their table. "Hey, you ladies are married right? I've got something for you to take home to your husbands."

Three of them were married, but Jessica didn't correct him. She wanted to see what Travis had.

He pulled tiny, clear objects from his pocket. Here's one for each of you. He laid the circular things on the table, one in front of each woman.

Connie picked hers up and studied it. "What is it?"

Travis took one and rolled it onto his pinky finger. "Condoms."

Jessica choked. Connie howled. Soon the entire table was in stitches. Travis, the little sucker, smirked and sauntered off.

Casey stared at hers as if she was afraid to touch it. "What the heck is it?"

"I think it's a rubber fingertip. It's used to sort papers or to count money."

Keri rolled one on her finger. " Hey look. It has bumps."

"That's for added pleasure," Connie said seriously. Everyone laughed.

"I'm taking that boy home."

"Don't forget to take…" Connie tapped Keri's finger. "…your husband's condom." That set them off again.

This was just what Jessica needed.

She couldn't remember the last time she'd had this much fun.

***

"For Christ's sake, lower your voice."

"Why. We're in an alley where drunks puke and dogs come to piss. No one can hear us."

Seth glanced down the dark alley. Carl was right, but that didn't make Seth feel any better. They had a new problem to deal with. "You forget why we're here? The blonde bitch overheard me."

"You don't have to worry about her. She's toast."

Seth glared at Carl. "She should have been." Seth was there when Carl put the bomb on the woman's car. "She escaped."

Carl stumbled back, holding up his hands. "No fucking way."

Yes, way. The blonde bitch was still alive. "She wasn't in the car."

Seth watched the expressions on Carl's face, as his confusion quickly turned to acceptance. Then dread. Yep, he was scared. Rightly so. Seth was not one to forgive, and Carl knew it. He correctly was expecting Seth to punish him. Carl's shoulders slumped, then he stood straight, ready to take whatever penance Seth was going to dish out.

"Now what?"

Seth had to admire Carl's courage. And his loyalty. But Seth also had to admit it wasn't Carl's fault. There was no reason for Seth to exhibit his authority, or vent his displeasure. How could Carl have known the bitch would take off with someone else.

"You're off the hook."

Carl's eyes looked like they might pop out of their sockets. He breathed a sigh of relief. "You can't do this without me?"

Anger simmered under Seth's skin. He didn't need anybody. He got along fine on his own. He thought about driving that point home when he remembered *he* had called Carl.

Seth tapped down his anger and gathered his thoughts. Planning and preparation would grant him victory. "We tried it your way, but you're right. I do need your help."

"I told you I was in. What you wanna do, boss?"

She should have minded her own business. The goddamn bitch had seen him. Heard him.

When it came to saving his neck, the obstacles in his way became mere nuisances. Like pests, they needed to be swatted away.

"We need a new plan."

CHAPTER 7

Jared scrubbed a hand over his face, wiping the sleep from his eyes. Five a.m. A firefighter never knew when the alarm might go off, so he had to get sleep whenever he could. The bunks in the firehouse were comfortable, so they could not be accountable for his restlessness. A beautiful blonde had earned the credit for that. Especially after he found out she wasn't married.

Of course there was a first time for everything, but his instincts had never let him down. He'd known there had to be a reason for his unexplainable attraction. Obsessing for a woman he couldn't have had damn near drove him nuts. Now, he obsessed freely in his dreams.

Ah hell. He might as well get up.

He donned the sweats he kept on the edge of the bed, slipped on his sneakers and stepped to the main room. He decided to put on a pot of coffee and wait for the shift change. As the smell of strong coffee filtered through the air, he leaned a hip against the counter and thought about the stabbing victim they'd lost last night.

Damn hoods. A mugging. The vic had told Mike he never carried more than ten dollars in his wallet. Guess because the man wore a suit, his attacker had assumed he had a wad of cash. Single, thirty, only a year older than Jared.

Christ.

"Couldn't sleep?"

Jared damn near jumped out of his skin. "Thought I was the only one up."

"Smelled the coffee," Mike said scratching his chest.

Jared took two mugs from the cabinet and poured them each a cup. Mike took his to the table and propped his big bare feet on the chair beside him.

"Thinking about last night?" Mike said before he took a sip of the hot brew.

"Yeah." Jared plopped onto the opposite chair. "He was only a year older than me."

Mike nodded. "Got you thinking about your job?"

"Naw. Not really. Hell, Mike. He was leaving a store. Not willingly heading into life threatening danger."

"Like we do every day."

Jared hadn't considered his life was being threatened every time he went out on the truck. He was simply doing his job. "I guess it goes to show it can happen anytime, anywhere."

Mike gave a nod. "There's only one thing sure in this life. We're going to die. We just don't know when."

"I don't want to know," Jared mumbled.

Mike lifted his mug. "I plan to live a long, happy life. I've got a woman to share it with now."

Yeah. Mike's schoolteacher. He was in love. Guess what they said was true. The bigger they are—the harder they fall. And Mike had fallen hard.

"Did you ever consider leaving the fire department?" Jared asked him.

"Never," Mike answered after he swallowed his coffee.

Jared felt the same way. By the way Mike was looking at him, Jared figured he better let Mike know what he was thinking.

"From the day I joined Station Eight, being a firefighter is all I've ever wanted to do. The adrenaline rush was a surprise at first. Now I thrive on it."

Mike seemed to relax. "We all do. Why else would we stay? There are a lot of ways to help people. It takes a particular individual to run into a burning building."

Jared agreed. He never considered himself a hero. But he liked the feeling he got when he saved a life. Not once had he questioned the force that drove him.

Mike narrowed his eyes. "Something else on your mind?"

"Maybe you noticed, I've been sleeping like shit."

Beep. Twang. The PA system blasted out a 911 call. Mike rose from his chair just as Cooper bounded down the hall. Jared met up with Shep at the top of the stairs. They hauled ass to the bottom where Laredo was jumping into his bunker boots.

"Let's get the lead out," Shep's voice echoed in the bay.

Jared opened the cab of the quint and climbed in. Laredo hopped into the driver's seat. The rigs arrived at the burning structure within minutes. A small market with an apartment above. Knowing Shep would want him to check the apartment first for survivors, Jared prepared himself for what he might find.

More sirens and trucks with firefighters arrived right on their tail. The Cap shouted instructions and the men hurried to obey. A pickup swerved in behind the rigs, scattering gravel across the parking lot. The driver jumped out and ran to Shep.

"I'm the owner." The guy looked like he just crawled out of bed. Guess he didn't take time to comb his hair. At least he had on clothes. He stared at the flames consuming the structure and kept running one hand over his head like he couldn't believe what he saw.

"Do you know what happened?"

"No. No. Someone drove by, saw the fire and called me. Hell, I thought it was a prank."

"Is anyone inside?"

The owner jerked his head up, gaping at the upper floor. "I rented the top floor last week. The tenant has been moving stuff in. I don't' think he's sleeping there yet. God, I hope not."

"Collins!"

"On it." As Jared turned to go check, the man behind him shouted.

"He has a private entrance in back."

Jared took off. Black smoke curled from the building. A stairway led to the top floor. Flames churned through the roof. Not a good sign. Station Nine had hoses lined around back. The lifeless, rubber-lined tubes came to life as water filled their veins. Jared darted up the steps.

"Let us get the fire under control before you go in there," one of the men yelled.

"Can't wait," Jared called back. "Possible vic inside."

Two firefighters slapped water on the roof while another hosed down the door. The windows were closed up tight. Jared swung his ax, breaking off the door knob, then he popped in the door.

The smoke was thick, and he could barely see a thing, though he could see well enough not to fall into the gaping hole shooting flames through the ceiling a few feet away. How was he going to get around this bitch?

Static came across the radio.

"Collins. Abort."

Jared froze. "Say again, Cap."

"The tenant is elsewhere. No one's inside. If you can safely confirm, do it. Otherwise, get the hell out of there."

"Copy that."

Jared took a final look. The apartment had an open floor plan. A doorway led to what he guessed to be the bathroom—the wall engulfed in flames. With most of the floor caved in, there was no place for anyone to hide. Feeling the heat beneath his feet, he figured he better get out before the section he was standing on caved in, too. He took a step backward just as the floor beneath him gave way.

The air left his lungs and a cloud of smoke filled his vision.

Pressure gripped his chest as steel bands latched around his torso.

"Thought you were a goner."

Him too.

No words could describe his moment of terror. He latched on to his life saver.

"Not today, big fella."

Mike helped him get his footing. "The tenant's not here. Let's get the fuck down."

A short while later, the flames were nothing more than hissing steam. While Cooper and Laredo rolled up the hoses, Jared stowed his gear and overheard Shep's conversation with Mike.

"Lots of speculation on how this fire started."

"Any chance the tenant smokes?"

"Nope. His kid came tearing in here like his ass was on fire. Said his dad rented the space. Then he called to make sure his dad wasn't in there."

"The fire started downstairs," Jared interrupted.

"You sure?" Shep pulled off his helmet. "The way the owner is spouting off, it seems like the landlord plans to blame the tenant."

"Unless he has access to the store downstairs, it wasn't his doing."

"Kid said his dad volunteered at the Mint Spring Fire Department. He occupies the place officially the first of the month, but the landlord let him move some stuff in early."

"Could be faulty wiring or old appliances. This store has been around a lot longer than I have," Mike added.

"It's history, now. Hope the guy had renter's insurance."

Jared glanced at the scorched timber. "Perfect location. Does a lot of business, being on the end of town. And with the interstate a mile up the road—a gold mine."

Mike kicked a smoldering hunk of wood. "You'd think the owner would put some money into maintenance and upkeep."

"That's the thing with old buildings," Shep said. "Doing that would cut into the owner's profits."

"You don't think he set the place ablaze?" Jared asked.

"I'm saying he might not want to spend money for upgrades when he could put the money in his pocket."

"He can't blame the tenant. He wasn't here, and we found nothing upstairs. It definitely started downstairs."

"Hooley will figure it out."

***

Seth shook his head as he saw the news.

Another one got away.

A bystander in his parked car. But then, just because the guy was in his car didn't mean he saw anything. He could have been waiting on someone. He could have been asleep.

"The guy was carrying stuff in. Looked like he was moving in the place. He left once and came back."

"Didn't you follow him?" Seth asked Carl.

"Sure, I did. But, like I said, he came back. Guess he slept somewhere else."

"Possibly his old apartment."

Carl cringed. "That rat trap is a shithole. Even I wouldn't stay in a place like that."

Seth glared at Carl. "Worse than prison?"

Carl shook his head. "'Bout the same, I guess. More rodents."

Seth fumed. His plan was not flowing as smoothly as it should. "I don't like loose ends."

"I know that. And I'm telling ya, there ain't no way he could have seen me."

Perhaps not. Carl was good at his game. Hell, even Seth couldn't follow Carl in the dark.

"Keep an eye on him. If he even looks in the direction of that investigator, then we'll deal with him."

"You got it, boss."

***

Jessica was watching the news on TV when there was a sharp knock on her door. She placed her ice cream carton on the table and padded over to peek through the peep hole. One of her nurses stood on the other side. Jessica flung the door open.

"Hey, Alicia, what—" Alicia had her arms wrapped around herself and she was trembling.

"Hi, Jessica. Um, are you busy?" Alicia's hand shook as she swiped a curl behind her ear. Then she did a quick, jerky look over her shoulder.

"Alicia. You look a wreck. What's wrong?"

"Can I come in?"

"Of course." Jessica stepped back, and a flustered Alicia hurried inside.

Her strained eyes darted about the room. Clearly something had happened.

"Alicia, are you okay?"

"Um, yeah. I'm just nervous."

Jessica had never seen Alicia like this. Nervous? Alicia was freaking out. "Why don't you sit down. Can I get you something to drink?"

"Do you have any alcohol?"

Okaaay. If Jess wasn't already worried about Alicia, her reply would cinch the deal. *Alcohol?* "I have some wine."

"Perfect."

"Alicia. You're shaking. Do I need to put the lock on the door?" What if Alicia was running from someone? What if someone followed her here?

Frightened eyes locked with hers. "Maybe."

Oh hell.

Jessica practically flew to the door, locked it and slid the chain in the metal slide. Of course, if someone really wanted to get in, that little thing wouldn't stop them.

She marched to the kitchen, grabbed the wine, and two glasses. She took two deep breaths to steady her own nerves.

"Have you had anything to eat?"

Alicia shook her head.

"Sit." Jessica poured wine, then went to the fridge to get some cheese and meat. Next, she grabbed a pack of crackers from the cabinet.

"I stopped at the donut shop." When Alicia started talking, even her voice was shaky. "While I was standing in line, I felt someone watching me. You know that creepy feeling you get when you know something isn't right?"

"Yeah," Jessica replied as she poured the wine.

"I looked around and no one looked suspicious. But several people were looking at me."

"You're a pretty girl, Alicia. Of course, people were looking at you. Especially men."

"Yeah. I get that all the time, but this was different." Jessica set a glass in front of Alicia and watched as she took a big gulp.

It was all Jessica could do to remain calm. *Shit.* It was up to her to keep Alicia calm. Jess hoped it was Alicia's imagination.

"It's not the first time. I've felt it before. I...I got scared and ran out of the café'. Without my donuts." Maybe she was paranoid.

"I've got cake." Jessica got up and pulled a container from the corner. "Abby brought this to work today for Stephanie's birthday, and she's on a diet. Everyone took a slice. This was left over. Too bad you were transferred to second floor. You miss out on celebrating with us."

"I like it there." Her eyes grew big when Jessica took off the lid. "Yum. Red Velvet is my favorite. And Abby makes her cakes from scratch."

At least Alicia had stopped trembling.

"Yum is right. Food—or better yet, sugar—is always a good pick-me-up when you've got problems. Chocolate is a given. But Red Velvet and cheesecake work miracles, too." Jessica licked her finger where she'd scooped icing from the container lid. She took two saucers from the cabinet, added a slice of cake, and slid the plate across the counter. "Goes good with *Cabernet.*"

"Even better." Alice took a bite and moaned. "God, this is good. Can she bake or can she bake?"

"As good as chocolate?"

"Are you kidding? Red Velvet is food for the soul."

"Mmmm," Alicia muttered and reached for a cube of cheese. Then she laughed. "I know. Good combination, right?"

"Feeling better?"

Alicia took a big gulp of wine and nodded. "Yeah. I guess it was my imagination."

"Maybe. Still, don't blow it off. Just be aware of your surroundings." Jessica came around to sit beside Alicia. "You know, when my mom was alive, Clint Eastwood was a big-time movie star. His bodyguard gave lessons on self-defense for women. My mom took the course. She said he said the most important thing was for women to be aware of what was around them. Like walking to the parking lot from the mall. Park in a well-lit area. Look for suspicious vehicles parked next to you, like vans. That kind of stuff."

"Sounds like good advice."

Jessica sipped her wine. "She worried about me and my sister. Every time we left the house, she drilled us. Didn't like it so much then, but now I'm grateful every day for her badgering."

"How long has she been gone?"

"My twenty-first birthday. She suffered for nearly a year, but she wanted to wish me happy birthday. Then passed away in her sleep that evening."

"I'm sorry, Jessica."

"God, how did we get so maudlin? It's been eight years. I still miss her, but I remember her with a smile. She wouldn't want me all weepy."

Alicia stared at her wine glass. "My mom is so far away. When I got out of college, I was lucky to find a job right away. So I stayed here."

"That doesn't happen often, but there is a high demand for nurses."

"I like it here. Mom comes to visit, or I go home when I can. It sure is nice knowing she's there. I couldn't imagine not having my mom in my life." A look of unease crossed Alicia's features. "Gosh, I'm sorry Jessica."

"Don't be. I loved my mom, and she loved me. I can talk about my mom and feel good. Don't feel bad because yours is still here. Be thankful, and see her as often as you can."

"You're the best, Jessica." Alicia leaned over for a hug.

Jessica hugged her back. When they separated, she asked, "Do you feel better than when you got here?"

Alicia held up her empty glass. "Another glass of wine might do the trick."

Jessica lifted the bottle. "I like the way you think."

Several glasses later, Jessica's ribs hurt from laughing so hard. They'd moved from the kitchen to the living room with a second bottle, and were now lounging on the floor. She gripped her stomach with one hand, and with the other, she placed her glass on the coffee table.

"You actually ate mud?" Alicia hooted. "I don't believe you."

"I swear. Cross my heart and hope to die." Jessica made a motion across her chest as she said the words.

"Your sister was mean."

"Well, to her credit, after my first taste, she smacked it out of my hand and said 'I can't believe you were going to eat that.' I was stupid. She tricked me and I fell for it."

"How old were you?"

Jessica frowned as she thought back and counted. We had just moved into the new house. Maybe four."

"Oh my God. You were a baby." Alicia refilled their glasses. "I never pictured you as a tomboy."

"You've only seen me in my nurse uniform. I climbed a tree faster than any boy. Jimmy, he lived down the lane, and Danny, he lived up on the corner; they tried, but they couldn't out do me." Jessica grinned with satisfaction.

"Boys to play with, that's why you were a tomboy."

"Those guys were closer to my sister's age. She played with dolls most of the time. I liked my firetrucks." Jessica leaned in close to whisper, but her voice was loud and strong. "I also had a crush on Jimmy."

Alicia sat up, sloshing her wine. "Speaking of which, word is you're dating one of the hot firefighters who put out the fire at the hospital."

"What? No .... I'm not."

"You hesitated."

Jessica shook her head, and quickly thought she shouldn't be doing that with the room spinning. "I met the guy twice. No, three times. And each time he was on an emergency call."

"Really? Give me details."

"You know I used my vacation watching my sister's kids. Well, Tiffany, the little stinker, called 911 to get her cat, Charlie, out of the tree. Aiden chased the cat up there."

Alicia burst into laughter. "Oh my God. That's hilarious."

"Well, the fire department came."

"For real?"

"Yes," Jessica nodded. "Jared, that's the fireman's name, gave me a lecture on how to raise my kids."

Alicia frowned. "Wait a minute. Your kids?"

Jessica shrugged. "He thought I was their mom."

Alicia took a sip of wine. "This is good stuff. You set him straight?"

"No. I was mad. Furious at him for giving me a lecture."

"Okay. When was the next time?"

"He showed up at the hospital when your car was on fire."

"Oh. That was freaky."

Seeing the fear come back to Alicia's face, Jessica felt bad for reminding her. "I'm sorry, Alicia."

"That's okay. My mom is helping me get a new one. Well, not brand new. But new for me."

"I'm just glad you weren't in it."

"You and me both." Alicia turned up her glass.

"I wish you would have told someone where you were. Nash had a stroke when we couldn't find you. God, we thought you were in that car."

"I'm sorry." Alicia looked down at her hands, twisting in her lap.

Jessica reached over and covered Alicia's hands. "Don't be. He's not your keeper."

"Nash is a good guy. I didn't realize he liked me. And I was with another guy." She looked upset, so Jessica had to ask.

"Do you like Nash?"

"Sure." Alicia shoved her long hair out of her face. "He's a dreamboat."

"Who is the other guy? The one you were with?"

"Oh, that's Greg," she replied with a wave of her hand. "He offered to buy me breakfast."

"You can tell that to Nash when you get back to work."

"What? That I left with Greg? Or that we're just friends?"

"Depends on how much you like Nash. You did say you like him."

"Duh. Yeah."

"Then tell him."

Alicia's eyes popped wide. "I can't tell Nash I like him. Gosh, what would he think?"

"Would you like to go out with him?"

"Of course."

"Then you've got to tell him something. Tell him you went with Greg to breakfast because you both were starved."

"We were."

"You've got to talk to Nash at some point. I can't believe you're being shy."

"Forget about him." Alicia scooted around to face Jessica. " Tell me what happened with fire guy?"

"Uh, that concerns Nash, too."

"Nash?"

"Yeah. When he finally found out you weren't in the car, he hugged me."

"Nash?"

"You're repeating yourself."

"Why did Nash hug you?"

"In relief, goofy. I told you he was having a stroke. We thought you were in the car. The burning car."

Alicia got a blank look on her face. Then, suddenly, she said, "Oh, I get it. Your fire guy saw Nash hug you. Maybe he got jealous."

"Ha. Fat chance."

"This time you set him straight, right?"

"Oh sure. He told me to keep my husband back. Or something like that. So no. I did not correct him."

Alicia smacked both hands down on her lap. "What is wrong with you, Jessica? You had ... Oh, wait. You said three times. Third time's a charm. Right?"

"Not exactly."

"Jessica. What the hell?" Alicia reached for the bottle and waved the other hand as she talked. "You cannot let this guy keep believing you're married."

Jessica held out her glass for a refill. "Remember the night Tiffany was sleepwalking? I called 911."

Alicia paused. "Don't tell me he was the one who showed up that night."

Jessica nodded her head. "He said something about her mom, meaning me, and Tiffany said 'Jessie's not my mom. She's Jess ie.'"

"At least someone in the family has some sense." Alicia put the bottle down. "Uh, just Jessie? Well? Does he know or not?"

"Yes. He knows I'm Tiffany's aunt."

"Woo hoo! About time. She took a sip of wine from her glass. "Then what?"

"We talked. A little."

"Enough to get things straight. Finally. So, when's the big day?"

Jessica frowned. "What do you mean?"

"When are you going out with Mr. Hot Guy?"

He didn't ask.

On their first meeting, they argued. Then the next time he'd seen her he yelled at her. The third time he'd come to her rescue. He more than likely thought her a hopeless case. Would he even want to see her again?

She certainly hoped so.

CHAPTER 8

Cooper slammed a cabinet door. Since the coffee pot was right in front of the kid, Jared eyeballed Cooper, waiting to see what he was going to do next. He opened the twin cabinet door, and after a quick scan, he slammed it too.

"Working on the door hinges, Coop?"

"Funny."

"They seem to work just fine. I could hear you from the bunk room."

Cooper opened the lower cabinet. "My turn to cook, and it looks like last shift cleaned everything out."

"What's in the fridge?"

"Not much." He stood and placed his hands on his hips.

"We can do a grocery run," Jared said.

"Mike will want chicken."

"Chicken? Thought he was more a steak and potatoes man."

"Hoss, right? I call him Hoss cause he's a big guy. My old neighbor used to watch *Bonanza*, a rerun from way back in his day. One of the cowboys was a big fella. His name was Hoss. Anyway, his favorite is fried chicken."

"Why don't you do that pasta dish with the chicken?" Jared moved in to get his coffee.

"Chicken Alfredo?"

"Nope," he replied as he lifted the pot. "The other one."

"Ahhh, you mean Chicken and Gnocchi."

"Is that the one with the red sauce?" Jared leaned his hip against the counter and blew across the top of his cup. Not that he needed to cool it. Purly habit.

"No, that's Mostaccioli."

"Tastes like lasagna."

"That's because it's made with the same ingredients. Only the noodles are different."

Jared wondered where Cooper had learned to cook. Cooper showed up at the station about two years ago. Never did own up to his background. Never volunteered any information about himself. Jared didn't ask. You'd think by now the kid would trust the guys.

"How come you know so much about cooking?"

"I grew up in a kitchen."

Vague answer.

"That explains a lot."

Immediately, the kid got his hackles bunched up. The men ribbed Cooper just for fun. Hell, they picked on everybody. But the kid was young and happened to be the newest member of the team.

"What's that supposed to mean?"

Jared held up a hand. "Hold on, pup. If you want to do a food run, let's go now."

"I told you not to call me pup."

Jared ignored him and strode to the bay. Laredo had pulled the truck through to the outside.

"Hey, where you guys off to?"

"Food run," Cooper answered.

Laredo's grin lit up his whole face. "Climb in, *amigos*." Laredo stretched his arm toward the truck. "The limo awaits. You cooking, Cooper?"

"Yep."

"What's for dinner?"

"Pasta."

Laredo rolled his eyes. "Why did I ask?"

Mike stepped through the bay door. "You guys having a meeting?"

"Hey, Hoss. You want to go on a food run?"

"If I get to pick the menu."

"No," Laredo and Jared spoke at the same time. Mike just raised his brows.

"It's always the same thing with you, Mike. It would be nice to have a little ... variety."

Cooper hiked a thumb over his shoulder. "Jared already said he wanted pasta."

"So, I have Jared to thank for you making pasta. Again," Laredo complained. "Throw some rice and beans in there, will you?"

Cooper planted his hands on his hips, "For once I'd like to have a big steak. Every time we plan steak, we get a call. I never get to eat one right off the grill."

"Since you're doing the cooking, why don't you fix what you want?"

"Thanks, big guy. But you cook the best steaks. Besides, I already agreed to make Gnocchi."

Mike's face screwed up. "What's that?"

"Pasta," Jared and Laredo said again at the same time.

Cooper placed a hand on Mike's shoulder. "It's got chicken for you, big guy. Pasta for Jared. And I'll throw in come chips and beans for you, Laredo."

"*Gracias.*"

Jared rode shot-gun. Mike and Cooper climbed into the back.

They always got a lot of stares when they took out the truck. No sirens or flashing lights, still people wanted to know where they were going. Pressed T-shirts with ACFD printed on the back, and uniform pants, they still got a lot of attention.

Cooper grabbed a shopping cart as Jared and the others strode inside the grocery store. He and Laredo did their usual surveillance, checking out the ladies. You could always find some fine-looking ladies in a grocery store. Shame most of them were mamas.

Mike headed over to the produce. He picked up lettuce and tossed it to Cooper. Those two made grocery shopping seem as if they were on a basketball court. Jared didn't mind coming along. That way he had a say in the dessert.

Just as he turned down the next aisle, he saw a blonde in a tight-fitting pair of jeans. He was about to comment to Laredo when the breath left his lungs. Damn, he needed to stop thinking about Jessica. He imagined seeing her everywhere.

"Are my eyes deceiving me?" Laredo slipped his sunglasses on top of his head, and wiggled his bushy brows. He'd zeroed in on the sexy blonde. He looked at Jared. "Well?"

"Well what?"

"I know you two didn't hit it off right away, but I thought you made up."

"What the hell are you talking about?"

Laredo flashed a grin and pointed. "Her."

Jared looked to his right and two aisles over stood another sexy blond. He recognized her right before she pushed her buggy out of sight.

Jessica.

"Yeah," Laredo breathed. "I thought so."

"Shut up, Laredo."

A dozen things raced through his mind. *It's her. She's really here.* He continued to stare at the empty spot like an idiot.

"I don't know you." Laredo turned his head away. "You're behaving like a man I do not know."

"Go away." Jared slowly stepped to the aisle where Jessica had gone. The last time he'd seen her had been when she called 911 for her niece.

Her niece.

Well, didn't that just make him feel all fuzzy?

"Excuse me, miss."

Jared jerked his gaze up to a man standing next to Jessica. *Shit.* He'd thought she was alone. Who was this joker?

"Yes?" Jessica answered the guy.

"I wanted to say, first that I'm not a stalker. But I couldn't help but notice your perfume. It's smells really good."

What the fuck. Some guy stepped right up to her? She didn't know him? Was this guy trying to pick her up? Jared decided to listen in on their conversation.

The guy plastered a big fat smile on his face. Jared immediately wanted to wipe it off with his fist.

"Thank you." Jessica was being nice. Too nice.

"I didn't mean to bother you. You know, some women you smell their perfume a mile away. But yours ... it kind of sneaks up on you. I mean, it's not strong, it's ... well, it's nice. Very nice. I've passed you twice and I just had to say something."

Jessica grinned. Dammit.

"I've had other people tell me the same thing."

I'll bet.

"I really like it. What's the name of it?"

Are you kidding me? This guy was trying to pick her up. In the grocery store.

Well hell. Wasn't he and Laredo guilty of the same thing?

"Touch."

"Pardon me?"

"Touch is the name. Like, touch me."

Oh hell, no.

The man blinked.

No asshole. She did not tell you to touch her.

"It's T-O-U-C-H." Jared went along in his head as she spelled each letter. "Touch. And I love it for the very reason it lingers. It's not strong, but you can't buy it north of South Carolina."

"Really?" The guy took a step closer.

Jared fisted his hands.

"Yes. I found it in Florida years ago. There is a perfume outlet in Myrtle Beach that sells it, too. Other than that, you won't find it in Virginia."

"I'll be."

Give me a fucking break.

It was time Jared made his presence known.

He reached for a can of what-ever-the-hell was in front of him to keep his hands from reaching for the fool's neck. Jessica had her back to Jared. He walked up to her, giving a glare to the asshat standing in front of her, making it clear that he should get lost.

"Hi there."

She spun to face him. Her eyes got big, then she smiled.

Thank fuck.

"Hi yourself."

Jared glanced at the guy who had taken the hint and was walking away.

He smiled at Jessica. "Fancy meeting you here."

She laughed. The sound carrying a reaction over his skin. He liked it.

And yes, she smelled good.

"I would say we have to stop meeting like this, but I'm glad to see you."

"Are you?" she cooed. Damn, she was flirting with him.

He felt like a teenager. "Yes."

"What are you doing in here?"

"Getting some grub for dinner tonight. The guys make a regular run for groceries, now and then."

"There are others with you?"

"Yeah."

And if they know what's good for them, they'll keep their distance.

"You know, we can fix this thing of running into each other. How about you go out with me. Nothing fancy. Just a drink. Meet my friends at The Pitt Stop."

"I'd like that."

His tense shoulders relaxed. "Good."

"Hey Hollywood!" Jared jerked toward Cooper's voice. There he was, down by the check-out.

"Guess the guys are ready to go."

"Hollywood?" The smile on her face was teasing.

"I'll explain when I pick you up." He reached for his cell. "Here. Put your number in there. I'll give you a call."

Jessica took his phone and punched some buttons, then handed it back.

"I look forward to hearing from you."

Jared grinned, thinking of the cat and the canary. "You won't have to wait long."

"We'll see."

No, not long at all. This woman lit a fire in his gut. He was actually excited about calling her.

Real soon.

CHAPTER 9

Jared must have pulled his cell phone out of his pocket a dozen times yesterday, speculating on how long he should wait before he called Jessica. A few hours? A day? Fate had a way of making those decisions.

The sun rode high by the time he got home. There had been moments he doubted if the team would make it back to the station. After the car accident on Route 250, all hell had broken loose. Every station in and outside the county had been on the scene.

A tire blew out on a car, causing the driver to lose control. He'd been headed up Skyline Drive, which was lined with trees on both sides. At least the guy hadn't made it to the Parkway, or they might never have gotten the fire under control.

Even so, when the car had caught fire, it was like a zipline shooting up the mountain. The dry woods torched in an instant. All units were called in. Every firefighter, every volunteer, every man available.

Station Eight fought the fire for an hour, then swapped out and the next group would take over. The brief moments when they could remove their helmets were precious, the much-needed water soothing to his dry throat. It seemed no time at all before it was their turn again to battle the flames. Each group had rotated until the fire was finally contained.

He was dragging ass when they had gotten back to the station last night. Or rather, the wee hours of this morning.

He stepped into his garage and considered stripping right there. He was exhausted, smelled like a chimney, and couldn't wait to take another shower. He could have stood under the spray at the firehouse until he fell asleep, but he'd wanted to go home to his own bed.

He pulled his phone out of his pocket and thought about Jessica. And the call he'd planned to make. The choice had been taken from him when the 911 call had come through.

Since then, there had been no time to think of anything but the fire roaring through the forest. He kicked off his shoes and padded to the bedroom. He placed his cell on the top of his chest of drawers along with his keys and wallet. He would call Jessica when he got his second wind.

An hour later, Jared sat at his kitchen counter feeling almost human again. The steam from the shower helped to clear his lungs, but the smell of charred wood still lingered in his nose. He'd already downed one glass of tea and was working on the second one. The roast beef sandwich disappeared so fast he had to make another one.

Man, he was beat. Forest fires were never easy. The longer the fight, the more ground you think you lose. They must have been successful; although, at the time, it was like working the same piece of ground.

With his stomach full, and his throat calmed down, now might be a good time to call Jessica. He ran a hand thought his wet hair as he padded to the bedroom where he'd left his cell phone. He opened the screen and checked the time, 12:07. He scrolled through his texts and messages, nothing important. He found Jessica's number and hit the call button.

One ring. Two rings.

His belly did a funny flutter thing. Hell. Maybe he should have waited until he got some sleep.

Three —

"Hello?"

The bottom fell out of his stomach. She sounded all sexy and sweet.

"Uh, Hi, Jessica. This is Jared."

"I figured. I sent myself a text when I entered my number in your contacts so I'd have your number."

"Oh." He hadn't even noticed. "Did I call at a bad time?"

"No. I'm off today. How about you?"

Did he go into the whole spill about the car and the woods? He'd rather yank her through the phone and talk to her in person. *Shit.* He needed to go to bed.

"Did you hear about the car wreck on Afton that started a forest fire?"

"Yes, I did. I was on duty when the driver came into the hospital. Were you working that fire?"

"Yeah. All night." Jared raised a hand and massaged the back of his neck.

"I was worried."

"About me?"

"Yes, and everyone else. Everything is so dry now."

"Yeah, went up like a torch."

"Are you okay?"

Tired. Worn out. Good. "Yeah, I'm good. Could use some sleep."

"Is the fire out?"

"It's under control, now. But there's a big cloud of smoke hanging over the valley."

"I saw it. It's terrible."

"You don't want to stay outside too long. You might want to wear a mask."

"How long do you think it will last?"

"I'm afraid it's going to be here for a while. At least until it rains or we get some heavy winds."

"You must be exhausted. Did you get any sleep?"

"Not yet."

She sighed. "You called me first?"

"Yeah, I guess I did. I told you I would call."

"That's nice."

"Hey, what do you say we give this a go and get together? Have a real conversation face to face."

"I'd like that."

"I have Thursday and Friday off. Some of the guys are going to The Pitt Stop, so I thought I'd call. Mike's taking Cassie. She's a schoolteacher. I think you'll like her." Maybe that way Jessica wouldn't feel pressured, or awkward, than if the two of them were alone.

"Sounds like fun. I'm off Friday and the weekend."

Talk about pressure. The weight on his chest lifted, and he hadn't even realized it was there.

"Great. Does seven-thirty sound okay? We can get dinner there."

"Sure. I'll be ready."

Jared grabbed a pen and some paper. "What's your address?" She told him and he wrote it down.

This was happening.

It surprised him how much he was looking forward to it.

***

Slow days were few and far between, but today Jared appreciated the slower pace, especially after being up all night last shift. Four hours at the station, not one call from dispatch. Usually by now they at least heard a minor scrape of some sort come across the scanner. No calls about the cloud of smoke floating above the county.

Jared decided to work on the inventory. Laredo had the radio blaring like always, which suited Jared fine. Cooper was taking his turn again, in the kitchen. By the look on Mike's face, Cooper was cooking something good.

Mike inhaled. "Mmm mmm, oven fried chicken."

"How do you know it's in the oven. Fried chicken means frying pan. Fried chicken in an oven. Who ever heard of such a thing?"

"Not the way Cooper fixes it."

Jared shook his head. "Shep still holed up in his office?"

"Yep. Been in there since he came in at five, according to Greg."

Greg worked the previous shift. Sometimes he'd hang around and ride shotgun with Mike on the squad. Cap locked up in his office for hours wasn't good.

"Wonder if he has an update on the Wimer explosion."

"Speak of the devil." Mike gave a nod over Jared's shoulder.

A gray SUV pulled up in front of the bay door. *Hooley*. So much for the day being dull. The last time the fire-investigator had come to the station he'd brought bad news.

A few weeks ago, five units from five houses were scheduled at the Wimer property for a training exercise. Five minutes into the drill, the house exploded like a fiery tornado. Unplanned, and should not have happened. The damn explosion had taken everyone by surprise. Firefighters scurried about the debris-littered earth, battling flames and dragging wounded men to safety. It was horrendous. But the real nightmare had come when Hooley suspected the explosion had been deliberate, and some maniac was targeting firefighters.

"Hooley," Mike greeted him first.

"Mike. Jared."

"Got any more news on the explosion?"

"I don't have a lot to add, but I still think you guys should be on alert."

Didn't need to tell him twice. Jared loved to play around, but when it came to his job, he took it quite seriously. Hooley had told them an arsonist was pretending to be a firefighter. That created a whole ton of questions. Not to mention it made the guy a lot more difficult to catch. If the perpetrator was walking in and out of firehouses like he belonged, the bastard could sabotage anything right before their eyes.

The police department Captain liked to throw his weight around, but Hooley had set him straight when he asked for Chuck to work with the investigation. Said Chuck was the only one in the police department who thought with the head on his shoulders. Jared would've liked to have seen that.

Chuck believed firefighters were being targeted. Why would anyone hold a grudge against a firefighter? Hell. They were the ones trying to put *out* the fires.

"Where's Shep?"

"In his office," Mike replied.

Jared watched Hooley climb the stairs to the top level. "Wonder why he's here," he said out loud.

"Shep will tell us."

Jared turned to Mike. "They still have the Wimer property roped off. How do you feel about a road trip?"

"We covered that ground pretty thorough last time. Doubt we'd find anything else."

"I guess you're right. I hope to hell he's wrong about some nut job coming after firefighters."

Mike's expression quickly turned to anger. "I wish the cocksucker would show his face."

Jared mentally shuddered. The perp wouldn't stand a chance going up against the big guy. Mike bench-pressed double his weight and had arms the size of hams to prove it.

"At least Hooley has Chuck helping with the investigation."

"Did you know Chuck turned down a promotion so he could play detective for Hooley?"

Jared was stunned. "Turned down— Is he nuts?"

"Well, I guess turned down isn't exactly the right word. Delayed. Hooley figures if Chuck stays in uniform, he has access to traffic. A traffic cop needs no explanation for pulling over a car."

"Yeah. Chuck mentioned he was looking for out of state cars—cars that weren't part of the normal routine around here. With the interstates connecting in our county, there's always out of state cars showing up."

"But then they leave. If there is a suspicious character, or an unusual car hanging around longer than the norm, Chuck will notice. Whether it's a routine stop or something suspicious, if he's in uniform, he'd just be a cop doing his job."

Made sense to Jared. "Under cover, so to speak."

"I guess."

"Well, Hooley did say, more eyes might see something different. Chuck will be good for a detective job."

"My blood still boils that I didn't notice a stranger at the training site. He should have stood out." Mike's jaw snapped from his clenched teeth.

"How could we see anything when all hell broke loose. Shit, we were damn lucky no one else got seriously hurt. "Have you seen Ryan lately?"

"The place on his leg where they took out that hunk of metal is heeling well. He's still in a wheelchair, but doing good."

"Last I saw him, he couldn't recall anything after the explosion scorched his eyebrows. He was right on top of the blast. He's a lucky SOB. I'm glad he's going to be okay."

"With time. He has one hell of an attitude. Can't say I would be, Jared. I'd want to kill the bastard who set it up."

Me too.

"His wife is dealing with a lot."

"She's a good woman."

"Seems like it. They make a good couple. I'm glad we went to see them."

Mike stared at the wall in front of him for several seconds. "Takes a special woman to put up with our chosen profession."

Jared thought about that for a minute. Guess Cassie was okay with Mike being a firefighter. How would Jessica feel about him—

Now why would he think a dumb question like that? It wasn't as if he was planning a future with her.

"You know Mike, if you don't treat Cassie right, I'll be right here waiting—"

The growl that came from Mike would be laughable if he didn't look so damn scary.

"You like it here at Station Eight?"

Jared threw up his hands in defense. "Hold on, big guy. You know I'm kidding."

"Cassie is mine. And soon the world will know it."

Did that mean he was going to put a ring on Cassie's finger? Jared damn sure wasn't about to ask. Not right now, anyway. He turned the subject back to safer ground.

"I never want to see a training site go bad again like that one."

"Let's hope Hooley and Chuck find this asshole before he kills someone."

"Like Hooley said, if a man goes to the trouble of stealing gear from a fire station, and wears it during a fire exercise, he'll do just about anything."

"If this guy is a pro, Jared, we have to watch our backs."

An uneasy chill quivered down Jared's spine.

CHAPTER 10

Mike and Laredo were members of his team, yet Chuck rated right up there with them as his most trusted buddies. The four of them were more at home fighting fires and chasing criminals than sitting on their asses, twiddling their thumbs.

Still, they needed to unwind, and their favorite place to do that was The Pitt Stop.

By the time Jared and Jessica arrived, the club was packed. On Friday nights, people didn't waste time starting off their weekend.

Jared wound his way thought the press of bodies, holding tight to Jessica's hand. He didn't dare let go in this crowd, stomping to the loud beat of some line dance number.

Christ. Who started that crap?

That's all people did anymore. He liked to hold a soft woman, real close, go for a slow sway, with her and him sealed together from head to toe. Before the night was over, he planned to do just that.

Normally bars were a playground, where he zeroed in on babes in short skirts and tight shirts, revealing lots of flesh and a promise of scoring. Once females discovered his profession, he didn't need a pick-up line of big fire hoses. The women were too eager to find out for themselves.

Tonight, he brought a date. Tonight, Jessica was the only woman on his mind. The guys were sure to rag him about that. Given his past, bringing candy to the candy store was way out of character.

In jeans and a button-down shirt, he looked pretty good tonight. Jessica was a knock-out in her short skirt. He could barely take his eyes off her long, long legs. When she'd opened the door to her apartment, he damn near swallowed his tongue. He'd hurried her out of there. If he'd stayed too long, he'd have her on her back in no time. It was their first date. He had to give a good impression. Besides, if things went the way he planned, he'd have her out of her clothes before the night ended, anyway.

Laredo spotted them first. "Hey, *amigo*. And the lovely *señorita*." He went into a spill of Spanish that had to be sexual flirting. Jared always got a kick out of Laredo hitting on women. This time, his gut didn't like it. "Back off, Casanova."

"But Jessica and I are old friends." He leaned close to Jessica. "I hear you are *Tia* Jessica."

She smiled at Laredo, and the green knot in Jared's gut tightened. "I can see where you thought I was Tiffany's mom."

"You would make a lovely—"

"Enough, Laredo. Jessica is my date."

Jared ignored the cocky gleam in Laredo's eyes.

"Bucket of beers?" Mike called out. Then he signaled the waitress.

Jared pointed to Mike, thinking she would remember him from the night she called 911. "Jessica, you know Mike."

"Hello, Jessica. How did you end up with this—"

Jared interrupted, "And this is Chuck. He's a police detective." Uh, maybe mentioning Chuck was a detective was too soon, but it wouldn't matter to Jessica.

"Hi, Jessica."

"Hello, Mike, and Chuck."

"You like beer? Or would you rather have something else?" Mike asked.

"What you're drinking is fine."

"Beer it is. Brittany is bringing another bucket."

Just then, the waitress lifted a silver bucket, full of ice and beer, onto the high table.

"That was fast," Jessica said.

"We're in here a lot. The ladies take care of us."

Chuck nearly choked. Jared glared at him. Single guys' minds stayed in the gutter, most of the time. Jared had meant the comment to be innocent. The girls did cater more to the first responders.

Jessica laughed. "I'm not touching that one."

So, she had caught on. "These guys are full of themselves. Don't pay any attention to them."

"Oh, I don't know. I might hear some good stories."

Jared loosened up. Evidently Jessica was comfortable enough to join in the teasing. He lifted a beer and handed it to Jessica. Then he took another one for himself. "I'll get the next round." Normally, Jared nursed one beer all night. He wasn't much of a drinker. Mostly, he joined in the fun while everyone else drank themselves stupid.

Mike raised his bottle. "To Jessica." He clinked the neck of his bottle to hers.

"Why thank you."

The others did the same. Jessica seemed to fit right in.

"Am I the only female with you guys, tonight?"

"You are not with these yahoos," Jared quickly answered. "You're with me."

"Cassie is with her mom, tonight," Mike said.

"Cassie?"

"His woman," Chuck said.

"I was going to say my girlfriend."

"She's his woman," Jared agreed.

It was perfect timing. The band played a slow song. "I believe this is our song, my lady."

"On your best behavior, Jared?"

"Can it, big guy." Jared took Jessica's hand and led her into the middle of the dancers. He'd been looking forward to this all evening.

He pulled Jessica in close, from shoulder to hip. She smelled delicious. For a quick second, he imagined her lying in his bed. All sweet smelling and sexy as hell. He gave himself a mental shake, steering away from sexual fantasies. She relaxed into his arms, and they swayed to the music. Finally. Jessica. In his arms.

"You like country music?" he asked.

"I like all kinds."

Immediately, he wished he'd kept his mouth shut. A rush of cool air hit him where her head had been. He wanted to grab the back of her head and bring her forward, urging her cheek next to his heart. She fit him perfectly. He ignored the nagging at the back of his neck, that she felt a little too perfect.

He didn't have to worry, for she buried her face into his shoulder. Like a rabbit, rubbing its nose to get cozy. He glanced down, and his lips brushed her temple.

Damn.

He was ready to grab Jessica and take her the hell out of there right fucking now.

He was sporting wood, for Christ's sake. She had to feel it. The guys could take a flying leap. He was leaving.

Calm down. This is our first date.

Jessica felt like a million bucks. He tried distracting himself. The firehouse. He and Cooper stocked the supplies in the—

Her fingers stroked the back of his neck.

Fuck.

Well, yeah. He'd like— *Shit Jared. Don't be a dick.*

He rested his arms at her waist, trying to ignore her cushy breasts against his chest. He tensed. Any moment now, sweat would trickle down his temple.

Jessica raised her head and met his gaze. "Jared. Are you okay?"

Never, and he meant *never*, had a woman affected him this way. Normally, he had to push the females away. Why was he acting like a teenager with his first hard-on?

"I'm trying to be a good guy, Jessica, but I can't help how much you turn me on."

She giggled.

Giggled.

He looked past her shoulder. "Not what I expected."

"I'm not laughing at you."

"Coulda fooled me."

"It's just that you're so cute when you pout."

"Pout?"

"I suppose you imagined I'd fall at your feet. Behave like a foolish girl who is taken with your good looks. I'm not like other women."

That was for damn sure. He took a breath and inhaled her sensual fragrance. "If you were, I wouldn't be acting like this."

She tilted her head. "Like what?"

"There's something about you that draws me. I'm very attracted to you."

"And that's new?"

"You bet it is. This place is full of sexy women. But the only one I want to look at is you." Even in the darkened bar, he could see her face flush. "It's not flattery. I was attracted to you even when I thought those kids were yours. I thought you were married."

A big grin lit her face. "I'm glad we got that sorted out."

Me too.

"Would you like to go someplace a little quieter?"

She almost looked shy when she nodded.

The second the song ended, he took her hand and led her to the booth. He planned to grab her coat and head out. When they got back to the table, Jessica's phone went off. He used the time to cool down. There was no reason to act like a wild stallion.

"I'll be right there." Jessica turned frightened eyes to him.

His gut twisted. "What is it?"

"Alicia. I have to go. She's hysterical. Someone broke into her apartment."

"I'm going with you."

Jared drove double time to Alicia's apartment. Once there, Jessica raced up the stairway, with him hot on her heels.

"Alicia," she called out as she knocked on the apartment door. "It's me, Jessica. I'm here." She knocked harder. "Alicia, open the door. Jared is with me. Please—"

The sound of a chain scraping a latch, then the door opened. A hurling body slammed into Jessica.

"Thank God!" The woman was sobbing uncontrollably.

Jared didn't like the idea of a burglar lurking close. "Let's get out of the hallway, shall we?"

He guided the two women inside, and ... let out a low whistle. The room was a mess. Cushions off the couch, furniture turned over, obviously an intruder had entered Alicia's apartment.

He closed the door and noticed the chain looked securely attached. No splintered wood. No sign of forced entry. So how had the burglar gotten inside?

"Alicia. Calm down. Tell me what happened?"

"Nash dropped me off. He's been taking me to work and bringing me home since my car burned."

So this was the nurse whose car caught fire at the hospital.

When I came up stairs ... The door was still locked. I always lock the door." Her voice rose with anxiety. "I freaked, Jessica. I saw this and I freaked!"

"We're here now," Jessica tried soothing the girl.

"Did you call the police?" Jared asked.

Alicia's eyes were wild as she jerked her head to him. She grabbed Jessica's arms as if she was drowning. "No. After what happened to my car ... I don't know. I ... I called you."

"That's okay, Alicia. I'm here. Remember I told you about Jared?"

"The fire guy?"

"Yes. This is him."

Jared smiled, hoping to ease her tension. "Are you okay? Did you see the person who did this?"

Alicia shook her head. "No. Oh my God. I didn't look to see if he was still here."

Seeing the woman was about to become hysterical again, Jared quickly tried to reassure her. "There's no one here. But, is it okay if I go through your rooms to be sure?"

Christ, he hoped the bastard was gone—for Alicia's sake. As for him, if he caught the SOB, he'd break the guy's neck.

Alicia nodded.

After a thorough search, Jared found no one. The only room that had been turned upside down was the living room. Clearly this was an attempt to scare Alicia.

Jared took out his phone. What he needed was help from a cop he trusted.

Chuck.

Jared called Mike first. Not only was Chuck working quietly on the arson and accidents, but he was good friends with Mike.

"Hey, Mike. It's me."

"What the hell is going on? You guys okay?"

Jared glanced at the bedroom doorway and slipped inside. "We're good. I need some confidential police advice."

"Doesn't sound to me like you're good."

"Later. Is Chuck still with you?"

"Nope. He left the same time I did. I'm on my way home."

"Can I get his number?"

"Hang on. Let me pull over."

Jared glanced around the bedroom. Everything seemed to be in its place. It didn't look like the living room.

Mike came back on the phone. After getting Chuck's number, Jared quickly dialed again.

"Detective Winston."

Thank God, he answered.

"Chuck. This is Jared. I need a favor."

"Stand in line."

Jared didn't have time to waste. "Sorry, this is important."

"It better be more than a parking ticket."

"I need your help. It's urgent."

Chuck must have recognized the anxiousness in Jared's tone. "You've got my attention."

Jared had a straight line of sight from the bedroom into the living room. The girls couldn't hear him. "Jessica's friend is in trouble."

"The chick who was with you tonight?"

"Yeah. That was Jessica. A subject for another day."

"Okay. What do you need?"

"It's her friend, Alicia. She works at AMC. Some guy has been stalking her, and he just broke into her apartment."

"Did she call the police?"

"No. Um … it's … touchy. We need someone we can—"

"Where are you?" Jared hesitated, then gave Jessica's address. "I'll be there in ten."

Jared left the bedroom and found Jessica still at Alicia's side. "I have a friend. I think he can help. First, I'm getting you girls out of here."

He'd turned on the coffee pot as soon as they got to Jessica's. Coffee was the wrong thing for any of them to be drinking. They were wired enough as it was. He thought Alicia would be calmer at Jessica's apartment. He didn't know what else to do while they waited for Chuck.

When a knock sounded on the door, Alicia damn near jumped out of her skin. "Who is it?"

Jared made sure he looked through the peephole to appease the woman. "My friend." He watched her for a moment to make sure she accepted the idea before he opened the door.

"Hey, man. Thanks for coming."

"You said urgent." Chuck caught sight of the two women on the couch.

"You remember Jessica." Jared held out a hand toward her. "This is her friend, Alicia." He didn't know her last name. "This is the policeman I told you about."

"Hello, Alicia." Chuck didn't even move.

Alicia stared at Chuck as if she was sizing him up.

"It's nice to meet you, even under these circumstances. I heard you might need some help."

Jessica spoke up, "Can I offer you some coffee. Or iced tea?"

"There's cold beer, if you'd rather not have coffee." Jared thought they all could use one.

"I was on my way home when Jared called," Chuck answered Jess. "A beer sounds nice." His steady tone and warm smile seemed to make Alicia relax.

"I'll get it." Jessica stood, but Alicia had a tight grip on Jessica's hand. He didn't think Alicia would let go, but she gave Jessica a nod as if silently telling her she was okay.

"Can I have one, too?" Alicia surprised them all, except maybe Chuck.

"Of course. It might be good for you." Jessica strode to the kitchen, and Jared quickly followed close behind. With the open concept of Jessica's apartment, it was as if they all were in the same room.

"Mind if I sit down?" Chuck asked Alicia. When she gave a nod, he took the chair next to the couch.

"May I call you Alicia?" Chuck's quiet, strong voice held her attention, but at the same time soothed.

Alicia nodded.

"Are you all right?"

She nodded, again.

"Were you hurt?"

She shook her head no. Jared locked gazes with Jessica, wondering if Alicia would talk. Jessica got glasses while he got the beers from the fridge.

"Should we wait here? Give them a chance to talk?" Jared asked Jessica.

"I don't know," she whispered back.

They waited and watched.

"Alicia, you don't have to tell me anything you don't want to. You don't have to talk to me at all. But sometimes, when a person gets a jolt like you have, the shock lessens when we talk about it. Then, the problem doesn't seem as big."

If Jared didn't know better, he'd think Chuck was coming on to Alicia. Charm oozed out of him in spades. But then, he most likely was trying to make her comfortable. She'd already been scared to death.

"The good thing is, you have friends to help you. Jared is my friend. He called me and told me you needed help. I'm just here to listen. You can tell me anything you like."

The entire time Chuck spoke, Alicia stared at him in a daze. Good Lord, the woman was spell-struck. At least it was better than the terror he'd seen on her face a short while ago.

"I like the sound of your voice."

Bingo.

Jared released a sigh. Evidently Jessica had been holding her breath, too.

"You do?" Chuck asked gently. Then he said, "Thank you."

"It's nice. If you are Jared's friend, I guess you're a nice man."

Chuck's face lit up like a neon sign, and he gave her a smile to make any woman tear off her panties.

"I try to be a nice guy. My mother taught me manners, and to respect women." Chuck obviously had experience with this sort of thing. If the situation weren't so dire, Jared would have laughed. This was probably Chuck's way of gaining her trust. Alicia had been hysterical earlier. Maybe Chuck didn't want to set her off again.

"I miss my mom."

"When Chuck looked toward them, Jessica quickly spoke up, "Alicia's mom lives in Tennessee.""

"Tennessee is only a few hours away. I bet you visit your mom every chance you get."

Again, Alicia nodded.

"You can call me Chuck, if you like."

"Okay."

Jessica bumped Jared with her elbow and handed him a beer. She took the others to Alicia and Chuck.

"Chuck, did you know Alicia's car caught on fire at the hospital?"

He turned back to Alicia. "That was your car?"

Another nod.

"I'm sorry. Perhaps it was something mechanical, but won't ever happen again."

"No. The police said someone did it. Set it on fire, I mean."

Chuck knew before this. They had discussed it. Jared was sure Chuck wouldn't mention that to Alicia.

Jessica spoke up. "This could be just a hunch, but ..." Jessica turned to Jared. "Jared and I wondered if the same guy who broke into Alicia's apartment could have been the one to set it."

"Dumb luck I wasn't in it," Alicia said distractedly. "It's only two years old."

"What do you mean, dumb luck?" Chuck asked.

Alicia recounted the entire story while fiddling with the bottle in her hands. Chuck was working with Hooley in the fire department, so he was familiar with most of what Alicia elucidated. He would know if the device on her car was like the one used at the training site.

"Alicia, do you mind if I ask you some more questions?"

"Sure. I mean, go ahead."

"Why didn't you call the police? Instead of Jessica."

"I was too scared. Jessica is the first person I thought of, and I knew she was dating a fire guy. So, he had to be safe, right? This stalker could be anyone. I didn't know what to do."

Jared was glad Alicia had accepted him. He interrupted, "She had to get away from there. We brought her here to Jessica's apartment."

"What if he's out there?" Alicia cried. "What if he followed us? I don't want to get Jessica into trouble."

Chuck covered Alicia's hand and spoke in that calming voice that could have melted stone. "Leave that to me. I don't want you to worry. Okay?"

Alicia looked at Chuck with doe-awed eyes, and calmed immediately. "Okay."

"I need to make a call. I'll step over there for a moment." Chuck waited for Alicia to absorb his words, then he went to the kitchen.

"Oh, Jessica. I'm sorry. I didn't know what else to do. I told you someone was following me."

"Shhh. I know. That's okay, Alicia. Chuck will sort this out."

"I'm sorry I ruined your date." She glanced to Jared, then back to Jessica.

Jared felt the need to speak up. "There's no need to apologize. I'm glad I was with Jessica when you called."

Jessica raised her gaze to him. Their eyes met and a warm sensation speared his chest. Damn, she was beautiful, and she was looking at him as if he was her everything. A wave of lust gripped him in the gut.

Chuck rejoined them in the living room. "The police are going to your apartment." They will check for fingerprints and go over everything with a fine-tooth comb."

"Oh." Alicia dropped her head. Chuck sat on the couch beside her.

"It will be all right. They won't break anything or—"

Her head jerked up. "Oh, it's not that. I have um ... personal stuff."

Chuck grinned. "There will be women there too. They'll handle the female things."

Alicia's face went from pink to fire-engine red. For a quick moment, Jared wondered what she had that she didn't want anyone to see. He shrugged off the thought.

"Is there anything there you need? By need, I mean absolutely must have. Life threatening, like insulin."

"You believe me?" Alicia's big eyes locked with Chuck's. "I've had this creepy feeling for a while now. I'd be walking down the street, and the hair would stand on my neck. You know, the kind of feeling when you know someone is watching you."

"Yes, Alicia. I believe you. And tonight, your apartment is proof. Now, is there anything there you cannot live without?"

She shook her head. "No."

"Anything you need you can get from me," Jessica said.

"Next question. Is there any place you can stay for a while?"

"Right here," Jessica said firmly.

"No. I mean away from the city. Relatives?"

"Are you kidding? My mom would freak? There isn't anyone else." Alicia chewed on the end of her fingernail. "I don't want to bother Jessica."

"It's no bother."

"I'd rather she stay somewhere that has no connections."

The first thing Jared thought of was his brother. Perhaps—

"I know a place." All eyes turn to Chuck. "It's my uncle's place. Eighty acres that join the National Forest."

CHAPTER 11

Several miles out of town, Chuck took the lead. He'd been behind Jared looking for anyone who might be following them. They drove through Deerfield to a lane marked 'private'. Chuck unlocked the gate and motioned them through. The mile-long lane, lined with trees on both sides, opened up to a space with a nice cabin planted right in the middle of the lot. Hell, it looked more like a house than the country shack Chuck described. Jared shoved the gearshift into park, then got out and opened the truck door for the girls. Alicia wasn't going anywhere without Jessica, and Jessica wasn't going anywhere without him.

"This is it." Chuck pulled a set of keys from his pocket and strode to the log cabin.

Alicia shivered as she and Jessica followed Chuck up the pathway to the empty house belonging to his uncle.

"We have running water, electricity, most of the comforts you'd find in your apartment. You won't be able to turn the lights on until I go to the circuit breaker out back. I want to close all the blinds, too."

"Do you think it's safe to turn on the lights?" Alicia's eyes were haunted, and she tensed up even more at Chuck's words.

"We're in the mountains. The lights won't be unexpected. As for the blinds, there shouldn't be anyone out here, but no sense in advertising your presence."

"Do you think he followed us?"

"No," Chuck answered clearly and directly. "Whoever it was, he missed you. You did the right thing by calling Jessica and going with them. I didn't see anyone following us."

That seemed to calm Alicia a bit. Jared wondered how Jessica was holding up. She had jumped right in and took care of Alicia like a mother hen. Kind, attentive to her friend in need ... another quality that impressed him.

The girls had been quiet on the drive. Jared liked the mountains. Fresh air, green trees, and given the chance, he could lose himself in nature's beauty. When they stepped inside the cabin, Jared gawked at the picturesque space. Whoever had designed this layout had done a magnificent job. An open room, the living area was separated from the kitchen with a counter that blended the room as one charming space. Windows on the far side opened to majestic mountains and stars in a dark sky. With a large stone fireplace, wood logs for a wall, the place was incredible. Definitely a man cave. Jared would move in here in a minute.

Even the furniture had been handmade, possibly from the same logs as the cabin itself. Only the kitchen looked modern. Because of the appliances, he supposed.

Chuck was a hunter. He showed them his trophies, animal heads and such. Jared didn't kill animals. Not that he was gun-shy or weak. He just preferred other sports. Hunting had never interested him.

Hunting for a criminal like the asshat who had a grudge with the fire department, he'd have no problem putting the fear of God into that man.

"I like your idea of a *cabin*," he said to Chuck.

"My uncle believed in being comfortable, and he made this stuff himself."

"It shows."

"Only one bedroom, though. He liked sleeping out here in the main room."

"I can see why." Tall windows covered the upper level, giving plenty of light to the big room.

"The bedroom is back here." Chuck led Alicia to the back, Jessica followed. Their voices dulled as Jared studied the detail of the room. Large beams crossed the ceiling. Chuck's uncle must have been a hell of a carpenter.

"You'll be safe here. Nothing to worry about," Chuck told Alicia.

"I don't want to stay by myself."

"I don't blame you," Jessica said. "I'll stay with you."

Well, that was unexpected.

She turned to Jared with pleading eyes. Was she asking him for his understanding? Or did she want him to stay, too?

"If it will make you feel better, I can stay tonight. I'll have to get back tomorrow morning for my next shift, though."

"That would be great." Jessica's smile was like a lighthouse beacon. And didn't that just make him tingle all the way down to his toes.

"This couch pulls out," Chuck said stepping to a big leather sofa. "There's plenty of sheets and stuff. I'll turn on the hot water tank. Give it a bit to heat up. There's always coffee. You can raid the cabinets for something to eat. Not sure what's up there. Been a while since I've been here."

"How often do you come out here?" Jared asked.

"Not as often as I'd like. At least once a month to check on things. I stay as long as I can; sometimes it's only one night. I try to stay two weeks in November and a week or two in January. Make a lot of day trips during the summer and fall."

"Man, I'd live out here."

Chuck laughed. "Me too, if my job wasn't so demanding. When I retire, I plan on living here."

"It's beautiful, Chuck," Jessica said.

Women normally wouldn't like to live this far from the city. Jared had figured Jessica was one of those women, but she seemed to like this place.

"Thanks. You guys get settled. I'll head on back." Chuck gave a nod to Jared, which meant he wanted to talk privately. Then Chuck stepped to Alicia. "You'll be safe here."

"I don't know what to say. This place is beautiful. Thank you. For everything."

"My pleasure."

When he turned, he caught Jared's gaze. "I'll walk out with you."

As soon as they stepped onto the porch, Chuck stopped Jared. "I'm kind of glad you're staying," Chuck said.

"Why?"

"Nothing's wrong, ... she seems really fragile."

"You mean Alicia? Guess seeing her home tossed shook her up pretty good."

"That and being stalked. Did you know about that?"

"Heck, no," Jared said with a shake of his head. "I just met her tonight. You think this guy is out here?"

Chuck scrubbed a hand over his jaw. "No. I didn't see any headlights. I'm glad you're here because she's wired. She could do something stupid. If she panics and no one is here, she could hurt herself."

"Yeah, I know what you mean. I've seen it. Once the shock wears off, she should be better."

"Hopefully a night's sleep will do the trick." Jared checked his watch. Two A.M.

Chuck got into his car and drove off. Jared stood there watching his taillights fade out, wondering what the next twenty-four hours would bring.

Jessica had found some sheets and blankets. At home, Jared slept naked. Couldn't do that tonight. Even though he knew sleep might be impossible, he took off his shirt and stretched out on the couch in his jeans.

Erie quiet, with only the sound of crickets and their rhythmical chirping sounds. Moonlight shined through the upper windows. He grasped why Chuck's uncle preferred sleeping in the big room. Stars glistened in the dark, night sky. Now this was sleeping under the stars.

Jared could enjoy the peace if his mind didn't race over recent events. Too many questions, lately. Some jerk targeting the firehouse, and now some guy after Alicia.

The bedroom door creaked open. His senses on alert, he tensed as he heard the sound of padded footsteps.

"Are you awake," Jessica whispered.

"Yeah," he answered as he sat up.

Jessica sank onto the cushion next to him. "I can't sleep."

"How's Alicia?"

"She finally dozed off. She was pretty upset."

"That's understandable. How are you?"

"I'd be lying if I said I wasn't scared."

His first impulse was to drag her close. Wrap his arms around her and tell her everything would be okay. He hoped it would, but since they were hiding out and no one knew who was after Alicia or why, he couldn't promise her a damned thing. Still, the urge to hold her churned his guts.

"I think we're okay. No one knows where she is."

Jessica chewed on her bottom lip. He could tell she wanted to say something.

"Jessica. You don't have to worry. I'm right here." Her beautiful almond eyes captivated him.

"Will you hold me?"

He wanted to check his ears to see if he'd heard right. Was he asleep and dreaming? He sure as hell hoped not.

"Come here," he said, opening his arms. She scooted to his side, and he drew her close, wrapping his arms around her warm flesh. Soft and smooth. He inhaled her scent, sweet, but not too sweet. Mouthwatering, it reminded him of sugary gingerbread. He wondered if she tasted as sweet.

He tucked her head in the crook of his neck and rested his chin on her hair. For a minute, the world drifted away. There was only him and her. His body relaxed and he simply enjoyed the feel of her warm, womanly body snug next to him. God, she felt good.

No words were necessary. He loved the feel of Jessica. Loved knowing she trusted him enough to curl up beside him, with him—totally unaware of how she affected him. His body reacted, but he resisted the fire burning in his belly.

After a while, her breathing evened out. He listened to her soft breathing, astonished at how contented he was. He leaned back, kissed her temple, and then held her while she slept.

He could get used to this.

His playboy lifestyle was taking a hard hit.

Forgetting everything else, he let himself sink into the moment.

***

Jared's eyes flew open at the sound of an engine. It should be Chuck. He eased his arm from under Jess's head and slipped to the window to take a peek. He released a breath as he saw Chuck get out of his car. Jared ran a hand through his hair, then met Chuck at the front door.

"Hey, man. You brought food."

Chuck handed Jared two bags of groceries and went back to the car for more. Jared placed the bags on the counter, then saw Jessica stirring on the couch.

"Good Morning," she said, stretching. Her hair all mussed, her sleep-filled gaze ... he swallowed. At that moment, he wanted to take her back to bed.

"Good Morning. We have food."

Her soft laugh had tingles dancing in his gut. Before he could explore the feeling, another head appeared in his vision.

"Good Morning, Alicia."

"Hi," she yawned. She gasped when Chuck clomped in and kicked the door shut with his boot.

"Whether or not you guys are glad to see me, I know you're glad to have some food." Chuck set the bags on the counter and the women dug into them.

"What you got in here?" Alicia asked. "Hope you don't expect me to cook."

Disappointment replaced the smile on Chuck's face.

"Got you," she said, smiling at Chuck. Seemed like Alicia had bounced right back after her ordeal last night.

"I can vouch for Alicia," Jessica said. "She can cook."

"My mama taught me." Alicia said, waving a pound of bacon as she spoke.

"Good. Cause I'm hungry." Chuck gave her a wink.

Alicia placed one hand on her hip. "What makes you think I'll cook for you?"

"I'm a big boy," Chuck said with a wide grin. "I can take care of myself. My mama taught me how to cook, too."

Jessica took the empty bag from Chuck. "Why don't you two go do manly stuff, and we'll get things going in the kitchen."

Sounded perfect to Jared. He figured the safest place for them was outside. He got Chuck's attention and gave a nod toward the door. He waited until the door was firmly closed behind them.

"Hear anything while you were in town?"

"Let's walk."

Jared figured that was a good idea, so the women wouldn't hear. He followed Chuck down the porch steps onto the rough ground. Twigs crunched under his shoes.

"Did a thorough search of the premises. Forensics dusted for prints and hair and other fibers. The living room was the only area that had been tossed. But they're going to dust the other rooms, too."

Jared frowned as he put his hands in his pockets. "You think it was a robbery?"

"No, I don't. Alicia said someone was stalking her. I ran a few names through the database. Dudes checked out. It's puzzling."

"What?"

"No reason to suspect anyone. But someone is after her. I need to find a connection."

"Your job sucks. If there are no leads, how in the hell do you catch your man?"

Chuck followed a path around to the back. "I had it easier when I was walking the beat. Since I joined Hooley with his investigation, it's all kinds of crazy. I'd still rather have my job than yours. Running into a building on fire is insane."

"Yep. That's me. Nuts." He and Chuck both laughed. When Chuck stopped, Jared did too. He took in the beauty before him. As far as he could see, nature was all around him. Green grass and tall weeds, all the way to the tree line. "I think you're the one whose nuts. You must like playing cops and robbers. I'd rather be here."

"So would I."

Silence stretched between them. "Can't have everything, can we?" Jared shrugged. "Gotta eat. Gotta work."

"It's our chosen profession that makes people speculate."

"I was trained for my profession. I know you were trained for yours."

"I've had more than my share of flying bullets since I joined the force. Though, I am smart enough to hide behind cars and buildings. At least it's not every day."

"I guess I'm dumb enough to charge right into flames."

"Still wouldn't trade places with you." Then Chuck faced Jared. " I saw Mike while I was in town. Told him where you were."

Damn. I should be at the station.

"Thanks. No cell service out here. I was supposed to report for shift today."

Chuck scrubbed his neck as if he had razor burn. "Yeah, guess I should have warned you about that."

Jared shrugged. "Doesn't matter. Unless there's an emergency." Chuck strode to the back deck. "There is a landline in the bedroom. I need to hook it up."

"Oh," he said, stepping up on the stained wood. "You do this? Nice color." Chuck gave a nod. Jared went back to their original topic, "Well, that would be good. Incase Alicia needs it."

"Rather she didn't use it. No need to alert anyone where she is. How'd she do last night?"

Jared leaned a hip against the porch railing. "No screams or nightmares. I guess she slept okay."

"I don't like this, Jared."

"What part? I don't like any of it."

"The fire, the explosion, the burglary ..."

The back door of the cabin opened. "You guys ready to eat?"

Jared turned to find Jessica in the doorway, a delicious smell floating out behind her. Right on cue, his stomach growled.

Chuck slapped him on the back. "Hope you made plenty. You've got a couple of starving men on your hands."

Bacon, eggs, and biscuits sat in bowls on the solid wood table. Jared's mouth watered. He dug into the food and groaned at the delicious flavor. Conversation flowed, staying away from the topic of why they were there.

While the women cleaned the kitchen, Jared helped Chuck gather wood and secure the cabin. He had no idea how long Alicia might be there, but Chuck wanted to be prepared. When the time came to leave, Jared wondered if Alicia would stay by herself. There wasn't another option.

Jessica said goodbye and Chuck gave Alicia instructions.

"Sit tight and stay out of sight. Okay?"

"Do not open the door for anyone," Jessica added.

"Okay, I won't." Alicia chewed on the end of her finger. Jared expected her to jump in the car and go with them.

"Well?" Chuck said to Alicia.

"Well, what?" she asked looking up at him.

"Close and lock the door."

"I will."

"Do it now?"

The timid little woman turned into a warrior. "Oh, good grief. Command much?"

"Huh?"

"The way you order people around," she said rolling her eyes. "You're not the boss of me."

"I am today. Now, do what you're told." Alicia was still muttering when she slammed the door.

Chuck stood there for five seconds and knocked on the door. Alicia opened it.

"I told you not to open the door."

"Are you kidding me? I thought you forgot something."

"Just close the door and lock it."

"Okay." Alicia closed the door again.

Jared and Jessica descended the porch steps and went to the car. Chuck stayed at the door.

He knocked again.

Alicia opened the door.

"What did I tell you? You didn't even ask who it was?"

"I knew it was you."

"If you open this door again, I'm going to make sure you won't be able to open it."

Jared and Jessica glanced at each other. This was getting almost comical.

Alicia placed one hand on her hip and cocked her leg to the side. Her eyes narrowed, and the glare she gave Chuck could have roasted marshmallows. "And how do you plan to do that?"

"I'll tie you up," Chuck growled.

"Promise?" she said with a smirk.

Jared laughed out loud. The scene looked ridiculously close to sexual foreplay. Except, the thunderous expression on Chuck's face suggested he might burst a blood vessel.

"Shut. The. Door. Do not open it. Period."

Alicia gave Chuck a two-finger salute, twirled on her toes, and gave him a saucy wink. Then sharply slammed the door.

"Women," Chuck said, stomping down the porch steps.

CHAPTER 12

Jared dropped Jessica off at her place and made a beeline for Station Eight. He was late. He'd never been late. An ass-chewing was sure to come his way.

On any given day, the front bay doors would be open and the rest of the building locked up. Today, all doors were open wide. Laredo and Cooper had pulled the trucks out and Greg from the previous shift was still there. Guess he'd stayed to help clean up the inside.

Jared drove to the back parking lot and shoved the gearshift into park. He should have known there'd be a welcoming committee to greet him.

"Look what the wind blew in."

"Cap's looking for you."

Jared kept his head down and marched up the stairs, ready to take whatever Shep would dish out.

Leaning back in his office chair, his feet propped on his desk, Shep had his fingers laced together behind his neck. Jared stepped inside.

"I don't suppose you care to tell me where you've been."

"I thought Mike would have told you."

"He said you might—or might not—make shift."

"Well, here I am." What else could he say. He hadn't called in. Didn't matter that there was no cell service where he'd been. There was no excuse for not showing up to work on time.

Shep dropped his feet to floor. "Care to tell me what's going on?"

Jared shook his head. "You don't want to know."

Shep hiked his brow and gave Jared, a look that said—"you did not just say that to me." Shep didn't like vague answers, and he liked nonsense even less. Jared figured he'd better start explaining.

"Actually, it's a friend, or I guess you could say a friend of a friend." When Shep continued to stare, Jared added, "It involves a woman."

"Are you in trouble?"

Jared ran a hand through his hair. "No. It's not what you think."

"What should I think?"

Damn. Shep staring at him like that made him want to leap out of his skin. "Look, someone broke into Jessica's friend's apartment. Tossed the place. Probably tried to scare her."

The expression on Shep's face eased to one of concern. "Sounds like that would do the trick."

"We took her someplace safe."

Shep rubbed the stubble under his neck. "Ex-boyfriend?"

"No," Jared replied, shaking his head. "The thing is, she's the owner of the car that caught on fire at the hospital."

The stern expression was back. "Let the police handle it."

Chuck was already on it. But ... "That brings up another problem."

"My problem?" That damn brow hiked up to his hairline again.

Jared shrugged. "Maybe."

Shep shoved his chair back and crossed his boots at the ankles. "All right. Sit down. This conversation needs more explaining."

Chuck's words kept running through Jared's mind. Too many coincidences. He dropped down into the chair in front of Shep's desk. "Maybe it has nothing to do with the fire department, but … there may be a connection."

"I'm listening."

"What if—and I know this sounds way out there—but what if this is the same guy?"

"Same guy," Shep repeated inquisitively. "That tossed her apartment and set fire to her car? Sounds like an ex."

"The same guy responsible for the training site explosion."

It took less than a minute for Shep to absorb that information. He jackknifed in his chair. "How in fuck's sake did you connect this girl's incidents with the department?"

"I don't know, Cap. But Chuck is working on it."

"And how did Chuck get involved with this … break-in?"

"I called him."

Shep shook his head as he placed his hands upon the desk. "Do you know what you're doing?"

"Chuck is in charge."

"I assume you don't want to provide details?"

"Not yet."

Shep seemed to think things over. "If I can't talk you out of it, don't get caught whatever the hell you're doing. You heard Chuck. Our fire bug is a pro. We better hope this is not the same guy."

Jared didn't tell Shep that Chuck was the one who provided a place to hide Alicia. Jared figured the less people knew, the less likely to involve them in a dangerous situation.

Who knew what they were up against.

***

Across the street from Station Eight, Seth watched several fire trucks roar out of the bays, sirens wailing. A large fire required all the engines, which was exactly what he had counted on. The firehouse stood empty. He could be in and out before the hero boys returned, none the wiser. Not that he wanted to hang around any longer than necessary, but the fire boys would be gone for a while. Carl had made sure of that.

Staying in the shadows, Seth looked in both directions, not a car or a person in sight. He quickly slipped to the building, fell to his knees and rolled under the barrier just before the last bay door closed. Timing was everything.

He pushed to his feet and swiped at his shirt sleeves. Didn't need any dirt or evidence on his clothes. The station looked empty. He doubted anyone had stayed behind. Still, he cocked his head, listening for any sound that would alert him to another's presence. Hearing nothing, he took a guarded step forward, making a cautious sweep about the bay, taking in the wide space where the trucks had been parked. Cabinets, shelves and equipment lined the walls. A tall table held lots of books and papers, and there were diagrams scattered on its surface. His gaze landed on an iron rack with tanks.

The breath eased from his chest as he smiled in triumph. He had deliberated long and hard, trying to decide his next move. Carl mentioned the air tanks, but the firefighters would check them regularly. No way of knowing which tank would be the one needed to do the deed. And he sure as hell couldn't tinker with them all. It was not his intention to take out the entire fire department.

No. Only one significant man would receive the proper amount of due diligence. Seth was determined the man responsible for his brother's death would suffer the same fate. A brother for a brother.

Slowly, he climbed the steps, keeping his eyes and ears alert for any movement, any sound. It appeared the building was empty, but he prepared himself in case someone was there. He'd never been one to go forward without precaution. Too bad his brother hadn't learned the same traits. Shawn had lived in the fast lane, sped through his days on full throttle. Always hatching some new plan to get rich quick. His last adventure had gotten him arrested and his partner had something to do with it.

Anger boiled inside. His brother's partner.

The bastard would pay. *His* brother would pay.

See how *he* liked losing a brother.

Seth shook his shoulders and cleared his mind. He needed to focus on the task at hand.

A balcony overlaid the bay with three doors and a hallway. The first room appeared to be an office. Most likely the captain's. The next door opened into a lounge. These guys had it pretty cozy here. He hadn't expected to see a pool table. The last doorway opened into a hallway that led to more rooms. Stepping into the hallway, he found a weight room containing equipment much like a gym. To the left, bunks. His chest tightened in eagerness.

Imagine how they would feel knowing he'd been in their precious space. He took in each bed and noted there wasn't much along the line of personal items. Since several shared this room, Seth figured personal shit was kept at home.

Easing from the room, he listened for any sound that would tell him of someone entering the firehouse. Still nothing. He continued down the corridor. A beam of light flooded into the hall from an open doorway. He froze. The alarm had sounded a major fire, all firefighters were expected to go. He carefully stepped close to the wall.

Slowly and carefully, he peered inside. Empty.

A large living area joined an open kitchen. They'd left in a hurry. Two coffee cups sat on a counter right beside a charger stand for walkie talkies. The slots bare, the guys must have taken the radios with them. Next to that sat a computer with the screen lit, as if someone had just left it. A phone and a notepad sat on a table, with a few pens.

Turning to the side, he saw a glass and a bowl of chips on a table in front of a sofa. Other than that, the place looked as sterile as Seth's sergeant had made his squad keep the barracks. Even the pool table looked new.

Must be nice, pampered assholes. The stuff in here was better than anything he ever had. Shawn was the one who bought brand name stuff and liked to show off his possessions. Seth had been happy being a grunt in the Army. Until the Colonel had shot his world to hell, informing him about his brother's death.

An eye for an eye.

A brother for a brother.

Seth was in no hurry. *He* would pay.

Seth backed out and flicked on the lights of each room as he strode down the corridor making his way back to the balcony. He moved down the stairs and strolled to the lockers. He was in luck. Little black squares with silver letters identified the person who possessed the locker. He scanned each one until he found the name he'd been looking for.

Pay dirt.

His pulse leaped. His chest swelled with his increase in breathing. A sense of urgency propelled him. He licked his lips as he lifted the latch, releasing a sigh of satisfaction when he found it unlocked.

Whatever he hoped to find, he was disappointed. A change of clothes, personal shit. Nothing of importance or useful to him. He closed the locker in disappointment.

He wandered around for a bit and then figured he better not waste too much time. After all, he was on a mission.

When he'd first thought to mess with the tanks, Carl had suggested tampering with a face mask would be less likely to be noticed. And look what just happened to be here.

Masks were lined in precision above each tank. No way to tell which belonged to who or if the men chose them at random. Seth had missed his target before.

Like moving chess pieces on a board, he was caught up in the game. Messing with the fire department intrigued him. Whether he got the right guy or the wrong one, it would still send a message. The men in the station would feel invaded.

They would wonder how he'd gotten in.

Wonder when the next time would be.

And he would be one step closer to his objective.

CHAPTER 13

The last shift had run into his day off, and now Jared was back on shift. It was as though he never left. He shrugged his air tank on over his heavy coat and checked his breathing apparatus. The tanks were good for thirty minutes. By the looks of this building, the team would use air fast. Flames shot out of every window and towered above the roof. Most of the employees had left hours ago, and the ones who stayed were standing in the parking lot watching the turmoil. There was always a possibility that someone was still inside. He hoped not. He and his team were about to enter the belly of the fiery beast. No one could survive without the gear they carried.

He glanced back to see Laredo standing on top of the quint ready with the high-powered gun. Jared stepped into the inferno while Laredo and Coop directed water into his path. He trusted the fire-retardant suit to see him through. Flames licked the walls and crawled across the ceiling. He worked his way about, scanning everything in the room. His vision blurred.

Something was wrong.

Very wrong.

Jared tore at his mask and stumbled backward. Heat blasted his face and smoke caught in his throat. He turned with his arms reaching blindly forward, instinctively searching for the way out. The sound of the devil roared in his ears; his eyes burned like a bitch. He opened his mouth to yell and coughed up a lung. Someone grabbed him and helped him to stand. He stumbled as a teammate pulled him free. He felt the air on his face as soon as they cleared the burning structure.

Jared fell to his knees.

If he could just shake...

The weight of the tank suddenly lifted from his back. Voices cut through the fog while hands turned him over onto his back. He couldn't draw air into his lungs.

Someone tried to put his oxygen on, and he fought with everything he had in him. *No. Not the mask. It's ... its ...*

"What the hell is wrong with you man?" That was Cooper's voice. Had he pulled Jared to safety?

"You don't take your helmet off inside a building."

"Cooper! What happened?"

Cap.

"Don't know, Cap. Jared is fighting like a demon jumped in his path."

"Get that oxygen mask on."

No! Jared couldn't see, but he flung his arms and pushed it away. "Puh ... sun."

"See what I mean?"

"Wait. Listen. He's trying to tell us something." Shep's voice was close to his ear. "What is it, Jared?"

"Pu ...sun." Then he gasped.

"Get a new can of oxygen!" Shep shouted.

Jared heard more commotion. Teammates shouting. Fire hissing. The loud pump shooting water through the hoses. Voices ... Voices.

"Put the apparatus over his mouth and nose."

A black fog swirled around him. He couldn't fight anymore.

"Come on, buddy. Stay with us."

"Is he okay?"

"He's breathing. Don't touch that. Leave it. Call Hooley."

Then the black cloud he'd been running from surrounded him, and swallowed him whole.

***

Jessica stood beside the bed of an unconscious woman in the recovery room. After a near fatal heart attack, she'd been rushed to surgery. With no family in the waiting room, Jessica promised herself she would stay with the woman until she woke. The woman's eyes fluttered. A sign the anesthesia was beginning to wear off.

I'm right here, Mrs. Landis. Jessica patted the woman's hand. "The surgery is over. You did well. You're in the recovery room."

"Jessica?"

"Yes, ma'am. It's me. Your vitals look good. You're doing wonderful. Are you feeling any pain?"

Mrs. Landis smiled, her body relaxed and then she slipped back into sleep.

Anxious voices buzzed in the hall. Some sort of commotion had the nurses in a tizzy. Jessica went to see what all the fuss was about.

"He can put out my fire anytime." A nurse giggled. Either a new patient or a handsome visitor had triggered the group's interest.

"A hot celebrity land on our floor?" Jessica asked as she walked up to the group.

"Hot is right." Karen waved her hand in front of her face. "Three of them. Just came into ER."

"One was hurt. The other two sashayed in like they were the only men in the building," Wanda added.

"I always loved a man in uniform."

"Military?" The emphasis on SEALs lately had a lot of women talking. The ditzy nurses ignored her and went on with their dramatic swooning.

"According to Marsha, one is the size of Paul Bunion."

"That one guy, the big one. He must be six-four. Or six-six."

"At least," Wanda agreed. Jessica guessed Wanda had been in ER when the *hot* men entered the building.

"Oh man, they had some pretty impressive abs."

"Reckon they get those on the job?" Grace only recently graduated from nursing school.

"Carrying big hoses," Karen giggled again.

"By their size, I'd say their hoses are big." Wanda laughed.

"I'd be game to see the big—"

"Hoses?" Jessica interrupted Grace as the word registered. "Would you please tell me what you are talking about?"

All three giggled. "Should we tell her?

"You're not that naive, Jessica," Karen smiled irritatingly.

"Well, to be fair, we weren't exactly talking about *fire* hoses."

Fire?

"They are all hot. *And* friendly."

Jessica wanted to scream. "Who are you talking about? Who's in ER?"

"Just the hottest fire guys I've ever seen."

Jessica's heart leaped to her throat.

"The blond one could be on the cover of *Top Ten*."

"Hold me back. I was ready to climb on the table with him." Karen made a grand gesture of climbing.

"What happened? Do you know who? What station?"

"Calm down, girl. I have first dibs."

Jessica was in no mood for games. "I'm not joking around, Vickie." Seeing the expression on Jessica's face, Karen quickly realized she was dead serious. No longer laughing, Karen scowled in puzzlement.

"Three firefighters. One was hurt."

"His name, Vickie. What was his name?" Jessica grabbed Vickie's arm.

"Jared," Wanda burst out. "I didn't get his last name, but one of the firemen called him Jared."

Pain crushed the air from Jessica's lungs. All sorts of imaginings flooded her mind. Burned. How bad? Was he breathing?

Please, God. Don't let him die.

Help me to face whatever it is.

Frantic, Jessica ran down the hall. She punched the elevator button repeatedly, then darted for the stairs. Her feet flew, careless on the steps, unconcerned she might fall and break her neck. The only thing on her mind was Jared. Getting to him as fast as she could.

Mere seconds had passed when she barged through the door of the ER. She searched frantically for uniforms. Scatters of conversation seeped through the haze in her brain.

A firefighter—hurt at the scene—brought to the hospital—smoke inhalation—poison.

Poison?

She spotted Marsha, the ER nurse, and ran to her side.

"Jessica. You look like you've seen a ghost. What's wrong?"

"I'm looking for the firefighters."

A big smile lit her face. "You and every other nurse—"

"Where are they?" Jessica blurted.

Marsha stopped and gaped. "Are you okay?"

"Where are they?" Jess's voice sounded panicky. Marsha's face sobered. She must have guessed Jessica's state of mind.

"In there," Marsha pointed to a doorway. "Do you know him?"

Jessica didn't answer. She wasn't sure she could. Pain crushed her chest, squeezing her lungs.

Calm down. She was a nurse for God's sake. It would not do for her to have a panic attack in the middle of the emergency room.

***

Jared woke with a gasp that stung all the way to his lungs. His chest burned like fire and his throat hurt like a bitch. The last thing he remembered was seeing Laredo on top of the quint. Cooper behind him with a hose, and Mike in the lead.

Man, he was thirsty. He tried to swallow and conjure up some spit. Razor blades scraped his throat. The skin on his face tingled like a sunburn. He better pay attention to where the flames were. All he saw was black. Something smelled funny.

His mask.

Christ. His mask.

He tore the tubbing from his face and fought to sit up.

"Eey compinche. Espera."

Laredo?

"Hey, man. You're in the hospital." Cooper's image came into focus. "Don't fight the oxygen. This one is okay."

"Your mask was tampered with," Laredo explained.

"No wonder you acted crazy. When you tore off your mask and charged me like a wild man, I thought you'd flipped your lid."

"Some...thing...mask." Christ, it hurt to talk. He didn't recognize his own voice. "Poison."

"We figured that out," Mike said from the end of the hospital bed.

"He was standing right next to me. I couldn't believe it when he yanked off his mask." Cooper raked a hand through his hair.

"Damned lucky."

"Good thing you jerked off your mask. If you'd breathed that shit any longer—" Mike broke off in mid-sentence. His gaze fixed on the door.

Even in her scrubs, the woman took his breath. Whether Jessica meant for him to or not, he noticed her eyes light up when her gaze locked with his.

"Welcome back." Her voice sent a charge though his system.

"Hey, beautiful," he croaked.

"Don't try to talk. You swallowed smoke and you probably burned your vocal cords."

"He's toast. What do you say, *querida*? Are you finally ready to give me a chance?"

If glares could maim, Laredo would be crippled.

Mike laughed. "Watch out, Laredo. Maybe Jared can't speak, but I'd put my money on him getting out of that bed and opening a can of whip a—" He broke off with a cough.

"Shep would be here, but he's meeting with Hooley about the mask and tanks. Going over everything with a fine-tooth comb."

"Don't pay any attention," Jared whispered. "These yahoos won't let me go home until I get checked out."

"No indeed. You're in the ER. A doctor is going to look at you."

"A nurse just went to get him," Cooper said.

Jared gave Jessica one of his sexy grins. Damn, he felt better already.

"Are you in pain?"

"My throat hurts."

"What happened?"

"I'm not sure," he tried to answer, but whatever he'd breathed in the mask must have burned his throat.

"The ass—

Mike coughed interrupting Cooper and smacked him upside the head.

"Ouch! Uh, sorry."

It hurt to laugh.

Cooper tried again. "Jared here, took off his mask in a burning building."

Jessica glared at him. "Doesn't sound like a very smart thing to do." She might sound calm now, but her hand shook. She was not as calm as she pretended.

"Dumb idiot," Cooper mumbled. "Nearly gave me a heart attack."

"Gave you a heart attack? I was the one strangling." Jared rubbed the back of his head, trying to recall from memory. "I smelled something. My vision blurred. Had to be the mask."

"Knocked his, uh, butt out."

"The captain is having it tested just in case," Mike added, then he turned to Jessica. "We tried giving Jared oxygen. He fought us."

"I told you," Jared tried to shout, but his voice croaked like a damn frog. "Something was wrong." His eyes burned and his vision was still blurry.

"Shep is the one who figured it out," Laredo said to Jessica.

Man, all the guys were here. Kind of gave him a warm and fuzzy.

"Once we got Jared to understand it was a different oxygen mask, he calmed down. Then he passed out."

"Passed out? I'm telling you there was something fishy about that mask."

Jessica met his gaze. "You are right where you need to be." She seemed all tender and caring. Her hands were busy as she looked after him.

Warmth seeped into his bones. Seeing Jessica made being in a hospital seem worth it.

"You guys caused quite a stir in the hospital." Jessica broke eye contact and scanned him as she paced to the side of the bed. He hoped he didn't look as bad as he felt.

"Yeah." Cooper's grin reminded him of that damned Cheshire cat in *Alice in Wonderland*. The kid loved the attention. Couldn't blame him.

"One of the nurses took blood," Mike said.

"Only one?" Jessica asked with mock surprise. "With the buzz in this hospital, I assumed there'd be a dozen in here by now."

Jared captured her hand. "The only one I want is you." The guys probably thought he was flirting, but he meant every word. Jessica filled his thoughts daily. He went to bed thinking of her, woke up with her image in his mind. Hell, his dreams couldn't get any more erotic.

Her velvety brown eyes filled with wonder. Yeah. He meant it. Her reaction made him swallow. Had he shocked her? Did she believe him?

"Think you guys ... can give me a minute?" He glanced at each one, silently asking them to leave.

"We have to get going anyway. Get ready for the next shift."

"What? Like tomorrow morning?" Cooper stated.

"One day I'll explain things to you."

"You explain to me? Big guy, I hate to break it to you, but Jared here is my idol. I've been taught by the best."

"Come on, pup."

"You got to call me that in front of women?"

It was a thing with them—back and forth. Their voices grew distant as they strode down the hall. Laredo gave a wink just before he closed the door.

Jessica looked down at him and smoothed his hair back from his face. Her hand felt cool and heavenly on his temple. "Do you hurt?"

"Will it get me sympathy if I say yes?" His voice came out as a whisper. And if it caused Jessica to lean in real close, all the better.

The expression on her face melted his insides. He could tell she was struggling not to cry. Her eyes were glassy, and he could sense she'd been worried.

"Hey, beautiful. I'm fine."

"No, you're not fine. If you were, you wouldn't be in ER."

"You can kiss me and make me better."

She straightened. "You inhaled a lot of smoke."

"Then give me some mouthwash." He tried making things light and not so serious. What he really wanted was to kiss her. Right now.

The door to his room swung open, and a flashy white coat sailed through it. "Hello, Mr. Collins. I'm Doctor Muncie."

Shit.

"I understand you passed out. How are you feeling now?"

"Fine. Can I go?"

Or better yet. Get the hell out. He and Jessica were having a moment.

"I know you're anxious to leave the hospital. I'll not keep you any longer than necessary. Let's have a look."

The doctor did a little poking, and Jared cooperated, wishing the man would hurry up.

"Nothing showed up in your blood work. No concussion. Looks like you'll be fine with some rest. Any more dizziness, and I want you to follow up with a doctor right away."

"I've never had a dizzy spell. Still think something was in the mask."

"Even so, be on alert. Keep your throat wet. Try not to talk. After a few days' rest, you'll be good as new."

"A few days?"

"Thank you, Dr. Muncie," Jessica interrupted. "I'll make his friends aware of that."

Traitor.

"Thank you, Jessica. I'll leave him in your capable hands."

Damn, he'd like to be in her capable hands. The thought pulsed blood to his groin.

The doctor gave a nod. "Mr. Collins."

"Thanks, Doc."

The good doctor shut the door as he left.

Jared captured Jessica's hand. "Now what?"

"Now you can go home."

"Will you come with me?"

"You heard the doctor. You need rest."

"You said you'd make sure I got it."

"I said, I'd make sure your friends knew doctor's orders."

He screwed up his face into the most pitiful expression he could muster. "They've already gone. I'm stranded."

Her smile melted his insides. Damn the woman was beautiful.

"Please," he whispered. "Come with me."

CHAPTER 14

The *please* is what did it.

If this was a bad idea, Jessica didn't care at the moment. Jared had asked, and for whatever reason, she couldn't deny him. So here she was at his apartment.

"Welcome to my home," Jared said with a wave of his hand for her to enter.

When he first pulled up to the garage, she'd thought he owned this large house. Then he explained it had been divided into condos. The large open living space connected the living room with the kitchen. A shiny granite top drew her attention to the high back chairs and stainless-steel appliances. Neat, just like him.

"Very nice. I wasn't expecting something so big. And tidy, for a bachelor."

"I might live alone, but I'm not a slob. I picked this apartment because it's just like living in my own house. And it's close to the station."

Silence lingered. He held her captive with his gaze. Jared triggered every nerve in her body. Finally, he spoke. "I'll be right back."

She watched him saunter down the hallway with a dry mouth. *Mmmm.*

She fled to the kitchen to find something to occupy her mind—other than thinking of him removing his clothes in his bedroom. Imagining him naked shot her hormones into overdrive. She searched the refrigerator for something to drink. Beer. Cold. Orange Juice. Cold. Bottled water.

Hmmm.

A kettle sat to the left of the fridge. So, he either had coffee or tea often. She'd been thinking of getting a kettle for herself, but that meant instant coffee. And she liked her pods that gave her a fresh cup of java every time.

There had to be tea bags here somewhere. A glass container was behind the kettle.

Aha.

With a flip of the switch, the kettle began to boil, and in no time, she had tea. Being a guy, he probably liked it sweet.

The water in the bathroom stopped, which meant Jared was getting out of the shower. A little devil crawled up on her shoulder and jabbed her with his pitchfork. She wouldn't mind seeing him in the buff.

She quickly turned on the faucet and splashed water onto her cheeks. He tempted her to want things she'd be better off without. Of course, that's what the nagging voice in the back of her mind told her. She wanted to ignore that little voice. Kill its very existence.

What had her sister told her? Live in the present. Not the past.

Remembering the past was what kept her from making another disaster. To her credit, she'd been young. It'd happened years ago. Every once in a while, the pain returned. Reminding her of her foolishness. The heartache had grown more tolerable, but the memory would always haunt her.

"Hey, did I lose you someplace?"

Jessica quickly turned off the water and shook off her melancholy. A hot man stood behind her and she preferred to concentrate on him.

"Uh, nope. Right here," she said as she turned around. And nearly lost her breath. Wow, Jared looked hot. Hair wet and all slicked back. Well-fitting jeans showed his thick thighs, and a tight T-shirt stretched across his chiseled abs. She checked to make sure her tongue wasn't hanging out of her mouth.

"You looked a thousand miles away. If you have something else to do, I won't keep you." He looked so serious, and so woeful when he said that. Clearly, he wanted her to stay. And she wanted to stay.

"The only thing I had planned the next two hours was work. I'd much rather be here." His megawatt smile generated a heat in her chest like a hot furnace, making her glad she'd told him what he wanted to hear.

"You may have made me the lesser of two evils, but I'll take it."

"Oh, I didn't mean ..." The sound of his laughter set off sparks in her lower belly. A whirlwind of emotions battled her from all sides. "I'm glad you invited me."

"My throat is feeling somewhat better. Is that for me?"

He motioned to the glass on the counter that she had poured for him. "Yes."

"Thanks." He took a drink, and she watched the protrusion in his neck bob as he swallowed. A tingle went from her chest, down to her belly.

"Do you feel sorry for me?"

Hot for you is more like it.

She brushed off her silly attraction and tried to be witty. "Who in their right mind would feel sorry for a man who kept a leering grin on his face most of the time?"

"I guess I'll have to work harder on my pitiful expression. I thought that was what got you to agree to leave with me."

"No." She breathed. "It was the tone of your voice when you said *please*."

She wasn't going to say that. Now she was glad she had. She'd shocked him. He took a deep breath and let out a long sigh. Then his eyes darkened as he just stared at her. She stared back, feeling the current between them. Heat. And more heat.

"I saw your kettle," she blurted, then motioned to the thing.

"Yeah. It's different, but I like it. It's quick."

"I didn't know if you might prefer something cold or hot to drink. I turned on the kettle in case you wanted tea." She shoved her hair behind one ear.

"You can check the refrigerator, but I think all I have is beer. And maybe orange juice."

"Orange juice is good for you."

"How about wine? I have a bottle or two up there." He pointed to a cabinet. "Before you tell me I can't have that, I'm not on any medication and I feel fine."

She chewed her lip for a moment, then thought a glass of wine might calm her own nerves. "All right. If you promise to sit down and don't go moving about. We can't have you falling."

"Anything you say, doc." God, he was a heart breaker when he smiled. She would need to guard her heart.

"Have you had any food?"

He lifted a bottle of wine down to the counter. "We can order. What do you like? The glasses are over there."

She found the goblets and picked one with each hand. "Pizza is fine."

"I have menus for China City, Little Maria's, even a Mexican restaurant in the drawer under the phone. Take your pick."

"A man with a landline. I'm impressed. So many people depend on their cell phones."

"I need to be reached if there's an emergency. So, I have both."

He had stepped close to her and spoke in a sexy voice that shot tingles to her toes. His eyes were so blue she could imagine floating in the sky as she gazed at him. His blond hair was short, but still long enough to sift her fingers through. Oh man, she was in deep doo-doo.

She picked up the paper leaflets and scanned through them. "I think I'd rather have Pizza. I love Cirro's."

"Then pizza it is." He poured the wine while Jessica called in the order.

"Delivery in twenty minutes."

He handed her a glass of wine. "Let's go into the living room."

"Okay."

He fell onto the sofa and patted the space beside him. He was as tempting as the devil, and she knew what she was getting into.

She sat next to him, close enough to feel his warmth. Actually, she was more excited with anticipation than nervous or afraid. He didn't pounce. He didn't ask her to do anything. He was comfortable. And cozy. And she'd already fallen asleep next to him once. That right there proved she could trust him.

She took a sip of wine. "This is good."

"I don't spend a lot for wine, but I'm not too cheap either."

"Stella Rosa," she said reading the label. "I like it."

"Goes with just about anything. Even pizza."

He took a sip from his glass, watching her over the rim. She watched him, her gaze following the little bob in his neck as he swallowed. For some reason that looked sexy. Heat spread through her middle. Jared looked delicious.

And she wanted a bite.

"I never dreamed I'd be sitting here with you drinking wine," she said.

"I know. Our first meeting more or less gave a completely different idea of how things were bound to go."

"You weren't nice to me."

He chuckled. "Yeah. Not one of my better moments. You want to hear a confession?" At her nod, he continued, "I was attracted to you, and I thought you were married."

"So, Connie was right." She'd mentioned that when Jessica had been fuming in her kitchen.

"Who?"

"Connie. The woman who was outside with me. She lives in the house next door. She said you thought I was the kids' mom."

"I did. That I could handle. Married woman—off limits." As he brought his glass to his lips, Jessica wondered at his statement. She'd bet there was a story there.

She watched him again, tilting the glass and his lips caressing the rim. A fire started in her tummy and spread to her cheeks. He must have noticed. Desire flared in his eyes.

The doorbell rang.

The moment broken, Jared rose to his feet. "I guess it's the pizza guy."

Jessica mentally shook herself. Is this what she wanted? Jared was hot, but his exceptional looks and profession labeled him a playboy. Surely, she was nothing more than a good time to him.

Did it have to be more?

She wished she could turn off her thoughts. Just go with the flow. Damn, he did things to her insides without even touching her. Months ago, she would have taken flight. Now she craved to be in a man's arms. This man's arms. Jared enthralled her. His eyes hypnotized, making her want to leap into their depths. His cocky grin enchanted her. She'd never wanted to jump a man so much in her life.

"You made the right choice."

What? Had she spoken out loud?

"Pizza was the perfect choice. I'm starving."

Oh.

"It smells delicious."

He threw open the lid. "Dig in."

"How about some napkins?"

"Sure thing." He grabbed a slice and took a bite, carrying it with him into the kitchen. He came back with paper towels.

She took a bite of the hot mess. "Oh, God. This is so good." She wiped a string of cheese from her chin. When she met his eyes, desire filled them again.

Oh God. He'd taste better than pizza.

She reached for her wine and took a healthy gulp.

"Don't choke. There's more. I promise I won't eat it all."

She blushed. Now everything he said made her think dirty thoughts.

He placed his pizza slice on the table. "Come here."

"What?" Her eyes widened in confusion.

"Let's get this over with." He held out his hand for hers.

"What?"

"If I don't kiss you right now, I'm not sure I'll be able to finish this pizza."

"You looked like you were doing a pretty good job."

"And you looked like you wanted me to kiss you."

I do.

Instead, she said, "Eat your pizza."

"Just saying." He shrugged, and grinned that panty-melting grin, then stuffed half a slice into his mouth. She stared at the sauce on the corner of his lips.

He noticed. "You sure?"

His teasing made her heart melt. All the warnings in the world wouldn't take this moment away from her.

The pizza gone, she licked the tips of her fingers, then scrunched up her paper towel. Jared poured her more wine.

"I'm glad we sorted everything out." She ran her finger around the rim of her wine glass,

"Did we?" His voice so close to her ear startled her. He smelled like man, and her overexcited hormones had her prattling.

"Yes. You came when I called for Tiffany. I was so scared."

He laced his fingers with hers.

"That's the night I found out you were single." She tightened their grip. "And I didn't need to feel guilty anymore."

"Guilty?"

"I had some pretty rousing thoughts about you."

Right now, she was having a few of her own. "Really? Are you trying to destroy my hero image of you?"

"I'm not a hero."

"You put your life on the line to save others." Thank God, he'd been there for her.

"I'm only doing my job. I'm not perfect by a long shot."

She met his gaze. "I didn't say perfect. You're a good man."

His brow shot up. "How do you know? You just met me."

"I've met you four times. You insulted me the first time." When he opened his mouth to speak, she held up her hand interrupting. "You explained why. In each of those instances I saw strength, confidence, and caring for the safety of the people in every emergency situation. Those are important credentials."

"Credentials?" he murmured with his eyes saying entirely something else. He released her hand to place both of his on her waist. Heat seared her where he touched.

"I ... think I'd like to know about your rousing thoughts."

Slowly, he leaned in, keeping his gaze locked on hers. She held her breath, waiting for the moment his lips would touch hers. His movements fluid, he gently brushed his lips from left to right, teasing her in a torturous dance. She sighed with delight and in anticipation.

He ran his tongue over her lower lip. The touch so erotic, she yearned for him to take her. He nibbled, then pulled the flesh of her lip out and lightly sucked. So smooth, so sensual, desire pierced her lower body.

After a few moments of floating bliss, his tongue slipped between her lips, inviting her to open. Then he gave her a kiss unlike any she'd ever shared in her life. Soft, sensual, demanding, she gave her all. Things heated up fast.

She clutched him, her fingers tightening in want. Her body ached with desperate need. His hands caressed her with a sensual touch, rising higher, and higher, taking her breath with each stroke. She climbed the desire ladder with him, losing herself in the kiss.

When he eased back, she found herself panting. He leaned his head against hers. Forehead to forehead, she waited for her breathing to return to normal. Along with that, some of her sense returned as well.

"Jessica," he whispered. "You kiss like an angel. I want you. If I don't stop now—"

She placed her palm over his mouth stopping what he was going to say. She wanted this. She wanted him.

He licked the center of her palm with his tongue. She shuddered.

Jared was the most attractive man she'd ever met. His touch turned her inside out. A pretty boy. A player. A big-hot-pulsing man.

How could she trust him? Trust herself? She couldn't have a fling. He already had too much of her heart.

"I can't. I'm sorry. I can't."

***

"Oh, Jessica. You didn't."

How embarrassing the evening had turned out. She was so torn, she had to tell Raven about her date with Jared. She propped her elbows on the island, as she released a harsh breath.

"Don't judge. I didn't leave him hanging." As soon as the words left her mouth, she realized that didn't sound right.

Raven propped a hand on her hip. "What the hell is that supposed to mean?"

"Such language from your mouth."

"The kids are at school. Now explain. You didn't go to bed with him, but you didn't leave him hanging?"

"Raven!"

"Jessica!"

Well crap.

"I just meant we talked. He thought he had upset me. I couldn't let him think that. So, I tried to tell him, but I—"

"You didn't trust him," Raven said setting her mug on the counter with a bang. "You still don't trust yourself. How many times do we need to go down this road. I've been very patient with you, Jessica."

"Patient?" What had she done to make her sister so mad?

"Yes, patient. It was a long time ago. Hear me repeating myself? I've let you cry on my shoulder, sympathized with your pain, assisted you with your struggle of getting back out there. It's a big world, Jess. People are different. So many personalities. Give the guy a freakin' chance."

"Wow. Tell me how you really feel." She lifted her coffee and blew across its surface.

"I'm tired of taking baby steps around you. You're an adult. For God's sake, act like one."

Jessica stared at her sister with an open mouth. Raven didn't cuss. She'd never talked to Jessica that way. Maybe about someone else, but never to her about … her.

Raven counted silently; Jessica had seen her do it a hundred times. Not knowing what to say, she kept her mouth shut.

Seconds ticked by that seemed like twenty minutes.

"Okay. I'm under control." Raven straightened, walked around the counter and slid onto the chair beside Jess. "I'm your older sister. I don't know everything, but I do know you can't keep doing this. Life is full of risks. If you don't take a few, you're not living."

"I've taken risks. I do things."

Raven propped her elbow on the countertop and propped her chin in her hand. "Yeah? Like what?"

"I'm a nurse. I see trauma in the ER every day. I've seen some things—"

Raven smacked her hand down on the counter. Anger filled her eyes. "That's not what I'm talking about, and you know it."

Jessica hung her head, staring at her cup. Raven was right. "I just want a normal man and a normal relationship."

"How do you think you're going to get one if you push men away?"

"I'll find and ugly man. Maybe a nerd. He won't have a string of women."

A very unlady-like sound huffed out of Raven's mouth. Her sister was getting disgusted. Jessica wasn't earning any brownie points.

"Look at Chad. He signed up for a job that puts his life in danger, but he took the risk. I can't stand the thought of him being in a hostile country. Maybe getting shot or even killed. That's my choice, and I live with it every day. I don't dwell on it. I love the man, and he is my life. I took a chance on him."

"Raven, I'm so sorry. I never thought—"

"Stop. I'm fine with my life. And if I had never taken a chance on Chad, I would not be this happy."

"You are happy." Raven glowed with happiness. Well, maybe not right this minute, but most of the time. She worked hard, took care of three kids and never complained. Oh, she did the normal, "I'm going to hang them, or I'll kill them" crap. But that was just her being witty. She never criticized or grumbled about her life.

Not like me.

"Jared takes risks every day."

"Tell me something. What bothers you more? Jared being a firefighter, or that he is attractive?"

"What kind of question is that?"

"Answer it."

Well, shit. Jessica braced her elbow on the counter and propped her chin on her knuckles. Being a firefighter is a daring profession. The fact that Jared can laugh and be as charming as he is, he must handle the stress very well. He must love his job. Yes, she would worry. But that was beside the point.

"Jared is good at his job. If he wasn't—"

"You're evading the question."

"No, I'm not. Firefighting is his profession, I'm okay with that."

"Um hmm. Go on."

"Well, he is hot. Any girl would love—"

"We're talking about you." Raven got in her face.

"Damn it, Raven. Will you let me finish a sentence?"

"Be my guest," she answered, leaning back. She picked up her coffee cup while keeping her gaze locked on Jess.

"Look, you know what happened before."

"You keep reminding me." Seeing Jessica's glare, she put up her hand. "Sorry. Continue."

"Jared is damn attractive, and he's attracted to me. Gee Raven, he set my pulse racing, and I got hot. I felt lust. Are you satisfied? Lust, Raven."

Raven calmly put her cup down. "Have you ever had these feelings before?"

"Even with—I refuse to say his name—I was willing, but I never felt the stirring, gut wrenching sensation I felt when Jared kissed me."

"Voilà!"

"Huh?"

"He's the one. Even if he's not the one you marry, he is definitely the one to get you out of your funk. He aroused you. Sounds like you've never been aroused before. From what I'm hearing, you wanted him to make love to you."

"Make love?"

"I was being nice. Have sex."

"But sex for sex is—"

"Don't knock it. If it's good, go with it. Why not try out the stud to see if you even want him in your stables."

Jessica laughed. "Raven, you're terrible."

"I know it seems like I'm talking crazy, but this is the most excited I've seen you in years."

Jessica swiveled on her chair, took a deep breath and released it. She rubbed her palms over her jeans to steady her nerves. If she said how she felt out loud, it would become real. Raven was her sister, her best friend in the whole world. She had to get it off her chest.

"I like Jared. As in falling for him. I'm scared, Raven."

"Well." Raven stared wide-eyed at Jessica. "I didn't expect that."

"What did you expect?"

"I hoped you would give him a chance. A real chance. Sounds like it's gone beyond that."

Jessica hung her head, letting her hair fall in her face.

"Don't hide, Jessica. Don't hide your feelings. Embrace them. I know you're worried, but like I said, if you don't take a risk, you'll never know what you can have. It might seem like things are happening fast, but that could be because this is real. Maybe Jared has feelings, too."

Jessica moved the hair out of her eyes and faced her sister. "I want to trust him."

"Then give him a chance. If he turns out to be an asshole, you learn from your mistake. Use it to make a better choice next time."

"If I blow this, what makes you think there will be a next time?"

"You can't hide from life." Raven placed her hand over Jessica's. "Get back on that horse and ride, girl."

"You're hopeless," Jessica said, with a shake of her head.

"Seriously, Jessica. Stop worrying. Love is wonderful. There is no experience like it. One day I hope you find it." She pulled Jessica in for a hug.

"Until then, ride that horse."

Jessica laughed. "How did you get to be so wise?"

Raven sat back, picked up her coffee, and met Jessica's gaze, eye to eye. "I'm your bigger sister. I know everything."

They laughed together. The lighthearted moment reminding Jessica of their younger years. When they had put their heads together and giggled until their sides ached.

CHAPTER 15

On a normal day, stress was not in Jared's vocabulary. With a certain blonde filling his every thought, he wondered if he'd lost his mind.

Women. He loved women. Although he never had to chase them, he sure enjoyed watching *their* maneuvers in trying to catch *him*. His actions, now, bewildered him. The only woman acquiring his interest was Jessica, and she remained outside his reach.

Last night he thought he'd broken the ice.

She had smiled at him, as if she needed him to touch her. Kiss her.

And he had.

A quiet moment, a kiss that rocked his world. He'd been totally lost in her, but he knew the moment her body language changed. Something had made her pull back. He'd worked harder in seeking approval from this woman than he had any other woman in his life. He'd thought his efforts were paying off. Until Jessica pushed him away. Was it her tendency to be distrustful, or had something happened to make her that way?

If it had been another woman, he'd think she was playing a game, eluding him and then inviting him with her eyes. But Jessica had melted in his arms—then back-peddled, as if she'd regretted being there. The kiss had been real. He'd bet his life on that. He'd seen her battle a conflict within herself. After all, he had his own problems to contend with, so he recognized the signs.

He didn't want to lose her.

Wasn't that a big surprise?

Keeping him at a distance would do her no good. Giving up was not in his character. Some men would pursue her for the thrill of the chase. No, it didn't have a damn thing to do with her resisting him. Or wanting something forbidden. Jessica fascinated him. From her scalding temper right down to her spellbinding eyes. He wanted her. And he usually got what he wanted.

Tonight, he would meet her sister.

Family.

When a female introduced her family, it was time to cut and run.

Problem was ... he didn't want to. Maybe he'd learn something from her sister.

"Parade starts at six," Mike said tapping his watch.

"I'm coming."

The fire department held a carnival every summer, and it just happened to be this week. Events and rides were open each night, but on Friday, the entire county flocked to Main Street for the parade. School bands, little league ball teams, even horses marched in the parade. But the finishing touch would be the fire trucks with flashing lights and sirens blaring. The kids loved it.

Jessica promised to bring the rugrats. Afterward, he would meet her sister.

"You look a bit put out? Everything okay?"

If what he felt resembled a noose tightening around his neck ... "Yeah. Fine."

Mike laughed. "You have that look."

"What look?"

"The one I had when Cassie was messing with my head."

Jared couldn't resist. "Which one?"

"Take your pick."

Jared grinned, then thought about how he couldn't go a moment without wanting to be with Jessica. Mike's observation was dead on. Granted, the big guy had been in the same boat a few weeks ago. Jared remembered Mike's frustration when he was trying to sort out his feelings. Jared had pried and had a lot of fun ribbing the big guy.

"At the time, I thought you two were perfect for each other."

Mike's chest puffed out, which was easy to miss since he could be mistaken for a tree. "Now you don't?"

Hearing Mike's tone, Jared quickly explained himself. "Not what I mean. She's perfect for you. I knew it then. You didn't."

The big guy crossed his arms and looked down his nose with a stern expression. "Is this where I'm supposed to tell you Jessica is perfect for you?"

"Tell *her* that. She's not convinced."

Mike shook his head. "You're slipping. Since when have you had trouble with women?"

Jared glared at Mike. "Don't let anyone else hear you say that."

"Like Cooper? That kid idolizes you."

"Well, maybe he'd be better off hanging around Laredo for a while."

Mike stared at Jared like he'd sworn off women.

Not a chance.

Mike pointed a finger at Jared's chest. "You know what he's learning from Laredo?"

"What?"

"Hit and run sex."

Oh shit.

When had Cooper told Mike about that. Maybe Laredo wasn't the best one for Cooper to be hanging around. Laredo wouldn't hurt the kid. Kid? What was he, twenty-two? Twenty-three?

"Cooper's not a kid."

Mike grunted. "Jessica coming to the parade?"

"Yeah." Jared lifted his coat off a hook. "She's bringing her sister and the kids." No need to tell Mike how he felt about that. The kids he didn't mind. It was the sister that made him nervous.

What if she didn't like him? What if she told Jessica to stay away from him? She couldn't be all bad if she was Jessica's sister. And her kids were something else.

"Laredo said those kids were full of energy. You straighten out that little girl yet?"

"Huh?"

"You know." Mike grabbed his crotch. "Tell her she doesn't have any balls."

He'd forgotten about that. Tiffany was a pistol.

"They'll have fun at the carnival," Mike said slapping him on the back. "Time to head out."

Of course, Laredo had the trucks lined up and ready to go. He was like a little kid. Shep ran over the schedule and gave a recap of their duties. At least they didn't have a dunking booth this year. He'd nearly drowned at the last carnival. Some guy, who thought he was a baseball player, had pounded Jared into the water a dozen times. Mike eventually had enough of the braggart and convinced the jerk—with one of his glares—to move along.

Now, Jared climbed into the ladder truck, riding shotgun with Laredo. You'd think the guy was aiming for a blue ribbon in a rodeo the way he sat in the driver's seat. Jared wondered if *he'd* ever been that green and proud of the quint.

A big no. The day an engine outshined a good-looking woman, he'd check himself into a looney bin.

Laredo pulled in line behind the squad and flipped on the siren. He got as much of a kick out of this as the kids. Jared scanned the faces of everyone lined up on either side of the street. He was looking for a certain blonde and three rambunctious kids.

***

"I want to ride on the firetruck," Tanner shouted in Jessica's ear.

"Me too."

Jessica needed to tell her sister how Aiden copied everything Tanner said. But then, she probably already knew.

"Who wants to see boring stuff?"

"It a parade, Tanner," his mother scolded. "And it's not boring."

"Is too."

"When's the fire truck coming?"

Bless his heart. Ever since Jessica told Aiden the fire trucks would be in the parade, he asked that same question every two minutes.

"Can we go to the carnival now?" Tanner was impatient.

"No."

"Why can't we go now?"

Raven had the patience of a saint. "It opens after the parade."

"When's that gonna be?"

"After the firetrucks."

"Will Laredo drive his big truck?" This time, Tanner directed this question to Jess.

"I'm sure he will."

"I want a hotdog." Tiffany's voice surprised her since Tanner had been chatting nonstop.

"Me too." Aiden's face brightened up.

"I want cotton candy," Tanner insisted.

"I want cotton candy," Aiden copied his brother.

"How come he wants to do everything I want?"

By the look on her sister's face, it was clear Raven had enough.

"Tanner. If you keep on, I'll take you home and leave Tiffany and Aiden with Aunt Jessie."

Tiffany stuck her tongue out at Tanner. Jessica covered her mouth to keep from laughing.

"Just cause he's a baby he gets to—"

"I'm not a baby. I'm this many." Aiden held up four fingers.

"How many is that?" Jessica asked him, the teacher in her coming out.

He touched each finger as he counted. "One. Two. Three. Four."

"That's right." She gave the little booger a big smile.

A loud horn blast had her jumping in fright. A firefighter with a huge grin leaned out of a firetruck window and waved. *Jared.*

"Laredo!" Tanner yelled and jumped into the street. Raven's hand shot out and yanked him back. "It's Laredo! In his truck!"

Both men laughed and waved like they were having fun. Even though Jared waved at the kids, Jessica felt his eyes on her. Her heart pounded, but she suspected it was more from seeing Jared than the startling horn. He looked better every time she saw him. She remembered the melting kiss and his hands on her body. Her belly tightened and her face flushed. Thank God, no one knew what she was thinking.

"Another horn screeched and a siren wailed. The engines held nothing back. The crowd cheered and objects flew through the air.

"Wow! Candy!" Tanner ran forward.

Tiffany and Aiden snatched the candy at their feet. Again, Jessica admired her sister's forte in managing three children. After the carnival and all the sugar, they were bound to consume, Raven would be dead on her feet.

Jessica had to admit. The children's energy was infectious. She was ready to tackle the carnival right along with them. "Okay, kids. Let's hit the carnival."

When the kids saw the rides, they forgot all about food. Raven headed to the kiddie rides, but Tanner refused to get on with Tiffany and Aiden. While Raven dealt with him, Jessica searched the crowd for Jared.

"Looking for someone?"

His voice sent chills over the back of her neck. She spun around. "Hi."

"Jared!" Tanner spotted him.

"Hi, champ."

"We saw the firetrucks."

"Yeah. I saw you guys, too. Where's the other two?"

Jessica pointed to the car ride where Tiffany and Aiden laughed and waved.

"Where's Laredo?" Tanner asked Jared.

"He's over at the cake walk."

"Mom, can we go over there?" Tanner pulled on his mom's elbow.

"Tanner. Wait just a minute."

Jessica jumped in before he could say anymore. "Raven, this is Jared. The firefighter you saw in the truck. Jared, this is my sister Raven."

"Hello, Jared." Raven looked like a sly cat. Jessica would elbow her, but Jared would see it.

"It's nice to meet you," he said with a sexy grin.

"I'm sure you had your reservations after meeting my children."

"They're great kids."

Jessica knew her sister. Raven gave Jared a smile that said *bullshit.* She leaned close to Jessica and spoke in a loud mocking whisper. "I like him."

The kiddie ride came to a halt and Raven gathered Tiffany and Aiden.

"Hi, Jared."

"Hi, Jared." It would seem Aiden mimicked both his siblings.

"Hi, guys. Did you have fun?"

The two jumped excitedly and told Jared about their ride.

"Mom. I want to ride that." Tanner pointed to the Bullet.

"I think that's too big for you."

"I'm growed up."

"Not that much."

"What about that?" He pointed to a stand-up ride.

"You're too—"

Ignoring Raven, Tanner looked straight at Jared. "Will you take me on that?"

Jared glanced at Jessica, then Raven. By the alarming look on his face, he didn't want to get between Tanner and his mom.

"Tanner. Manners. Jared is with Jessica, and I'm sure he has other things to do."

"Do you, Jared?"

"Uh, I don't mind, if it's okay with your mom." Jared kept his eyes on Raven, asking her permission.

"See, Mom!"

"If Jared takes you on that ride, when it's over you have to come back to the smaller rides with Tiffany and Aiden."

"Sure thing. Come on, Jared." Tanner grabbed Jared's hand and tugged him off.

"Well. He's something else."

"That he is," Jessica mumbled as she watched Jared and Tanner disappear into the crowd. He'd offered, gone willingly, and with a smile on his face, too. Her heart lifted at the gesture; Jared wanted to please a little boy.

"Mommy, I want to ride, too?"

"Me, too," echoed Aiden.

"Sure thing, honey." Raven glanced to Jess.

"They'll find us," she answered the unspoken question, allowing the kids enthusiasm to sweep her away.

Tiffany and Aiden laughed and waved as the little carousal circled around and around.

"He seems like a nice guy," Raven spoke while keeping her eyes on her children.

"Good looking with smart moves."

"Jessica. Not all hot guys are out for one thing. Look how he is with Tanner."

"Yeah," she said glancing over her shoulder. "Could be part of his game."

Raven faced her, with a concerned expression. "He's not a teenager, and neither are you."

"Not now, Raven."

"It's been five years. I know it still hurts. Don't compare every man with—"

"Do you have to bring that up?"

"Only if you're still living in the past."

Jessica stared down at the ground. "I don't want to make another mistake.

"Honey. We learn from our mistakes. Don't let them cripple us. You were hurt. You lived a horrible lesson. But, look how you are with my kids."

Jessica stared at Tiffany. A little girl with long blonde curls. A beautiful laugh. They could have grown up together. She buried the sting before tears came to her eyes.

"I am past it."

Raven gave her a look that said she knew Jessica wasn't past anything.

"Jessica. Jared seems like a really good guy."

"I want to believe that."

Jared. Hot, most definitely. The caring side she'd seen tonight, warmed her more than his sex appeal. Watching him with Raven's children tugged at her heart. The play-boy image she'd labeled him with was non-existent this evening. She'd been rash and unfair. Jared surprised her more and more. Her defenses were beginning to crumble.

"If he's still interested in me after a taste of this ..."

Raven gave her a squeeze. "Atta girl."

Jared's heart did a flip as he spotted Jessica standing with her sister and the two kids. Tanner was excited and couldn't stop talking about the ride.

"Mom, that was awesome." Tanner slid to a stop next to his mom. "Can I have a soda?"

"It's probably time for you guys to eat."

"I want a hotdog," Tiffany squealed.

The little guy did too, and then Tanner started asking for everything. When Jessica rolled her eyes at him, Jared covered his mouth to hide his laugh.

He took Jessica's hand and followed the bunch to the hotdog stand, all the while thanking Cap for letting him have the time to spend with them.

All the guys took a turn helping out with different areas of the carnival. He'd put in overtime all week, hoping to spend tonight with Jessica.

He pulled out his wallet and treated the family to hotdogs and drinks, waving off Raven's protest.

"Please. I'm happy to do it."

With the kids as a buffer, meeting Jessica's sister had been a breeze. His unease vanished as soon as she'd said, "hello." So much like Jessica, Raven was easy to talk to, and fun. She had a handle on her kids, too. With love and patience, she expertly managed her children.

"Hey, Jared. How do you spell relief?"

Thinking of the Rolaids commercial on television, Jared knew he had this. "R-O-L-A-I-D-S."

"Naw. F-A-R-T."

"Tanner!"

Jared laughed and wanted to fist-bump the kid. That was a good one. One glance to his mom said she wouldn't approve. Although, before Jessica had turned her head away, he saw her smile.

"Can you fart with your arm?" Tanner lifted his arm in demonstration. The kid was a hoot.

"Okay, I'm ready to call it a night." Raven had a hand on Tiffany and Aiden. The woman must take vitamins to keep up with all three kids

"Aw, mom."

"You've each had ten rides a piece. That's enough. Now, thank Jared and tell him good night."

"Thanks, Jared," Tanner and Tiffany said at the same time.

"You're welcome, guys. High five." Each kid took a turn smacking his hand.

"Fanks, Jared." The little guy was winding down. He'd probably fall asleep in the car on the way home.

Jared leaned down and scooped up the kid. "Hey, tiger, want a ride to the car?"

His tired eyes lit up. "Sure."

Jared propped him on his shoulders. Raven gave him a grateful smile. She had to be pooped.

"Mommy, are we going home now?"

"Yes, Tiffany. I think it's everyone's bedtime."

"Jessie, too?"

Jessica's gaze shot to his. He wanted her to stay with him. *Bedtime* gave him all sorts of ideas.

"Yes, sweetheart. It's time for me to go home, too." Her words said one thing, yet her eyes promised him another.

Hot damn.

Jessica reached out for Tiffany and lifted the little girl in her arms. A funny feeling swept through his chest. No matter what he'd said before, Jessica would make a wonderful mother.

As they waved bye to the kids, Jared was achingly aware of the woman standing beside him. He was dangerously close to yanking her to him and devouring her. Before he acted on his powerful hunger, he calmed his mounting desire. Jessica created intense emotions within. Longing, craving, being with her had his passions on overdrive. Being near her tested his limits.

"You're a good sport."

He released a deep breath. "What do you mean?"

"Three energetic kids clinging to you. Demanding your attention for the past hour."

Jared shrugged with an indifference he didn't feel. "They're cool kids."

"Tanner is a mess."

"He's a typical boy." Even knowing her touch would only feed his craving, Jared still had to touch her. He reached for her hand, enjoying the warmth spreading up his arm. "You don't really want to go home do you?"

"Not really," she breathed.

"Come on, let's ride the Ferris wheel." Anything to keep her with him.

"The Ferris wheel?"

"Don't tell me you're afraid of heights?"

"Bring it on."

Only two people stood in line. The motor hummed, and the cars moved forward. A man pulled a lever, and another man opened the bar. With his hand on her back, Jared guided her.

"You're not going to shake this thing if we stop at the top, are you?"

"Me? I want to woo the girl, not scare her off."

Jessica laughed at his expression. "Right answer."

It felt perfect to put his arm around her, drawing her close. His heart thudded double-time when she nestled right up next to him. Her tantalizing scent swamped his senses. Keeping his hands from roaming would be harder than he'd imagined.

The wheel stopped a few times before it reached the top. When the bucket swayed, Jessica gripped his thigh. He would have enjoyed the sudden heat in his groin if she hadn't looked so scared.

"Jessica?"

"What?" Her breath short, she didn't look at him.

"Hey. I've got you." He tightened his arm around her back and placed his hand over the one on his leg.

She buried her face in his shoulder. *Damn.* She was really scared.

He placed a finger under her chin and raised her face to his. When their eyes met, heat replaced her fear. Then longing. He brushed his lips over hers, and was lost.

The kiss began soft and coaxing, a way to relieve her fear. The idea was for her to concentrate on him and not her anxiety.

Never had anything tasted sweeter. Never had a woman grabbed him by the balls with just a kiss. He enveloped her within his body, gently rolling his tongue past her cotton candy lips. A little noise of pleasure escaped her, turning his desire to sweet agony.

CHAPTER 16

The moment he kissed her on that Ferris wheel, there was no turning back.

When Jessica had first met Jared, he'd been testy and rude. Even so, he'd attracted her. He had that sexy glint in his eyes that made him hot. Oh yes, he'd been completely aware of his sex appeal. He didn't like her. Then he did. Little by little he had wormed his way through her defenses.

And now ...

The click of the lock echoed down the hallway.

"This place is really nice. It suits you." When Jessica was nervous, she said whatever came to mind. She knew little about him, so how would she know if the place suited his personality? Her mind whirled. Would he pounce on her now that they were alone? Would he rip her clothes off? She couldn't very well push him away after agreeing to come to his place. The kiss on the Ferris wheel had melted her brain.

"Would you like something to drink? I can put on a pot of coffee, or maybe you'd like a beer."

Jessica took a deep breath to calm her nerves. Rolling her shoulders, she turned. Seeing him standing there with his windblown hair and his blue, glittering eyes, all her inhibitions drifted away. Could he read her thoughts? Did he know how much she craved his kiss again?

Unable to move, she stood there, not knowing what to do. Apprehension held her in place. She wanted this. She wanted him.

He took a step closer, and then another. She licked her lips in anticipation. Willing him to take her in his arms and crush her insecurities. Take away her indecision and demand her surrender.

His chest mere inches from her face, she had to raise her head to see his eyes. She trembled in amazement. The gentlest expression greeted her.

"You're safe with me. I won't hurt you. If you want to sit and talk, that's fine by me. If you want to leave, that's cool, too. I'm just a guy, Jessica. I'm very attracted to you. That kiss … Can't help wanting another one. But you set the pace. I'm—"

She placed her hand on his chest, and he stopped talking.

"I want another kiss, too."

Intense longing filled his eyes, stabbing her insides, flooding her with a craving she'd never experienced before. The kiss on the Ferris wheel must have affected him as deeply.

Sparkling blue eyes stared down at her, as if he was giving her time to understand the upspoken current between them. He wanted her. She was saying yes.

Tunneling his fingers into her hair, he cupped her head, then tilted it back a little. His penetrating gaze pierced her. She opened to him, allowing him to see into her soul.

Chemistry flared between them, raw and carnal. A magnitude of sensations consumed her.

Stimulating—inflaming—arousing.

Then, ever so slowly, he dipped his head.

Her eyes closed and she tightened her fingers, gripping his shirt. His lips dotted her cheeks with the gentlest of kisses. Whisper soft, his touch so tender, she marveled at his control.

Finally, his tongue slid over her lower lip. His teeth nipped the tender flesh, then soothed it with his tongue. She shuddered, nerves tingling throughout her body. More. She wanted more. Opening up to him, she welcomed his advances, letting his tongue explore the sensitive areas of her throat. The indentation between her neck and shoulder. God, this was wonderful.

His lips were as soft and seductive as the first time. He melted her insides along with any restraint she might have left. She slipped a hand around his neck and pulled him closer. She was falling freely, no doubts, nothing holding her back.

Her body hummed. He slid his tongue into her mouth, tangling with hers. Her fingers bit into his shoulders as their tongues did a mating dance. He shifted, sliding his hands down her body, pulling her tighter against him. Desire shot to her core. She wrapped her arms around his neck and melted into the solid wall of his muscled chest. Nothing existed but this glorious kiss.

It went on and on. Slow, deep, enticing. Tongue, lips, breaths. Until he finally came up for air. Her mind was in a whirl when his mouth traveled down her neck. Delicious. Oh, so delectable. His tongue circled behind her ear and flicked the lobe. How amazing, such a little thing could give such a large kick to her belly. His lips caressed her lobe, then he gently sucked, melting her entire body into a pool of goo.

Her feet left the floor, and she realized he had lifted her. One muscled arm held her snug against his hard chest, and the other one under her knees.

"Jessica. I want you. Please say yes."

Dragging her gaze to his piercing one, she caught her breath. Scorching intensity burned in his eyes. How could he think she would deny him? Her lungs ached; she could barely breathe. She gave a nod and burrowed her face in the curve of his neck, licking him, kissing him for her answer.

He tightened his hold, his steps as powerful as the arms carrying her. He sat down and cradled her on his lap. As he rubbed her back, the tightness in her chest slipped away with each stroke of his hand.

"I know I've been sending mixed signals, but I want this."

He gave a soft laugh as he slightly shook his head. "You're amazing, Jessica. I love having you in my arms. I can't get enough of touching you, kissing you. But I'm sensing something."

She placed a hand on his cheek. "I want you to make love to me."

"Then why am I getting the feeling you're holding back?"

"You scare me." Seeing his anxious expression, she quickly pressed on. "*This* scares me. You make me feel things I don't trust. When you kiss me, I lose myself. All I can think of is you kissing me and I want more."

Jared grinned like a tomcat that swallowed a gallon of cream. "I like what I'm hearing so far. More? That's a good thing. Right?"

"I'm used to being in control, and I'm not when you touch me."

Jared pressed his forehead to hers. "Can I tell you a secret?" he murmured. "I feel the same way."

Her eyes widened and she leaned back where she could see his face. Him? Jared?

"Yes, me," he said as if she'd spoken her thoughts out loud. "Since I turned eighteen, I've been in control of everything. My life, my emotions. Since I met you, I've been on a roller coaster ride. You're the first woman that's made me act this way. You're the first woman who's mattered. I want to impress you, in a good way. Not just get you into bed. I want you to like me. The man I am."

"You continue to surprise me, Jared. I've kept walls up for so long, I feel vulnerable having you knock them down."

"Am I? Knocking them down?"

Jessica nodded.

Flickers of desire darkened his gaze. He slid a hand up her back to her neck. Heat traveled from his warm palm over her sensitive skin and flowed throughout her limbs.

"No more walls?" he asked.

"None," she whispered.

Before she could think, Jared lifted her and held her, just as had before. He carried her down the hallway, and she was sure he headed for his bedroom.

Once inside, she was amazed at the décor. Everything was in its place, but the colors were definitely male. With her in his arms, he sat down, then placed her beside him on the bed.

"You are a beautiful woman. I promise not to hurt you."

The tips of his fingers caressed her throat, causing her breathing to hitch. The lids of his eyes drooped, giving him a sensual, smoldering look. Sexual tension held them both in its clutches. The drugging rush of desire coursed down her spine.

"Sweetheart," he said as he dipped his head. "You sure know how to mess with a man's ... uh, mind." He nuzzled her neck, his throaty whisper hummed through every nerve in her body.

Jessica clutched his head, threading her fingers though his silky, short hair. His mouth. She needed his mouth. Tugging his head, she took what she wanted.

Jared knew a thing or two about pleasing a woman in the bedroom.

Fear of moving too fast with Jessica held him in place. He'd never been so worried about a woman's reaction before. It had been pretty obvious most women wanted the same thing he did: a good time, then to go their separate ways.

Jessica had a hold on him he couldn't explain. Of course, they'd had a rocky start, but the signals coming off her at the carnival had given him the idea of a full night of passion. He wanted to snuggle up to her real close. Kiss her until she lay pliant in his arms. The last thing he wanted to do was to push her before she was ready.

Her breathing quickened, and the look in her eyes was promising. Then she reached for him and gave him a kiss that proved she wanted him. The desire she poured into the kiss nearly knocked him on his ass. Honest to God, the woman dove him mad with lust.

Kissing a woman had never felt so good. He slid his hand up to cover one breast. She gasped and tightened her grip in his hair, which was encouraging. Now, his hands wanted to roam everywhere they could reach.

She tugged at his shirt. He paused long enough to tear the thing over his head and toss it somewhere. When she tugged at her own, he held his breath. God, she was more beautiful than he'd imagined. Full and plush, and oh so mouthwatering.

When her fingers went to the clasp of her bra, he stilled her hands.

"Let me," he whispered.

His fingers trembled; he was so damn turned on. Finally, he was going to see her. Touch her. His tongue stuck to the roof of his mouth.

He'd done this a thousand times, but he felt clumsy. Hesitant. Had he ever wanted anything so badly in his life?

He flicked the clasp and peeled the flimsy material open.

She was lovely, so damn sexy. He wanted all of her.

He lifted a finger and traced a path from her neck, over her luscious globe, and stopped just above her nipple.

"Breathtaking," Jared said, then he bent his head and took the tip into his mouth. Her moan was music to his ears. He licked and caressed and nuzzled her. Then he left her gasping as he moved to give its twin the same attention. He grazed the bud with his teeth, delighting in the cry from her lips.

Things were heating up. His hunger for her multiplied by the way she responded. Her body gyrated, her hands clutched his head, they both were spiraling into a pool of passion.

His fingers slipped between their bodies, to tug at her jeans. She quickly helped him remove them, and then she pulled at his. There were no awkward moments. Each told the other with their actions what they wanted. He grabbed her panties, tugged them off and immediately covered her entire body with his. Skin on skin. The blood pounded in his head. He tried to slow down, but his hunger drove him. Her pleading drove him.

He cupped her curls and slipped one finger inside.

Sweet Jesus.

"Uh, do you, ... I mean, are you on the pill?"

She blushed. "No."

That told him so many things. He took pleasure in knowing Jessica had not been promiscuous with other men. He felt on top of the world.

"Hold on." He grabbed his jeans, got his wallet and found what he needed. Then he took care of business real quick. When he rolled back over, her eyes were tightly closed.

"Hey," he said softly. She opened her eyes. "Did I lose you someplace?"

She bit her bottom lip. "It's just I haven't really dated anyone in years. Jared, I want you. I don't want to lose this moment. I've never felt this good, this sure, in my life."

Thank God.

He grinned. "I'm right here, baby. Are you okay?"

"Yeah, and I didn't mind how fast things were going."

Shit. That twisted his groin in knots.

"I love your tongue. I love the way you move it and the sensations it creates in my belly."

Holy hell, he felt like a smoke stack ready to blow.

"Jared, make me yours."

He slammed his mouth down over hers. Desire clawed his insides. Her squirming told him she felt exactly the same way. When her body started gyrating, he knew her need was as great as his.

"Oh, baby. You are so ready for me."

"Yes, Jared. Hurry."

He took her hands in his, dragging her arms over her head. Their eyes locked. He held his breath knowing that this moment was epic. He arched his back and slid into her in one erotic thrust.

Fuck!

Their deep sighs mingled together.

He'd never felt anything so delectable in his life.

Jessica's eyes rolled back into her head. His dick throbbed.

Suddenly, Jessica's body contracted around him.

Jesus.

He had to move. His blood roared in his veins. He shifted, pulled out and thrust back in.

"Oh my God, Jared."

"Yeah, baby."

Blood thundered in his ears. He couldn't think. He couldn't prolong a damn thing. All he could do was feel. His body demanded he thrust. Then, he thrust harder, sucking air through his teeth. Jessica's cries sent him spinning out of control. Her orgasm ambushed him with its power. He was helpless to hold off the quaking sensation hurling through his body.

He shuddered, pouring himself into her.

Seconds, hours passed while he held her. Thinking of nothing but the bliss he'd just experienced. Thinking of how right she felt in his arms. He relished the feel of her skin, and the sound of her breathing. The hard pumping of her heart had slowed to a soft murmur.

Absolute bliss.

If he never moved from this spot, from this moment, he would die a happy man.

The tightness in his chest was gone. A miracle. Only moments before he'd been terrified. Terrified that Jessica would not want him. Would see him as a playboy? He'd rather she didn't see his vulnerability, but he wasn't a jackass. He cared. And he really cared about her.

She felt like heaven in his arms.

He wanted to say more. To explain how incredible this had been. Confusion held him back. He liked it way too much. He liked Jessica way too much.

I don't do relationships.

I had an itch to scratch—she scratched it.

Who was he kidding? Now that he'd had a taste, he was hungry for more.

This couldn't be happening to him. Feelings. Deep feelings for a woman. Emotions. To the point of being content with *only one* woman.

Craving one woman.

He was a man poised on the precipice of a cliff where he was about to fall off. Hell, he was ready to jump off.

His life was about to change.

And he was scared.

***

Jessica stretched, feeling every muscle in her body come alive. Lying next to Jared was thrilling. Everything about him excited her. He was rousing stimulating exhilarating ... yet she felt ... solace? Comforted? Safe?

Just plain awesome. Good. Great.

Still, they had to come back to reality at some point. She only hoped he would want to keep seeing her. That he would want to remain in her life.

She tugged the sheet over her breasts. "Jared?"

His eyes snapped open. "Yeah?"

"I don't want this to be awkward."

"What?" He shifted around so he could meet her gaze.

God, he looked wonderful. Delicious. All fluffed and sexy. Her belly stirred and punched—I want him again.

Uncertainty crowded in, pushing away the contentment she'd been feeling.

"I mean ... uh ..."

"Hey," he murmured softly. "This was incredible. You are incredible." He swooped down to kiss her, and she melted in his arms again.

After a long lingering kiss, he sighed.

"I hope that's a good sigh."

"I won't lie to you. I'm out of my zone, here. You're great. You're perfect. This is the best se—uh, I can't say I have ever felt this way."

She caught his slip, but it didn't bother her. Still, she wanted to know what he was thinking. "Take a stab at it. What are you feeling?"

He ran a hand through his hair and laughed. "Pretty fucking great. Uh, sorry. I mean, being with you was fantastic." He rolled, shifting both arms under her. "I want to hold you and never let go of this moment."

Warm tingles floated through her body, making her all warm and cozy. "Aww gosh. You'll make my head grow."

"No kidding." He put a finger under her chin and met her eye to eye. "It was wonderful. You feel like you belong here."

Belong?

"I don't expect dying devotion, but what you're saying is pretty solid. I mean, I didn't expect you to admit you felt anything like that."

His brow hiked up. "You didn't?"

She smiled. "I feel the same way. I'm excited, and awed, and everything tingles. I'm, well, I'm surprised you feel it, too."

"I've had my share of women. But nothing has come close to what I just shared with you."

Oh, how she wanted to believe him.

She shoved that one little curl back from his brow. "I care for you, Jared."

"I know you do, or you wouldn't have gone this far."

"You mean, casual sex? No, I don't do casual sex. But I don't expect you to put a ring on my finger, either."

He stiffened.

"Don't look so scared. I was only saying."

"I'm not ... not scared."

She enjoyed being with Jared, and there were no regrets. The joy in her heart stunned her. She had to admit she felt pretty great, too.

"Is it okay with you if we just stay here a bit longer?"

He tightened his arms around her. "You don't have to ask me twice."

She snuggled into his side. "Good. Cause I'm loving the feel of you against me." She slid her hand over his chest, relishing the touch of his silky hair. Her hand roamed farther and drifted to his side. She felt a pucker and realized it was a scar. Quite a long scar.

"How did you get this?"

"Not how you think. It's a reminder of a moment of my stupidity in my youth."

"Care to tell me about it?"

"To make a long story short—"

She interrupted, "I'm not planning on going anywhere."

"I'm not planning on letting you." He squeezed her to make his point. "Anyway, I was mad at my brother, at the world, really, and went looking for a fight. I found one."

"How many brothers do you have?"

He took a deep breath before he answered, "One. We have the same father. Long story."

"Any sisters?"

"No."

"Sounds like maybe your life is full of long stories."

"Yeah." He remained quiet.

Maybe he didn't want to talk about his family. Maybe it was a sore subject. So, she switched topics hoping this one was safer.

"Why did you want to be a firefighter?"

"I left home. Another long story. I decided to drive as far as I could. I drove, got a place to sleep, got up and drove on the next morning. I needed money, so I found a job, found a house to rent. A real fixer upper. I was working on it late one night, and I smelled smoke. Looked out the window and saw a fire next door. I ran over to help. The people who lived there were asleep. I woke them up, helped them get out. I guess someone called the fire department."

"You probably saved their lives."

"I was pumped. As I watched those guys run into that house, I couldn't believe it. The thing was engulfed in flames. They weren't afraid. Those men were charging in to fight that fire. I watched in awe. Each man knew what he was doing, with precision. I think I was high on adrenaline. I liked it. I felt good about myself for the first time since learning about—uh, never mind that."

Darn. He'd been about to tell her something important. She didn't question him, just let him talk.

"I went to Sation Eight the next day, signed on, and I've been riding the high ever since."

"Where is home?"

"Here. Staunton is my home."

"So, you never went back?"

"Nope. Never went back. Never finished college."

She raised up and propped an elbow under her head. "So, you were a frat boy."

"I was a dumb kid."

"Hmmm You came here, got a job as a fireman, and—"

"Firefighter."

"Oh, uh, firefighter. And you stayed."

"When I was twenty-one, a permanent position came open and I took it. That was seven years ago."

"I can tell you like what you do, and you're good at it. I watched you when Alicia's car was on fire."

Jared chuckled. "When I told you to keep your husband back?" He scrubbed a hand over his face. "That was a land-mine."

"Blew up in your face, huh?"

"No comment."

She slid her hand up his chest and rested it over his heart. "You sure are fit."

"The guys call me *pretty boy* and *Hollywood* in fun. I'm not one of those preppies who spend hours in front of a mirror, obsessing about my looks. Although, I do like to keep in shape for the job. We get plenty of exercise on calls, but I work out, too."

"I can tell." She found his scar again.

"You thought I got that from fighting fires."

"The thought crossed my mind."

His chest rose and fell with his sigh. "I was eighteen. Thought I had it all. A life most guys would give their right arm for. I was just a dumb kid. Couldn't appreciate the home I had. I don't know why I'm telling you this."

"Please don't stop."

"What I believed to be the truth all my life, was nothing more than a lie. I found that letter ... my world got yanked out right from under me. Self-pity can warp a young man's mind. I became bitter, resentful. Went out looking for trouble. Got into a fight with a knife."

"With a knife?"

"I deserved a punch from the guy. By the time I saw the knife, it was too late."

Jessica closed her eyes, visualizing a big man with a knife waving it at Jared. The image nearly choked her.

"I was lucky. Missed my important organs. A scar kind of adds a hero quality, don't you think? But, in reality, it keeps me grounded."

"Grounded?"

"A reminder. Never to let myself fall into a mindless void. While I was feeling sorry for myself, there were people out there who lost a whole lot more than their aspirations. People lost homes, loved ones. People who needed help."

"I would never have guessed. You come across as though you don't have a care in the world."

"Hey," he said with a shrug. "Lots of practice. Besides, I've got it good. I'm healthy, good looking." He waved his eyebrows at her causing her to laugh. She punched him. "I have a job I love. What more could a man ask for?"

"Nothing, I suppose."

He flipped to his side, facing her. "Wrong. I could ask for a good woman. Not sure I deserve one. I know I don't deserve you."

She lifted a hand, stroking her fingers from his forehead to his cheek. "Flattery will get you everywhere."

"It will? How about here?" He nuzzled her neck, and she didn't want him to stop. "How about this? Will it get me this?" He cupped her breast and lightly squeezed. Desire shot between her thighs.

"You've got a damn good chance..."

He covered her mouth with his and gave her the kiss she'd been longing for.

Hot, pulsing man. Caring. Loving?

Only time would tell.

But she already knew he had her heart.

CHAPTER 17

Though his team had labeled Jared a ladies' man, he suffered doubts of a real relationship. His father had cheated. A chip off the old block, Jared lived his life fearing he might be destined to do the same. Could it be in the genes? Passed down from one generation to the next?

So, he'd played the field and never got serious about one woman. He liked women. Loved them, in fact. He just couldn't give his heart to one woman. Yet now he could only think about one. He suspected Jessica already had a piece of his heart.

God, he wished he'd never found that letter.

"Pretty boy is getting all domesticated."

Jared blinked and glanced at the men around him. While the team was eating, he'd gotten lost in his own thoughts. He tuned in to the conversation at the table. Evidentially, he was the target.

"That's Mike. He's the one talking marriage and shit," Cooper said.

"I don't know, Coop." Laredo gave a mischievous grin. "Jared looked pretty housebroken last night."

"What are you guys talking about?" Jared asked.

"Decide to come out of that trance you went into?" Mike joined in.

"Yeah, big guy. You don't have any room to talk." Since Mike had met Cassie, the two acted like turtledoves.

Laredo stared at him in surprise. "*Mierda*, Jared. Are you admitting you're smitten?"

"I don't know, Laredo. He was riding the Round Up with the boy, not the woman."

Jared didn't have the fortitude to keep up with the idiots. Then Shep gave his two cents, "Come on, guys. It was a carnival. There were lots of kids there."

"Is this the mother of the kids where you and Laredo went to save a cat?" Mike asked.

"Are you dating a woman with three kids?" Cooper's shocked expression was overkill.

"I thought the woman was married. Laredo said her husband is in the military." Mike pinned Jared with his stare, his eyes twinkling with laughter.

Cooper dramatically placed a hand over his heart. "Jared, you're my idol. You can't be seeing a married woman."

"Better watch out, Jared," Laredo taunted. "He's going to kick your ass. Military guys know some bad shit, *amigo*."

Jared tossed down his fork. "Will you guys give me a break?"

"She's one sexy mother—"

Everyone's pager went off right along with the PA system.

"Shit," Cooper sputtered with his mouth full.

"Tough luck, Cooper," Mike said shoving away from the steaming pasta.

The code referred to a domestic situation. Cooper's turn to assist on the squad. A two-man team stood by in case they were needed, but first the police had to get the situation under control. After the all-clear was given, the EMTs could move in.

"I worked hard on this. You could stand to miss a few meals," Cooper glared at Mike. "Besides, one look at you and the bad guy would back off."

"I'll take this one, Cooper. Make sure you save me some of that shrimp."

Cooper looked like a dog that had been given a bone. Jared shook his head as he got up to go with Mike. At least the guys weren't razing on him anymore.

Jared was revving up the Midi when Mike jumped in.

"132 Ridgeway Court," Mike said as he programmed the GPS.

Jared put the shifter into gear and pulled out of the bay. When he turned onto Ridgeway, two police cars were angled in front of a house, their flashing lights bouncing around in the trees. Jared pulled next to the curb. One officer led a man in handcuffs toward a cruiser while his partner motioned Mike and Jared inside.

"He's drunk. Took a knife to his wife."

Mike crossed to the woman who had a gash on the back of her shoulder. Her husband must have gotten her when she ran from him. Good thing the police had gotten there first, or Jared would have been tempted to beat the shit out of the drunk. Mike's gaze locked with Jared. The big guy felt the same way.

"Hello. My name is Mike. Mind if I take a look at your shoulder?"

She didn't say a word as she turned her back to him. She removed the bloody towel she had pressed to her wound. Mike bandaged the woman's shoulder while Jared took her vitals.

"She need an ambulance?" Mike glanced at Bill, the cop who had followed them inside. Jared stood and motioned for Bill to follow him, so they could speak privately.

"It's up to her, but it's a scratch." Jared glanced back a he woman. "She's lucky. She doesn't seem too scared. Wonder if her sorry ass husband has done this before."

"The neighbors called us. Heard them screaming and yelling at each other. When we arrived, the husband opened the door, and when I saw the knife ..." Bill's voice drifted off.

"I can imagine. He come at you?"

"Todd was in front. He got the brunt. Took him down in two seconds. I had my hand on my gun, ready for him, but I didn't need it." Bill nodded toward the woman. "She was hiding in the bathroom. Her husband tried to break down the door. When we put the handcuffs on him, she cried. Didn't want us to arrest him."

"But you did."

"Had to. He came at us with a knife."

"You probably did her a favor. A lot of women are afraid to press charges."

"If he hadn't threatened Todd, there would be nothing we could do."

"You mean if she didn't press charges, he'd get off Scot-free?"

"You got it." Bill shrugged. "The way the system works."

That sucked. The guy would have gotten away with attacking his wife because she didn't want the police to arrest him. Jared shook his head.

Todd had been speaking in a radio. He clicked a button and stepped inside. "A social worker is on the way. She'll take care of the woman."

"Thanks for your help, Jared," Bill added. "We'll wait until the social worker gets here."

"What about her husband?"

"Colin and Travis took him down to the station," Todd answered. "They'll book him and keep him overnight." He shrugged. "Tomorrow? It's another day."

CHAPTER 18

When Station Eight was built, doors were put on both sides. The idea was to always have the engines facing forward. So, the trucks entered through the back, facing the front bay doors. That way drivers did not have to worry about room to back up or turn around.

Most days the bay doors were kept open on both sides. The front of the building had five doors. Only the rigs needed were sent out, and on big calls they all went. Today, only two of the back doors were open.

Jared's pager went off on his side. He rushed through the bay and met Shep ripping a paper from the printer. Cooper hustled to the row of boots lined along one wall with droopy pants folded over them. Laredo kept his boots in front of the maps. Even though Station Eight had a state of the art electronic first response navigation system, Laredo like to glance at the county roads and regions on the maps. He knew Augusta County like the back of his hand, but for whatever reason, he also took a gander at the ink detailing the area.

In the two seconds Laredo studied the map, he'd pulled up the bunker pants and snapped his suspenders onto his shoulders. Prepared to go, he grabbed his coat and raced to the driver's side of the truck. Jared hauled his butt into the back seat. As he closed the door, he saw Mike and the new recruit jog to the squad. Laredo flipped on the siren and the rig jerked as he pulled through the bay door.

"What is it, Cap?" Jared flicked on the GPS.

Shep had fought hard to get the Global Positioning Satellite technology. In an emergency, every second counted, and the GPS could track real-time movements of any equipped vehicle, helping dispatchers more accurately deploy emergency resources.

Riding shotgun, Shep glanced over his shoulder. "I-81."

"Shit. Another one?" Laredo spat in repulsion. "That's four in the last five days."

"Mile marker 245."

"When are they going to do something about that interstate? It's over-crowded. I-81 needs at least three lanes, or even four, north and south."

Damn. Jared recalled so many accidents close to the same spot. "Guess you don't need the GPS."

"The rig knows the way by itself." Laredo spun the wheel taking the ramp to the interstate. "When are the VDOT assholes going to do something to prevent these accidents."

"The big wigs in Northern Virginia use the funding up there. Shit, they have five and six bypass lanes in Alexandria."

"We can't even get three on I-81. And it's the main road that eighteen-wheelers use."

"I-81 doesn't affect the high-class politicians," Mike said. "Those people won't do anything about roads they don't travel on."

Jared snorted. "You'd think with most of the accidents happening within the first two miles after the rest stop, they'd do something. Wrecks every day, and too many fatalities."

"Every resident in Virginia has complained about the two-lane highway. Fuckers had the opportunity to lay four lanes, but could they do that? No. The good 'ole boys constantly fighting progress or anything that would make this area grow."

The new recruit gave his two cents. "If the plans for that Toyota factory had gone through, Congress would have had to widen the interstate."

"Good old Commonwealth," Mike grumbled. "A chance at jobs for hundreds of people, and they screwed that up, too."

"Don't get me started," Shep snapped. "Keep your eyes on the road and prepare yourselves. A tractor trailer went into the median and two more cars were involved."

Jared hated interstate calls. A burning building, he pretty much knew what to expect. But interstate roads had all kinds of crazies on them. Impatient crazies. Angry people who didn't want to wait. Business tycoons or regular asshats, and no idea of what they might do. With several vehicles involved, especially an eighteen-wheeler, traffic would be tied up for hours.

Five hours later, the trucks returned to the firehouse.

Jared rolled out of the rig, exhaustion cramping every muscle in his body. A bed and a bath. He didn't care in what order. The accident had been less severe than anyone expected. The wrecker had hooked up and pulled the rig out without any problem, but it had taken time to get a young mother and her child out of her car. Thank God both were okay. The driver of the other car had a spin-out. He'd be fine. The truck driver had not been as lucky.

The rescue group had waited for a wrecker and a flat bed, then helped to clean up. No fatalities, so it had been a good day. And he still had another fifteen hours left on his shift.

Moans, and groans, and a few curses echoed off the cement walls as the men stowed their gear. All Jared wanted was not to stink. As he put one booted foot on the first step, he stumbled from the blow to his back.

"Why so quiet?"

"Shit, Mike. I'd rather you knock me up the steps, not down."

He laughed. "You got something ailing you?"

For once, he'd actually been thinking of something other than Jessica. True, the woman stayed on his mind most of the time. She'd be at work when his shift ended …

"Hey!"

"Christ, Mike." Jared rubbed his ear. "I'd like to keep my hearing. What's with you?"

"Hollywood is redirecting your questions, hoss," Cooper said from behind them.

"I am not."

"Hmmm. You might be right, pup."

Jared glared at Mike and Cooper. "Were either one of you guys at the same place as me? I'm exhausted."

"How can you be exhausted? You didn't do anything."

Jared froze with one boot on the next step. He brought his foot back and slowly turned. If he wasn't so tired, he'd knock Cooper on his ass.

"Leave the kid alone," Mike said. "We both noticed you dragging."

"Something or *someone* … has Hollywood worn out. Come on, man. Is this what I have to look forward to?" Cooper pressed his thumb against his fingers like he was counting. "You're only eight years older than me. You mean, when I get your age, I'll be petered out?"

Mike busted a laugh that could have shaken the rafters. "Good one, kid."

Jared turned again, and continued up the stairs, his fists clutched at his sides.

"You still haven't answered my question," Mike boomed behind him.

"I'm tired and I stink. I'm taking a shower." He could hear Cooper laughing as he walked down the hall.

With one arm braced on the wall, Jared hung his head and let the beads of water pound his back. Damn, that felt good. He wondered if Jessica would give him a back rub. Her soft fingers kneading his back, his waist. That line of thinking was bound to lead to other things.

He finished off his shower and tied a towel around his waist. Shouts came from the break room, and he recognized the voice of one of the teenagers who had dreams of becoming a firefighter. He threw on his regulation pants and pulled a shirt over his head. A volunteer and the kid were playing a video game on the big TV screen. Jared gave a wave and headed to the refrigerator. Mike stopped him.

"Look, I know I took a long time in the shower. Make of it what you will."

"Hooley's here."

"What?"

Mike grabbed a water from the fridge, correctly guessing that was exactly what Jared wanted. He handed Jared the bottle and gave a toss of his head toward Shep's office. "He came in a few minutes ago. Maybe he has news."

Laredo stepped next to Jared, his normally black curly hair plastered to his wet head."

"What's going on?"

"Hooley's in with the Cap."

"Maybe he found something."

Jared thought about Chuck. "Anyone seen Chuck? Isn't he supposed to be working with Hooley now?"

"I heard he turned down a promotion to help with the investigation."

"You heard right," Mike rumbled.

Jared turned up his bottle and gulped half the water down.

"Got another one of those?" Mike opened the fridge, grabbed another bottle of water, and handed it to Laredo.

Cooper came down the hall. "You guys look like a group of cheerleaders with your heads together trashing the new girl in class."

"Get tired of watching the kids play *Halo*?" Jared glanced at the two boys with handheld controls, their bodies swaying back and forth as if they were trying to avoid getting shot. He played sometimes; although, he didn't get as involved as Cooper.

"*Destiny*'s my game now. More fire power. What you girls up to?"

Mike glared at Cooper. "Uh, now hoss. You know I didn't mean you."

"Better not, pup." Mike was only teasing the kid and Cooper knew it.

The door to Shep's office opened, drawing everyone's attention. Caught standing there in a huddle, he felt a lot like Cooper's comparison to a group of teenage girls. Shep counted heads the way Jared had seen him do a hundred times.

"You guys come in here."

Jared locked gazes with Mike, then followed him inside.

Hooley, the fire investigator, stood to the left, leaning against the wall. A sense of déjà vu hit Jared. Last time he'd seen Hooley in the Captain's office, the team found out someone had deliberately set the explosion at the training site. An eerie shiver ran down his spine.

Mike took one of the empty chairs in front of Shep's desk, so Jared took the other. Laredo and Cooper stood with their backs to the wall. Jared didn't like waiting, and this felt like he was about to get his ass handed to him.

"You find the person who set the explosion?" Jared asked.

Hooley pushed away from the wall and pursed his lips. "I'm afraid not. The evidence did prove arson. We're still working on the whodunit. The guy on the film is not with Station Nine or any other house."

"Guy has balls, stealing gear and blending in with the rest of the firefighters during a training. All the firehouses that were there, no one would recognize an outsider."

"We still don't know if he is targeting fire departments in general or individual firefighters," Shep said.

"Which brings me to why I'm here." Hooley stared at Jared. "Your mask was tampered with. We found traces of etomidate. It's used by anesthesiologists."

"Hell. I know what that is," Mike said, in a harsh breath. "Good thing you jerked it off as quick as you did."

"I knew something wasn't right."

"The perp got into our house," Cooper said.

"I'd like to know when," Mike growled.

"And how," Laredo added. "The bay doors are open most of the time, but one of us is always within sight."

"How did the fucker get by us?"

"How does this guy do anything?" Hooley grumbled. "It's obvious he is watching the houses. He's a clever SOB."

"Keep your eyes open," Shep said. "Watch your backs. Watch each other's backs."

"I like being a firefighter," Laredo said. "I never thought I'd have to worry about some guy shooting at me while I'm fighting a fire."

Jared spoke up, "How are we supposed to do our jobs if we have to keep looking over our shoulders? Checking and rechecking every piece of equipment, every hour.

"I understand your frustration. We'll get this guy."

Shep stood. "You heard Hooley. This guy is bound to slip up. Meantime, just do your jobs."

***

Jessica had the afternoon off, so she decided to drop in to see her sister. Of course, Connie was there. "Hi, guys."

"Hi, yourself," Raven said.

"Long day already?" Connie asked at the same time.

Raven said, "Coffee or tea?" She got up from where she'd been sitting at the island counter. "Or I could pour you a glass of wine."

"It's only half-past noon."

Raven shrugged. "The clock has its time; I have mine."

"Tea." Jessica climbed onto the bar stool next to Connie. She propped an elbow on the counter and Jared's image popped into her mind. Heat flooded her body, and she knew her face was turning red.

"Okay. Out with it."

"What?"

"You were a million miles away."

She could never hide anything from her sister.

"Oh, I don't know Raven. I'd say she was right down the block. What is the address of the fire station?"

"All right, you two. I merely came over to visit my sister."

"Uh huh."

Connie sat on the edge of her chair. "Do tell."

Jessica's throat burned with emotion. She wasn't ready to admit anything. Especially how much she enjoyed being intimate with Jared.

"Is it that bad?" Raven asked.

"Or that good?" Connie teased.

Raven leaned over to stare into Jessica's face. "Who is he?"

Connie caught on quick. "Have you found someone?"

Oh shit.

"That hot fire guy," Raven shot back.

"The one who insulted you?" Connie asked.

"The same," Raven answered.

"Don't talk around me," Jessica said. "I'm sitting right here."

"Then speak up," her sister scolded.

"All right. It's him. The fire guy. His name is Jared."

"He's charming."

"How would you know?" Connie asked Raven.

"He was great with the kids at the carnival. He's kindhearted. A real gentleman."

"Oooo, a gentleman." Connie batted her eyes. "So, you haven't gotten to the good stuff yet."

"Connie."

"What? I remember what it was like when I first met Rick. Wasn't long before clothes started flying."

Connie was too close to the truth. Jessica was embarrassed by her actions. She'd been acting like a prude, and then she'd turned right around and slept with Jared.

"Oh, honey."

Raven had the wrong impression. She evidently thought Jessica was on a sex guilt roller coaster. "It's not that, Raven."

Connie placed her cup on the counter and stood.

"I think it's time for me to butt out. This looks like a sister talk time." She leaned in for a hug. "If you ever need me, you know where I am. Anytime."

"Thanks, Connie."

As soon as the kitchen door closed, Raven blurted, "What is it?"

"Not what you think."

"You can't live in the past forever. Your guilt is dictating how you live."

And she'd been wrong before.

So much for the cloud Jessica had been floating on when she arrived. Telling Raven about her intimacy with Jared didn't appeal to her anymore. The mood had changed.

"Raven, we don't need to discuss this again."

"Honey. I'm so sorry it happened."

"I was in college."

"You don't deserve to live the rest of your life in regret."

Didn't she?

"I shouldn't have been messing around."

"You were a kid, in college. Young, ripe, peer pressure? Millions of girls have sex every day. You act like you're living in the dark ages."

"I'm not a slut."

"You don't have to be a slut to have a relationship. You were in love."

"I *thought* I was in love."

Raven froze. "You know the difference now?"

She certainly had not been in love with the boy in college. That was nothing compared to what she was feeling now. Jared was on her mind all the time. She kept thinking of how he had kissed her. How gentle his hands were when he touched her.

And when his mouth did its magic, she could not think at all. Only feel.

"Oh, Raven. I'm so torn. I really like Jared." She lifted her head to meet Raven's gaze, eye to eye. "I mean, a lot."

Raven smiled. "I think I know what you're trying to tell me."

"Yes, I slept with Jared." Jessica looked away.

"Do you think maybe it was more than that? Maybe what you feel for Jared is more than like."

"It's enough to prove my affair in college was not love."

"I know you well enough to know you didn't make the decision lightly."

Jessica flipped her long hair over one shoulder. "I've been so stupid. It wasn't so much making a decision as it ... it felt right. Jared makes me feel something I've never felt in my life." She met her sister's gaze again. "Does it sound crazy that I feel safe with him?"

"You trust him," Raven said cautiously.

"Yeah. I guess I do."

Raven covered Jessica's hand with hers. "Honey. I think you're finally getting over the guilt you've placed on yourself. If Jared makes you happy, I'm happy for you."

"I'm not setting myself up for a fall. I mean, I'm not expecting anything from him. We had sex. I don't expect him to marry me."

"You made love. Now you know the difference."

"Maybe I do love him a little, but I won't be devastated if he stops dating me, or whatever."

A corner of Raven's mouth lifted. "Got it all figured out?"

"Heavens no, Raven. I'm just not going to count on anything."

"You know, Jessica, it's okay to hope."

"Well then, in that case, I'm not ready to let him go."

CHAPTER 19

Usually, at night, things were relatively quiet. The ward settled down when the patients went to sleep. Most of the patients were elderly, had strokes or heart attacks, and the boy in Room 408 had been in a climbing accident. He had fallen over a hundred feet. He was lucky to be alive.

Tonight, Jessica had been called down to help in the ER. When she got there, she found chaos.

Teenagers in every cubicle or on stretchers in the hallway, IVs hooked up to several, and the rescue squad was bringing in more. The staff was scurrying about trying to access each one.

Good Lord, what happened?

"Jessica. I'm glad you're here. Jump in where you can. Kids overdosed. Charlotte went to get a tub of IVs from the storage room. We're going to need them."

Jessica examined the first young man she came to. "Bring this one in here." As she passed the next cubicle, a doctor was trying to revive a young girl. The loud beep of a machine told her another teen had coded.

It didn't matter what day of the week, patients who'd drug overdosed were a common occurrence. But on this night, a bunch of college kids had taken the same toxic drug and nearly died.

What was wrong with kids? They had their whole life ahead of them and were willing to just throw it away. Jessica wished every teenager could see what she saw on a daily basis. Would this be enough to stop students from frying their brain? She wanted to scream. Shout at the world.

All you dumbass kids that want to grow up too fast—you're risking not growing up at all.

Another young man did not survive. The girl standing next to him started screaming. The nurse had her hands full, so Jessica snatched a needle and vile from a cabinet. The girl had to be sedated.

Hours later, Jessica used her forearm to swipe the hair hanging in her face. Some of the students brought to the ER would never see another day. Their life was over. All at the waste of one decision. A careless decision to try a new drug.

She released a sigh as she stepped through the double-glass-sliding doors and squinted at the sun coming up over the horizon. Watching the sun rise was a humbling experience. A new day. A—

Out of the corner of her eye, a figure emerged from the shadows—in dark clothes, as well as a dark, sinister expression. Her heart skipped a beat. She wondered if this might be the drug dealer.

Before she could gather her wits and run back inside, he snatched her arm, his iron fingers digging into her flesh. A hand slapped over her mouth, and he squeezed, holding her firm against a brick wall of a chest.

She struggled to breathe through her nose. The man's musky cologne penetrated her senses. Her mind raced. Who was he? What did he want? The parking lot was well lit, but that didn't help her at the moment. The guard must be making his rounds. Suddenly, she recalled the night Alicia's car exploded. Did this guy have anything to do with that?

"If you don't struggle and you don't turn around, I won't hurt you."

Right. Like I believe that.

For a split second, Jessica decided to fight back. The more rational side of her brain told her to wait for the right moment. He said he wouldn't hurt her. Did she dare trust him?

Trust a lunatic? Are you insane?

She knew not to get into a car with an abductor. That would be sealing her fate. She would never get away.

"Stand still," the harsh voice at her ear whispered.

She forced herself not to move and concentrated on getting air into her lungs.

"That's smart. We don't want you. We want your friend."

Friend? Who could he possibly mean?

"Your co-worker. The pretty blonde nurse. Alicia. Alicia Fleming. Where is she?"

How did he expect her to answer with his hand over her mouth? She could barely breathe.

"I'll move my hand slowly. If you scream, I'll snap your pretty neck."

The blood in her veins turned to ice. She swallowed the fear rising in her throat. Seconds that seemed like hours passed. She thought she might pass out.

Finally, he slid his hand from her lips to her neck, a clear indication reminding her of his threat.

Terror clogged her brain.

The feel of his fingers grasping her neck paralyzed her. There was no doubt in her mind he was capable of ending her life as quickly, and as easily, as snapping a twig.

"I..." Her voice erupted in a croak. She tried again. "I don't know."

His fingers tightened, immediately cutting off her air.

"I haven't seen her," Jessica managed to mumble. "She hasn't been to work for weeks." At least that much was true. She prayed he believed her.

"I know that." The harsh voice thundered in her ear. "She seems to have disappeared."

It was on the tip of her tongue to ask why he wanted Alicia, but she didn't dare utter a sound. If he told her, then Jessica would know too much. What was stopping him from killing her?

"I saw you at her apartment. The next time you see your little friend, give her a message."

Anything! Just please don't kill me.

"What?" she managed instead.

"She can't hide for long."

Before Jessica could absorb his words, the arms holding her were suddenly gone.

She closed her eyes, stumbled and fell to the ground. *Dear God.* That was the man. Alicia's stalker. Jessica sucked air into her starving lungs. She couldn't believe the man had gone and left her alive. She froze and listened intently, trying to distinguish if her accoster was still close by.

The hospital doors slid open and she nearly jumped out of her skin. Two large shapes stepped onto the sidewalk, and she shrieked.

"Jessica?"

She gasped, and then sagged with a whimper. Strong arms lifted her.

"Hey. I've got you."

She recognized Jared voice and grabbed his shirt, clutching the material as though it was a lifeline.

"Are you okay?" The voice of the second man.

"Jessica? What happened? You're shaking." He brought her against his chest.

Her eyes darted to Jared and then the man beside him. "A man." She buried her face in Jared's chest.

"I'll check it out." The large man marched off with a confident stride. His size alone would intimidate, but the movement of his body looked like a man on a mission, and no one would dare get in his way.

"Honey. You're—" She burst into tears. Jared said something under his breath. "Come on. I'm taking you back inside."

"Wait," she said, still clutching his shirt. "Give me a minute."

His arms tightened around her. He held her without questions. Warmth heated her cheek and seeped into her bones. Her heartbeat finally calmed to a much slower rhythm, and she slid her arms around his middle. Hard. Solid. Safe. She wanted to burrow into him and absorb his comfort.

She needed his strength and protection, and he didn't seem to mind. He rubbed a hand up and down her back. When her trembling finally ceased, she released the death grip she had on him. She couldn't stand here all night, no matter how much she wanted to.

"Feeling better?" His deep voice sent another kind of tingling in her veins. One she liked.

Not trusting her voice, she gave a nod for an answer. Then she slowly pulled back.

"I don't normally fall apart like this."

"Ready to tell me what happened?"

"A man grabbed me from behind."

"I didn't see anyone." The big man was back, and she saw him clearly. *Mike.* "If there was a guy here, he disappeared fast enough."

"If?" Jessica stuttered.

Mike's expression quickly changed from anger to concern. "A mere slip of the tongue. I believe you. But whoever he was, he's gone."

"Thank you."

Mike assured her quickly. "No thanks necessary."

Jared leaned back, giving a bit of space between them. "Are you sure you're all right? Let's get you checked out."

"No, Jared. I'm fine. Just scared."

She realized she still had a fist full of shirt. She opened her hand and smoothed the material over his solid chest. Her fingers tingled and she forced herself to stop.

"What are you doing here?"

Jared's temples throbbed with his pulse. His heart pounded like a jackhammer. When he'd seen Jessica, it damn near jumped out of his chest. Her pale face distraught, and her body shaking. He wanted to pound his fist into the man who'd dared to touch her.

But even more, he wanted to gather her in his arms and never let her go.

Jared hiked his thumb at his cohort. "Mike and I brought in a patient with heart attack symptoms."

"More like a case of indigestion, according to his wife," Mike added.

"Routine. We handed him over and was on our way out."

"Good timing."

"Not good enough." He'd have liked to have been five minutes sooner. He could have saved Jessica from being scared to death. And he could have pulverized the guy.

"I'm glad you're here now."

"Me too. Are you coming to work or heading home?"

"I was leaving. I'd just stepped outside when … He covered my mouth and told me not to scream. Then he put his hand—" She lifted her hand to her throat.

His gut ripped. "Look, you don't have to say anymore. I think we should call the police."

"I want to go home."

Mike slapped Jared on the back. "I think you can handle this. I'll take the squad back." With a look of understanding, Mike gave a nod then walked off.

"If you don't want to go back inside—"

"No. I don't." Her fingers rubbed at her neck. Then she raised her gaze to meet his. "Jared. Would you please take me home?"

He would take her anywhere she wanted to go. He would protect her with his life. Damn if he would let her out of his sight. "I think we should call the police."

"The guy is gone. What can the police do tonight that they can't do in the morning?" she stared at him. "Please."

When she looked at him like that, he would do anything she asked of him.

"Of course.

She handed him her keys, and together they walked to her car. He entwined his fingers with hers, letting her feel a warm hand and a solid connection. She remained quiet the entire drive.

Jared followed Jessica up the steps to her apartment door. He liked that she lived above the first floor. If some thief wanted to break in, they'd have a harder time getting into the second story. Especially with a security-controlled stairwell.

She clung to him as he put her key into the lock.

She stepped inside and he stood at the doorway, not knowing if he was invited. Although, he would like to check out her apartment. Make sure no one else was there.

She slowly turned and her expression damn near stopped his heart. Lost. Afraid. His chest squeezed making his decision. He closed the door behind him.

"Thank you," she said in a much stronger voice. He was glad to see some spirit returning. "You want some coffee?"

She didn't need the added rush that caffeine would give her. He was sure her adrenaline was already speeding. But it gave her something to do, and it kept him here with her.

"Sure," he heard himself reply.

She had her hands at her throat again. He'd noticed her doing that before. His anger spiked again. Did that guy try to choke her? His arms shook as he thought of ripping the man's head off.

"Why don't I make the coffee while you go change?" He figured she would want to wash off the bastard's touch.

"Will you stay?"

"I'll be right here. I'm not going anywhere."

"Oh." She put her finger to her lips.

"That is, if you don't mind. I'll stay with you until you feel safe. Fall asleep. Whatever you need."

"Don't you have to get back to the firehouse?"

"My shift is over. Besides, Mike will cover for me."

She seemed relieved, then said, "You're probably tired if you've been up all night."

He took a step closer to her. "I'm used to surviving on little sleep. You've been up all night, too." She looked so lost. So vulnerable. "Come here." He pulled her into his arms.

"I want you to stay," she whispered.

He grinned. "That's good, because I have no intention of leaving you." She released a sigh that had to be relief. He held her. Surely, that was what she needed.

"He scared me."

"I've got you, sweetheart. I'm not going to let anything happen to you."

"I need you."

Those three words knocked the bottom right out of his gut. She needed him. That felt damn good. He worked his hands, massaging her back. After a while, he felt her tight muscles ease.

"If you planned on staying, why did you ask?"

He chuckled. "Manners. I don't expect anything just because we were, you know, together. I'm here for you. Whatever you need."

She raised her hand and cupped her palm over his cheek. "Jared. You are exactly what I need. I'm so glad you're with me."

His gut rolled at the emotion that brought.

"I need a shower."

He gave her a cheeky grin. "Want me to wash your back?"

"At this moment, I wouldn't object to anything you want to do."

Clearly, Jessica was upset. He needed to help her, not take advantage of her.

"Tell you what I'm going to do. I'm going to walk you to your bedroom, make sure you have everything you need, then I'll come back to the kitchen and fix something for us to eat. How does that sound?"

"Sounds perfect."

"And if you need anything, if you need me, I'll be right here. You won't be alone."

"Thank you." Her eyes grew glassy. He thought she might cry. Why hadn't she cried? Most women would be hysterical.

Jessica was strong. Then again, she could have a little shock going on.

As they walked to the bedroom, they held hands with their fingers interlocked. Jared watched her gather her pajamas, and then he stayed close until he heard the water running in the master bathroom. She'd left the door open a crack, so he could hear her if she called out. Still, he hated leaving her alone.

She seemed so vulnerable.

When he'd realized it was her crouched on the sidewalk, he was puzzled. Then, thinking she was hurt, his heart had gone into overdrive. His instincts kicked in. He wanted to hold her, protect her, kill anyone who came near her.

Man. He had it bad.

He strolled back to the kitchen and removed his boots.

Everyone loved omelets, so he took eggs, cheese, and he even found some peppers, from the fridge. He took a knife from the holder, found a cutting board, and chopped up the greens. He whipped up the eggs in no time.

While the pan sizzled, he checked a few more cabinets. Perfect. A bottle of wine. Much better than coffee.

He heard the shower turn off and hurried down the hallway. He stood at her bedroom door. "You doing okay in there?"

"Yes. Thank you for being here, Jared."

"Anything for you, doll. Breakfast is ready. As soon as you dress, come on into the kitchen. Okay?"

"Okay."

He was more than comfortable padding about in her apartment. He had the table set, the food ready, and the wine opened by the time Jessica entered the kitchen. His heart lurched. She looked like she'd been put through the ringer. The urge to kiss her was fierce, but he held back.

"Your table awaits." He made a grand gesture of waving his arm toward her chair. When she sat, he padded around to his side.

"You did all this?"

"The only thing missing is a rose," he shrugged. "Couldn't make one appear. So, we'll have to do with omelets, wine, and good company."

"I can't believe you did this. God, it smells good."

He grinned. "Dig in."

After a few bites, she lifted her wine glass. "I would never have pictured you a romantic."

He gave her a wink. "I know how to wine and dine a female."

"That's my point." She tilted her glass and sipped.

He leaned back, holding up his fork. "Oh, I see. The playboy image."

She shrugged. "This is perfect. I don't think you are as insincere as you pretend to be."

"You just used perfect and insincere in the same sentence."

"My first impression of you—"

"Here we go. Back to first impressions."

"Rude. Ladies' man. Behaves irresponsibly and has casual sexual relationships."

He carefully placed the fork down. "Not a very good impression of me at all. I do spend time enjoying myself, but I am not insensitive. Has your opinion changed?"

"Yes. You're kind. Caring. And you've been wonderful to me."

His heart warmed. "Watch it. You'll make my head grow."

He watched her finish eating, and relaxed when he saw that she was getting back to normal. Thank God he'd found her when he did.

She lifted her plate, and he stopped her. "Leave that. I'll get it later." He stood and came to her side. "Let's go into the living room."

She wandered over to the couch.

"Give me one minute." He slipped down the hall to her bedroom, and grabbed the blanket that was at the foot of the bed. "Here you go. I want you to stay warm and cozy."

"That's what you're for."

His body temperature jumped up another degree. He draped the blanket over her and sat down. She scooted over, snuggling against his side.

He realized everything in the world he wanted was right here. Her silky hair grazed his cheek, and she smelled divine. All he wanted to do was hold her.

Protect her.

Possess her.

"I love being in your arms," she murmured.

"I'll hold you for as long as you want."

A woman he'd been lusting after for weeks, here in his arms. If holding her was the only thing he could do, he was a happy man.

This just felt right.

CHAPTER 20

Closing her eyes tight, Jessica tried to clear the incident at the hospital from her mind. Thank God Jared and Mike had been there. She snuggled deeper into Jared's side. He had come to her rescue. Never mind that the guy had already gone. Jared was her knight. She was getting used to having him around.

From the first moment, she'd been attracted to him. Even when he'd insulted her, she had that disturbing niggle in the back of her mind that he was hot. But she'd thought Jared was a player. How wrong she'd been.

Heat came off him in waves. She loved the warmth. She slid a hand over his molded abs, feeling solid muscle. He tensed a bit, but she knew it had to be from desire. His reaction to her touch thrilled her. She smoothed her hand downward, over his taut stomach and firm belly. When she heard him suck in a breath, she smiled. Instead of going lower, she worked his shirt in her fingers, finding the hem, and slipped her hand underneath.

His skin was hot. She loved the contrast of silk and steel under her fingers. She stroked the fine hairs on his chest, caressing and fondling. It was as if she was making love with her hand. Before she knew it, she was rubbing her leg on his thigh. Her entire body was getting in the game.

"Damn, Jessica. You keep that up, and I won't be still much longer."

She smiled. "You can move if you want."

"I *really* like what you're doing to me, but I want to touch you, too."

"How long can you sit still while I have my way with you?"

He sucked in another breath. "That depends." His voice was almost a growl. She giggled.

"Vixen."

"I'm enjoying myself," she said as she steered her hand lower.

"I hope so," he growled.

She fiddled with the button on his jeans, feeling his hardness straining at the waistline.

Wow.

"That was fast."

He sounded out of breath. "All you had to do was touch me."

She got the button free and noticed the zipper was stretched tight. She pressed her fingers against the huge swelling, and grinned when she felt it twitch.

"Damn, that feels good," he said as he shifted. "But I can't sit still much longer."

"That sounds like a challenge."

"God, no."

"Oh, yes. You can't move." She had to use both hands on the zipper and had difficulty getting it open.

"You're killing me here."

"How's this?" She slipped under his boxer briefs and grasped his hard heat. He bucked. "Can we take this to the bedroom?"

"Please," she purred.

He growled. Then, he quickly stood, sweeping her up along with the blanket. His strides were long as he carried her down the hallway, and soon he stood at the side of her bed. He gently lowered her to the comforter, and then crawled onto the bed next to her.

"Now I get to touch you." He kissed her as if his life depended on it. She kissed him back with equal fervor, opening her mouth to his seeking tongue. Raw—passion—desire crawled between her thighs. He pulled back and she gasped for air, hating the loss of his mouth. But it was only long enough to remove her shirt and bra. Then he traced his thumb over her cheekbone while his eyes devoured her.

"Beautiful."

She blushed. Jared made her feel beautiful.

He leaned in and kissed her … and kissed her …. and kissed her. His mouth continued to plunder hers until she couldn't breathe. It wasn't enough. She wanted his heat. She wanted him inside of her. She twisted, gyrated, locked her leg around his thigh.

"Babe, you turn me on. I'm wound tighter than a spring." His mouth traveled down her neck, licking and nipping, sending shock waves to her center. His hands crushed the sides of her breasts, pushing them tight together as he lowered his head and buried his face. She didn't care about anything but how Jared made her feel.

"God, your skin is so soft. Like silk." He slightly turned his head and pulled a nipple into his mouth and sucked. Her breath came in sharp gasps. Gnawing hunger shot to her center and between her thighs.

"Touch me, again," he growled low in her ear.

She wrapped her fingers around his cock and relished the sound coming from his throat. Tingles vibrated on the back of her neck and raced down her spine. There was no thinking, only feeling.

"Damn." He sat up and tore off his shirt. He gave her a teasing grin, then jerked his jeans off, along with his boxers. His eyes glowed like a wolf lusting after Little Red Riding Hood.

"I. Get. To. Touch. You."

His thumb hooked in her pants, and he tugged them off. Then he pulled her to him, the feeling of skin on skin overwhelming. She sighed, and at the same time clutched him. Desire hit her belly like lighting, shooting streaks to her woman's center. She ached. She needed.

His fingers danced along her lower belly, searching for the spot between her thighs—right where she needed him. When his fingers dipped into her, she flung her head back and cried out.

"You're drenched, baby."

Pleasure speared through her and increased the ache in her belly. All she could do was go with the sensations attacking her body.

Jared. Jared.

"I want you," he groaned. "It scares me how much."

The throb deep within her grew more intense. "Take me."

He stared into her eyes for what seemed like an eternity. Then he dipped his head, ever so slowly, and ran his tongue over her lips.

With the gentlest of touches, he pressed his mouth to hers, his lips firm and warm. The kiss lingered, caressed. She squirmed, wanting more. Needing more. The kiss turned to fire. Hot mouths, twisting tongues, sensual desire raged.

She felt him there. And then, he thrust into her.

Oh, sweet heaven.

She wrapped her legs around his back, digging her heel into his thigh. She traced her hands over his shoulders, marveling at his rippling muscles. He withdrew and plunged again. She bit her lip when what she really wanted to do was yell.

Now. Take me. Harder. Yes. Yes.

He took her higher and higher with each stroke. She moaned, thinking her heart might burst. He growled, sparking her fire hotter. His strokes grew deeper. Faster.

The world around them faded.

And then…

Oh God…

Pleasure burst through her veins like exploding fireworks. Her center exploded while her heart raced, and she held tight to her anchor.

Jared. Jared.

Suddenly he stiffened, and she knew he reached his peak. The crest broke, and she felt his pulse inside of her. His arms were bands of steel, yet he held her with crushing tenderness.

I love you.

She never wanted this moment to end. Jared was with her. In her. And it was the most wonderful feeling in the world. When the last spasm eased, he went limp in her arms. She held him with wonder.

So perfect.

So right.

CHAPTER 21

Jared raised his hand, ready to knock on Shep's office door. Most of the time it was open. But he'd heard Hooley was back, again. He knocked on the door.

"Come on in, Jared, and close the door."

He did. Instead of Hooley, it was Chuck. "Good to see you, Chuck. What's up?"

"I wanted to be sure you didn't have any lingering effects from the face mask poisoning."

Damn. Whatever it was, it could have killed him. "Thanks, Chuck. Doctor said I'm okay."

"Quick thinking on your part. Shep, here, tells me you reacted fast, or you'd be dead."

"That's what they tell me. I'm just glad I sensed something before it got into my system."

Chuck gave a nod. "We can't afford to lose any firefighters."

Jared hated to think a perp was targeting them. "It appears that's who this maniac is after."

"Have a seat, Jared."

He sat in front of Shep's desk, and Chuck took the other chair.

"Any ideas yet how he got into the station?"

Shep answered, "We had a 911 call the night before Jared's incident. No one was in the firehouse. Everyone rode on that one. A large structure fire, right beside a nursing home. We couldn't let that fire spread."

Chuck scratched his chin. "That had to be when the perp came in."

"The place was locked up, tight. I saw the doors closing, myself." Jared thought back to that night. "I guess if someone was fast enough…"

"But you didn't see them shut all the way."

"No. They were closed when we got back."

"I'm grasping at straws here."

A spring snapped as Shep leaned back in his chair. "Usually, there are two recruits here twenty-four-seven. That's the only time the station was completely empty."

"Shep's right," Jared added. "The recruits rode with us that night."

Chuck shook his head. "We know this guy is a professional. He can probably enter any building."

"He could be a locksmith."

"We thought of that. Checked every locksmith out from here to the next two counties."

"Dammit," Jared said in frustration.

"Someone tampered with the equipment. I guess we should be more careful that the tanks are filled. Wouldn't do for a tank to go empty while we're inside a burn." Shep lifted his head to Chuck. "What about Jared's mask. You said you found traces of a chemical. What about fingerprints?"

"Like I said before. This guy is a pro. He wasn't stupid enough to leave prints."

"As far as I'm concerned, he's pretty damn stupid to target firefighters," Jared snapped.

"This guy is playing with us."

"If he was after me, or anyone particular, why doesn't he go after the one person? He's screwing with a lot of innocent people."

"Don't beat yourself up, Jared," Chuck told him. "We still don't know if he is targeting you."

"Think about it," Shep said. "The explosion at the Wimer property could have been any firefighter. We had several units there from different houses. He stole a uniform from Station Nine. That doesn't mean he was after someone at Station Nine. But the mask was in our house."

"And it was mine."

"You're not the only house he hit."

"And what about that fire at that store? Where the guy was supposedly moving in. I was up on the top floor when it collapsed."

"Then, explain this one. Mike's helmet was the one with the bullet hole."

Damn. The incident downtown where a shooter took pot shots at them. A car accident where the drivers were mysteriously absent. Mike had been hit. Chuck was fitting the puzzle pieces together. That's why he was the cop. Jared smacked a fist in his opposite hand. "This shit is driving me crazy."

"That's what we don't want. Firefighters need to keep their minds on their jobs. Not on a maniac they think is out to get them. Something has to be done, Chuck."

"I'm working on it, Shep."

"The only other incident where there could have been a fatality was the car fire at the hospital."

Chuck shook his head. "There was no fatality."

"But there could have been. What about the girl who owns that car?"

"What about her?"

Jared quickly replayed his conversation with Shep, trying to remember how much he'd revealed. Shep was the captain. He deserved to know everything. But Chuck wanted to keep Alicia's whereabouts unknown.

"She wasn't in the car."

"I'd rather not discuss her. She's in hiding."

"You're the expert," Shep said with a nod. "I'll leave solving this damn enigma to you."

"Every fire, every call since that training day is suspicious. If there is a connection, we'll find it."

"Do you have anything to go on?" Jared asked.

"I'm keeping my eyes open. Hooley and I are working on this together. I have access to police files, and have more experience with criminals, where he has more experience with crime scenes. While I'm in uniform, I can stop any suspicious cars. For any reason."

"Have you seen any suspicious traffic. I mean, well, out-of-state cars, or dark tinted windows? Virginia doesn't allow them."

"Not really. And I've pulled over more cars the past few weeks than I have the last six months. I still need all the help I can get on this one."

Shep placed his hand on the surface of his desk. "Everyone in the department is on alert, Chuck. All shifts have been inspecting the inventory daily. It's extra work, but the guys understand it needs to be done. We can't have another incident like the one Jared experienced. Or worse."

"I get the feeling this guy is watching our every move. If he'd taken a tank or any gear, you would have caught it, right?"

"Right," Shep answered.

"So, he tampered with it in the station. You wouldn't notice unless it was gone."

"Or moved," Jared added. "He put it back exactly where it belonged."

"Precise. This guy is meticulous. He's calm. Patient. I know you get tired of hearing this. You guys have got to watch your backs."

"We're the good guys," Jared shouted with frustration. "We put our damn lives on the line to save and protect. It pisses me off that firefighters have to protect themselves from someone who is trying to harm us."

Chuck stared at the floor. "It does boggle the mind."

"Boggle? Hell, it's downright insane? Who is this fucker?" Jared shoved out of his chair, nearly knocking it over.

"We all feel the same way," Shep told Chuck.

"We'll get this guy. It might take some time, but we will get him."

***

Jared drove home, tossed his keys on the counter and kicked off his shoes. Something Laredo said stuck in his mind. He booted up the computer and surfed the internet for the local news. Clicking on different television sites, each had their version of expressing events. Some with more drama, and certainly their own version, but they all related basically the same story.

Once the thought had been introduced, he couldn't dismiss the possibility of the incidents being related.

It seemed a natural assumption that the training site explosion was connected to the poison in his face mask. Who knew what the deal was with Mike's helmet. Now he wondered if the burning car at the hospital fit into the puzzle.

Since her car burning up wasn't an accident, can't help but wonder if it could be the same guy?

That's a long shot.

May be. But there have been a lot of unexplained accidents in the past month. Knowing some nut job is out there puts ideas in my head.

Alicia swore some guy had been stalking her. After seeing her apartment, Jared knew it was true. But no one could figure out who or why? No ex-boyfriends. No jealous lovers. So, who wanted her harmed?

If her incident correlated the ones with their perp, there had to be a connection.

Damnedest thing he ever tried to figure out.

Hooley was the best investigator at arson. Teaming with Chuck, the best cop on the police force, they were bound to find the culprit.

Nut job? Jared just hoped there wasn't more than one.

CHAPTER 22

To his surprise, Seth's brother had been a wealthy man. He'd hid his corruption behind a legitimate business, until his partner found out. Shawn had built himself a tidy fortune. Seth had used those funds to lease this warehouse property on the same street as Fire Station Eight. Not only was it secure, safe, and quiet, it was a perfect spot to spy on his enemy. The money also paid for the fancy security and surveillance equipment. Purchased on the black market, no less. Shawn had a list of his connections and business associates on a thumb drive, stored in a bank safety deposit box that was registered in both of their names.

Seth clenched his jaw in anger. Even with all that money, it had taken weeks to locate him. Then days of casing the area, studying the comings and goings. Picking the perfect time to strike, only to have the SOB escape his trap. Hell, they all looked healthy. No sign of anyone coming close to death.

"You sure that shit works?"

"I'm sure," Carl answered. "Should 'a knocked him out at least. You said since we couldn't be sure if it was his mask, not to give you enough to kill him."

"Must have the constitution of a horse."

"Hey. You might want to see this. Must be someone important."

Seth walked over to Carl standing at the metal barred windows. A black SUV had driven up to the station and stopped directly in front of the bay doors. Didn't the dumbass know you weren't supposed to block the trucks. What if a call came in? Serve the asshole right if the engine drove right over that fancy new Lincoln Navigator.

The hair stood up on the back of Seth's neck. He tossed a cigarette on the floor and ground it out with his boot. "Hand me those binoculars." He zeroed in on the two men getting out of the vehicle.

His hands tightened on the Razor HD binoculars. His fury nearly blinded his vision, but he forced his eyes to focus on the bastard responsible for his brother's death.

"Son-of-a-bitch!"

"What?"

"He's here."

"Who?"

Looking through the lenses, Seth gripped the binoculars so tight his fingers cramped. He ground his teeth together, choking on his rage. He had to count to ten. Otherwise, he might charge down the damn stairs and go after the bastard.

"You mean ...." Carl's voice trailed off in comprehension. "He's the one?"

Seth lowered the glasses. "What's *he* doing here?"

"Which one is he?"

Seth glanced at Carl and blinked. "Yeah." He pointed. "That one."

"Let me see," Carl said taking the binoculars. "Shit. Can't see his face, now."

Seth seethed. *A brother for a brother.* The man he hated more than any other was within his reach. His chest pounded with the force of his anger.

"What ya gonna do? Go after him or stick to the plan?"

Seth, paused, his hands fisting and opening. "He killed my brother. Sent him to that hell-hole with murderers."

"Uh, Seth?"

He continued to stare at the firehouse bay door.

"You taught me something, Seth, and I'm going to give you some of your own advice back. Don't let anger guide you. Only act when you're calm."

Seth glared at Carl.

"Yeah. That's not the look you have on your face right now."

Of course not. My fucking brother is dead. That bastard killed him.

Carl shrugged. "Just saying."

Seth fisted his hands, to keep from reaching for Carl. "My brother is dead. I just saw the man responsible for his death." Seth inhaled. *One, two, three, four, five.* He exhaled until there was no breath in his lungs. One thing Seth could pride himself on was his patience. Damned difficult when he saw the one person whom he was directing all of his hate. He calmed the storm seething within his body, knowing Carl was right.

"A brother for a brother," he murmured. He took back the binoculars for another look.

"What's the plan?"

Thoughts flooded Seth's mind on the different ways he could kill him. Make him suffer. He could take the bastard out in a quick minute. But then, where was the satisfaction in that? He wanted the bastard to suffer. There was no pain like the sting of a family member's agony. He knew that pain. He was determined to inflict that same sorrow onto his enemy.

Yes, Seth decided. The original plan was best. "We'll stay here and keep watch."

CHAPTER 23

The rigs were examined regularly, but after the meeting with Hooley and the captain, all the men at Station Eight were stepping up their game. Jared made a point of crawling under the engine frequently, checking things over for himself. Laredo had claimed the ladder truck. No one could get within ten feet without Laredo knowing. Even if the person was an employee.

After all, the perp had gotten the gear from Station Nine somehow. In broad daylight.

Mike knew a lot about engines, but the retired chief was the one Jared had learned his big engine motorized skills from. He'd found the older man under the quint one day and asked what he was doing. After that, the chief had spent his free time showing Jared the ropes.

Some days, like today, Jared crawled under the squad. It was a tight fit, but he liked the atmosphere under here. Out of habit, he looked for anything out of the ordinary—an oil leak, loose screw, or he just followed the line of the pipes and their connections. The sound of heavy footsteps echoed, and a pair of shiny shoes not belonging to any of the guys came into view.

"Is that a new method of fighting fires?"

Jared recognized that voice. He rolled the creeper from under the rig.

"Hey, man." Jared climbed from his knees, stretching out his hand to his brother. James grabbed it and hauled him in for a bear hug.

"Good to see you, Jare."

"You too, big bro."

"Hello, Jared."

Jared hadn't noticed Roger was with James. Roger was Shep's brother. Both men wore suits. As for Roger, the dark threads were a part of the dress code up in Washington DC, and of course James was CEO of his own company.

Jared stuck out his hand. "Hi, Roger. "Is this a family convention? What are you guys doing here?"

"When I told Roger I was driving down to see you, he elected to come with me."

Jared couldn't help but wonder what James was doing here.

"Figured if James could check on his little brother, I could check on my big brother."

"I take it Shep doesn't know you were coming, either."

"Nope," Roger answered. "We decided to surprise you both. He here?"

"Up in his office." Jared gave a nod over his shoulder.

"Thanks. I'll see you guys later." Roger climbed the stairs to the next level and Shep's office.

James stared at Jared all of ten seconds before he spoke, "Looks like you're eating well."

"Staying in shape. You taking care of my girlfriend?"

James got that pleasing look on his face he always got whenever his wife was mentioned. "She's fine. I take real good care of her. You should come for dinner."

"Looking forward to Thanksgiving."

A frown creased James' brow. "You could pay a visit before then."

Yeah, well. James wouldn't show up without a reason. Jared wondered what it was. "I don't have to, now that you're here. What's up?"

"Do I need a reason to see my brother?"

And there was that hard line for a mouth.

"Naw. But I bet there is one."

Every time Jared saw his brother, he was reminded of the sacrifice James had made. When their parents died in a car crash, Jared was still in high school. James quit college so he could take care of his little brother. Of course, Jared thought he was old enough to make his own decisions. James set him straight.

The plan had been to sort out things at their house, Jared would finish school, and then they both would go to college. While they were going through some legal papers, Jared had come across his birth certificate. And his adoption papers. His world had come to a screeching halt.

"Been hearing some things."

Jared jerked out of his musing. "What kind of things?"

"Accidents. Concerning the fire department." James tried for normalcy, but his body language said otherwise. The man was tense, and if Jared knew his brother, determined.

"There are always accidents in my profession. That's what I'm trained for."

"Explosions at training sites? Fire equipment being tampered with? Some psycho targeting firefighters?"

Made sense that James had learned about the occurrences at Station Eight. Must have heard from Shep's brother.

Jared wiped his hands with a rag, stalling for time to come up with an answer that his brother would accept. James was the most stubborn, pig-headed man Jared knew. He thought about the time James had tried to convince Jared they were still brothers whether they shared blood or not. Being the hot head he was, Jared couldn't see anything other than his anger.

His hurt.

You will always be my brother, Jared. You hear me!

James still acted like one, anyway.

"Let's just once again agree that my job is dangerous and there's no sense in discussing it." Jared walked to the back of the engine and tossed the cloth onto a counter, feeling James' presence right behind him.

"We will discuss it. You think accidents won't happen to you? That's why they are called accidents. Not planned. But now you have a deranged fucker out to get firefighters. Did you think I wouldn't find out?"

Jared whirled back around to face James. "I've done nothing but think about the crazy person out there. Yes, for whatever the hell reason, the bastard is seeking some sort of bizarre vengeance on the fire department."

"And that doesn't scare you?"

"I can't live my life in fear. If I did, I wouldn't be able to do my job."

James hesitated before speaking. "There are other jobs."

Jared fisted his hands. "I like this one."

"You could—"

Jared raised a hand and held it up with his palm to James' face. "Don't start that again. You've got to let me live my life the way I want!"

Dammit.

He'd shouted. He wouldn't be so angry if James would let this go. Evidently, James was as furious as Jared because his jaw tightened and he looked like a volcano ready to blow. He was worse than a snorting bull.

Too bad.

"I'm your brother," James said. "I'm concerned."

Stepbrother.

Damn it. Would the pain ever go away?

"Look," Jared said, shoving a hand through his cropped hair. "I've made a life for myself here. This is where I belong. You need to accept that."

"I thought I had." James released a burdensome sigh. "But you've got to understand my worry. The threat is real."

"I know."

James stared at Jared, and he stared right back.

Finally, James grunted. "You always were too damn stubborn for your own good."

"Look who's talking."

"Are you ever coming home?"

"Didn't you hear anything I said? Don't look so lost, bro. You have a wife and kids."

"If you say I don't need you in my life, I'll deck you right now." When James' temper flared, he was meaner than hell. He also was an inch taller, and had used that, as well as the reminder he was older, to intimidate Jared upon occasion.

Jared held up his hands. "Whoa, big brother. I'm just saying your life is there. Mine is here. Christ, James. I'm not going to change my life because you want to be a big brother. I chose to face the threat of fire every day. If I start worrying about that, I'll start second-guessing myself. Then, one day, I won't come out of a burning building. Same thing goes for this triggerman. I can't change the way I think, or the way I live. That would make me a danger to myself."

"I'm not in the mood for you to be reasonable." James pouted, but he had calmed.

"I love you, Delores, and the kids."

"Then why don't you come see us? Other than on holidays."

"I've made a life here."

James grew quiet. And thoughtful. Finally, he said, "You're the only brother I have."

"I know." They grew up as brothers. They would always be brothers.

Suddenly James' face curled up in anger again. "Why did I have to hear you were in the hospital from someone else?"

Well, shit.

"Who told you?"

"That doesn't matter. What matters is you were poisoned."

Yeah. He wished he knew the asshole who did it. "I caught it quick enough."

"What if you hadn't?"

"Here we go." Jared rolled his eyes. "James, I'm okay. It's part of the job. We don't even know if I was the intended firefighter."

"Part of your job? Some bastard tried to kill you! Or worse, got you by mistake!"

Jared had feared the same thing. But still, no one knew for sure. He placed a hand on his brother's shoulder. "Did you hear anything I said? I put my life on the line every day. Every man here is in danger. What are we supposed to do? Close the firehouse? The team of Station Eight is my second family. I trust every one of them with my life, and they share equal trust in me. It's my choice. Please accept it."

After a long silence, and a lot of grunts, James finally shrugged. "What choice do I have? It was worth a try."

Jared slapped his brother on the back. "Come on. Let's go upstairs and have a cool drink. Cooper is cooking tonight. It's bound to be something exceptional."

CHAPTER 24

Nausea teased Jessica's stomach. She'd been on edge since trying to call Alicia. It didn't matter that Chuck had told them there was no cell service at the cabin.

Still, she couldn't shake the feeling that Alicia was in trouble. She didn't dare go find out by herself, so she'd called Jared and asked him to drive. The closer they got, the more Jessica felt her muscles tighten. What started as unease had grown into impetuous panic.

"Breathe."

She jerked toward Jared, meeting his gaze before he turned his concentration back to the road. Thank God, he was with her.

"You're wound tighter than a guitar string ready to pop. What makes you think she's in trouble?"

"She didn't answer the phone."

He gave her a look that made her feel stupid. "Really?"

"She shouldn't be alone."

"Maybe she took a walk. Man, I'd love to be out here in this beautiful country atmosphere. This time of year is ideal for a walk. The leaves are changing color. The crisp air opens up the lungs."

"But what if—" Jessica suddenly halted. Finishing her thought would make it real.

"Jessica, honey. I know you're worried. Don't create trouble when the situation may be harmless. No one knows where Alicia is."

Jessica chewed on her lip. "I hope you're right."

"Her phone can't be tracked. There's no cell service out here."

Like she needed to be reminded again? "Have you heard of those wave signals?"

"Wave signals?" He glanced at her in confusion.

"Connie's husband, Rick, said sometimes a wave or a spurt of a signal can get through an area. You just have to be in the right place at the right time."

Jared shook his head. "I've never heard of such a thing."

"He said it's happened in some remote areas. What if Alicia turned on her phone?"

"That's a pretty far stretch, Jessica."

Maybe it was. Maybe pigs could fly. Until she saw Alicia with her own eyes, Jessica would not be satisfied.

"There's the turn off." Jared drove down the private road that would take them to the cabin.

Jared. Please hurry.

Jessica held her breath.

The sun was slowly disappearing behind the horizon when Jared pulled to a stop in front of the cabin. Jessica jumped from the car and ran to the front door.

"Jessica, wait!" Everything was quiet. Alicia had not come out to meet them, nor had she yelled through the door. He knocked hard before grabbing the door handle.

Unlocked.

He shoved Jessica behind him and eased the door open, searching the inside before pushing the door open all the way.

"Alicia!" Jessica yelled and tried to shove around him. He grabbed her arm.

"Wait. Someone could be inside."

"Oh God. Where is Alicia?"

"Stay behind me."

Splinters of wood littered the floor. Two chairs were overturned, and a cooking pan lay on the floor with a puddle of food spilled to the side. Signs of a struggle, but no sign of Alicia.

"Holy Shit!" Expecting an ambush, Jared shoved Jessica behind him again, as he stealthily stepped through the living room. Jessica called Alicia's name. After a few tense seconds, she ran forward. He grabbed for her arm and missed.

Dammit.

He caught up with her at the bedroom door. Nobody in there.

Dying rays of sunlight drifted below the trees. Whatever had happened, he didn't want to be here after dark.

"Let's go. Now."

Jared pulled Jessica to the door. Without sparing a glance in any direction, he tugged her to the car, only releasing her hand when he opened the passenger door. Blood pounded his temples as he stalked to the driver's side.

"Where's Alicia?"

He glanced at Jessica as he started the car. Her hand on his sleeve trembled. "I don't know, but we've got to get out of here in case the ones who did that are still lurking around."

"What about Alicia? Shouldn't we look for her?"

"We need to call the police. If we hang around here, the same thing could happen to us." He jerked the shifter into gear and slammed on the gas. Tires spun, throwing dirt and God knew what else flying. "Can you get a cell signal?"

"No. Not yet."

"Damn it." He hit the steering wheel with his hand. "This is where you need phone service. Out here in the boonies where's there's nothing. We've got to call Chuck."

Jessica's hand shook so hard he wondered how she could see anything on her cell. He wanted to reach for her, but at the speed he was driving, he needed both hands on the wheel.

"Jared. I'm terrified. Where is she?"

"Chuck will send a search team out. Alicia is smart. Maybe she got away."

"God, I hope so."

The highway loomed before them. He took a sharp turn to the right. The car slid sideways into the shoulder, and he steered it back onto the pavement. "You have on your seat belt?"

"Yes. Just don't run off the road. There's no way to call for help."

As if he needed reminding.

"Now! Now! I've got cell service.

Hell, he almost slammed on the brakes. "Thank God. Call Chuck."

"I don't have his number."

Jared dug in his pocket for his phone. "Here. Find Chuck's number."

She dialed and handed the phone back to him. A ringing tone buzzed in the car. Jessica jumped.

"Bluetooth," he said. "Come on. Come on."

"Detective Winston."

"Chuck. Alicia is gone."

"Jared? You sound out of breath. I can barely understand you. Got static too."

Jared took a deep breath and tried again. "Jessica and I went to the cabin. Alicia is gone."

"No one knows where she is. Are you sure she didn't wander off?"

"Looks like a struggle took place. Door is busted and chairs overturned. Someone took her."

"Son-of-a— Where are you now?"

"Route 250. About ten minutes from the cabin—"

A loud *crack* and a zip ripped through the car.

"Christ! Get down."

"Was that a gunshot?" Jessica fell back in the seat and scooted toward the floor.

"Jared? What the fuck's going on!"

Headlights glared from behind. Suddenly, the car jerked wildly as there was a loud crash. The vehicle hit Jared's back bumper, knocking them forward. Jared stepped down on the gas, trying to outrun the car behind them.

"Stay down. Hold on to something."

"Jared. Answer me!"

"Oh my God, Jared. Is it them?"

Them? The bad guys? The men who took Alicia? He didn't have a clue.

Maybe he didn't know who this guy was, but the dickhead meant business. The vehicle pulled alongside and rammed into the back fender. Jared couldn't see a damn thing as his car spun out of control. When it stopped, he was headed in the opposite direction. He slammed on the gas.

"They're turning around." Jessica was peeking over the headrest.

"I told you to keep down."

"You want me to be sick? All that spinning around, I had to get up."

Feisty even now. He might be in love.

"Chuck. Chuck!" They must have lost the signal. "I don't know this road or where it goes. I'm heading back to the cabin. We might have a better chance there than on the highway." He spun the wheel sharply, sliding sideways as he took the turn. Ready for the slide, he held the wheel and caught traction quicker than the first time.

Minutes counted when you had felons on your tail.

"Good Lord. I need to get up."

"No!" Jared yelled. "Stay down."

"I am. I am."

"Chuck's a police office. And he's a hunter. He might have a gun stashed away at the cabin."

"You know how to use one?"

"Dad taught us when we were ten."

"Good. Cause I've never even held one."

The car skidded to a stop, throwing rocks on the front porch. He jumped out and was around the car as Jessica met him at the front. They charged into the house and slammed the door behind them. A lot of good it did trying to lock it.

"Help me get that cabinet." He motioned to a large hunk of wood. Together he and Jessica lugged the thing in front of the door. "I'll look for a weapon. Grab that fire poker and see if there are any large knives in the kitchen.

A huge gun safe stood in one corner of the bedroom. No chance of getting in that. Jared prayed Chuck might have left one in a drawer someplace. The first place he looked was the nightstand. No luck. Guess that was too obvious. He stalked to the dresser, tossing things as he dug to the bottom.

Jessica came flying through the bedroom door, nearly giving him a heart attack.

"Someone's here. I heard a car out front."

"Get behind the bed." Jared shut the bedroom door, wishing there was more between them and the men outside. "Don't freak when I turn out the light."

Everything went dark. He pulled a laser light from his pocket and flicked it on.

"I want to keep searching for a weapon. I haven't found anything."

"There's a metal box under the bed."

Jared crawled next to Jess. "Let me see." A box with latches like a briefcase. Maybe a fancy gun case. He tugged it out and opened the latches. *Bingo.*

Jessica's gasp floated to his ear.

"Yeah. She's a beauty, isn't she?" A silver Magnum .44 revolver. A black grip. Satin finish. He lifted the gun, liking the feel and the weight. Nice piece. He slid the lever and opened the cylinder.

Where the fuck were the bullets?

"Jess. We have a problem."

"We don't need any more. There's one getting ready to kick our ass any minute?"

"No bullets."

"What?" she quietly shrieked.

He dug under the bed. "They've got to be around here somewhere." She scurried around the bed. "Where are you going?"

"Helping you look."

"I've got the light."

"So, look under the bed. I'll check under the nightstand."

Damn. What a fix. Dark as black and no sound from outside. What were the crooks planning? He knew in his gut there was more than one. Sweat trickled into his eye. He swiped at it with his arm.

"Hey."

Jared froze. "What?"

"There's something attached on the back of the headboard."

"What are you doing up there?"

"Bring the light."

Wood scraped in the living room. The criminals were coming in the front door. He and Jessica were out of time.

He craned his neck to follow the beam of light behind the top of the bed: a box duct-taped to the back of the headboard. He tore it from the wood. A box of shells. *Thank Christ.*

His fingers trembled as he tore open the box and quickly loaded the gun.

Let the fuckers come in now.

"Get back behind the bed."

"You, too. Don't stand out in the open."

Did she think he was going to walk right into the line of fire?

More scraping of wood and then silence. They had to be in the house.

"I'm going to fire a warning shot to let the fu—uh suckers know I have a gun. It's going to be loud. Cover your ears."

She did.

"You might as well come out. We don't want to hurt anyone."

Yeah, right. And I'm the Statue of Liberty.

On his knees, he leaned from the corner of the bedpost. "I have a gun. Go away, and I won't use it."

Laughter echoed through the door.

"If you had a gun, you wouldn't be saying you have one."

"Here goes," he warned Jessica.

He fired through the wall beside the door. He'd seen enough TV shows to know people hid at the side of a door.

"Motherfucker!" someone yelled.

Jared held his breath. At least he had a shit load of bullets. He just wondered how long he could hold them off before he ran out.

"Guess you do have a gun."

Jessica burrowed into Jared's side. "I won't bother you or interfere with your aim, but I have to touch you. I need your strength."

He had to hand it to her. She didn't scream. She didn't faint.

"Baby, I think you're pretty damn strong. You're helping me be strong." He thought he saw a flicker of a smile.

"You don't want to do this," the voice called out. "Throw your gun out here. If you do, we'll let the woman go."

No way in hell were those bastards getting anywhere near Jessica. He didn't trust them, and he knew they sure as hell wouldn't let her go. What did they want anyway? And where was Alicia?

"My gut tells me you won't let either one of us go."

"You won't like it if we have to come in there. You're dead if you don't come out willingly."

"You can't," Jessica whispered.

"I'm not that stupid," he whispered back.

"Fuck, man. Ya hear that?"

Jared and Jessica shot a glance at each other. Jessica shrugged, then said, "Wait. I think I hear sirens."

"Yeah. More than one."

"Get the hell out of here." Boots pounded to the beat of the criminals running. The sirens grew louder.

"Chuck," Jared said. "He sent the cavalry."

***

Once the uproar calmed down, Jared took Jessica home.

Damn. They could have been killed.

Jessica could have been hurt. A gun. The criminals had guns and weren't afraid to use them. What if the police hadn't showed up?

She went to change, so he sat on the couch and picked up the remote. Hell, there wasn't a damn thing on TV he wanted to see. He placed it back on the end table.

Jessica had created something inside him he thought he'd never feel. She was important to him. The ordeal tonight showed him how much. He hated the thought of anything happening to her.

He scrubbed a hand over his face and scratched the itchy beard forming under his chin. She was getting damn close.

"Thank you for waiting. I really don't want to be alone."

"No problem. Come here."

Jessica crawled beside him, and he drew her in close. Damn, she felt good. He would hold her tonight. At least for a little while. Then he had to let her go. It would kill him if she got hurt because the perp came after him.

"Jessica, I'm so sorry about what happened."

"It wasn't your fault."

"I need to talk to you."

There must have been something in his voice, because she stiffened. Or maybe she was reading the vibes coming off his body. If that were the case, then she must be confused. Because the battle warring within him could only end one way.

"You need to stay home where you will be safe."

"Are you forgetting that I am a nurse?"

"I know you have to go to work. Just stay away from me. Stay away from the firehouse."

Jessica tensed. She moved away, leaving entirely too much space between them "Jared, what are you saying?"

"Jessica, I mean it."

"Mean what? Alicia works at the same hospital as me. The guy who grabbed me was looking for her. That doesn't have anything to do with you or the fire department."

"Except her car was torched."

"Well, yeah. I'm not in danger because of you."

Jared thought of the creep targeting firefighters.

But you could be in danger because of me.

For her own protection, he had to end things.

God knew this wasn't going to be easy. He had to do it.

He captured her hands and squeezed. "I will always be here for you." God, his voice was ready to crack. He swallowed and willed himself to get it together.

"I know that, Jared."

"If you need me for anything, call and I'll be here."

"Why do I get the feeling you're saying one thing and meaning something else."

"I mean it." Seeing the doubt in her eyes made him stumble. "I think we need to ... cool it."

She jerked her hands free. "I beg your pardon?"

"Uh, I think we need to stop seeing each other. This isn't working out."

She practically leaped off the couch. "And you pick tonight to tell me?"

Part of him wanted to kick his ass and hold her forever. The other part, the reasonable part, told him this was his only recourse. Keeping her away from him was the only way to keep her safe.

He was dying to wrap his arms around her and kiss her until the sun came up tomorrow morning. She aroused him, sure, but somehow, she completed him. He wanted more. More of Jessica.

"I don't want you to get hurt."

"What do you think you're doing?"

Well, hell.

"I don't want to hurt you, but I'd rather have you hate me than cause you harm."

"What are you talking about?" she shouted, waving her hands about.

He stood. It was easier to talk with both of them standing. "Well, tonight for example. I put you in a terrible situation. You could have been kidnapped, or killed."

"You didn't put me there. I'm the one who called you. You can't control what a criminal will do."

"But I can keep you away from danger."

"How is you breaking up with me keeping me out of danger?"

Aww, hell.

He rubbed the back of his stiff neck. This wasn't going exactly as he'd planned.

"If my profession isn't enough to scare you off, then how about this? There is a maniac targeting firefighters, and I don't want you anywhere near him. He could come after me. Ryan almost died in an explosion that was set by the f—uh, guy. Mike got a bullet to his head. I was poisoned. What if you get caught in the middle—or heaven forbid—he comes after you?"

Her eyes shot wide. "Good Lord! When did all this happen?"

Shit. He'd spilled his guts. Too late now to change course. "The last several weeks."

"Have you forgotten Alicia?"

"Hell no. That's why I'm doing this. The bastard is getting too close."

She scrunched up her face and gave him a look that made him feel stupid. It didn't matter. He had to protect her.

"Do you know the man who is doing this to Alicia?"

"No," he said with a shake of his head.

"Then you don't know anything, and you don't know how I feel." Her pain-filled eyes grabbed him in the gut.

He was trapped. Caught between what he wanted and what he needed to do. She looked so achingly beautiful, he nearly faltered.

"You deserve so much better than me. It wouldn't have worked anyway."

She blinked. "What?"

"We can't be together. In time, you'll know this is for the best."

Jessica practically leaped from the couch. "I call bullshit."

His mouth dropped open. He couldn't believe her reaction.

"If you don't want to be with me, say it. Be a man and say it straight up."

She thought— He should let her think whatever she wanted. If she thought he was a dick, the break would be easier.

He struggled for the words, and prayed his voice wouldn't betray him. "I'm sorry, Jessica. This is the end." He shifted, thinking he had to get out of here before he changed his mind. "You won't be seeing me again."

"You're a real prick, you know that? You were getting sex. I was good for a few more turns before you had to toss me aside. What a shame. You're just like—" She stopped abruptly.

Who? Jealousy hit him hard. Of course, he had no right to ask since he was breaking up with her.

He opened his mouth to correct her. Tell her she had it all wrong. Instead, he kept silent. Her hatred was better than seeing her get hurt.

"Oh God" she moaned. "You're not even going to defend yourself?"

At least she wasn't crying. He wouldn't be able to stand it if she started crying.

"You're making all the decisions? You think you can tell me what to do?" Her voice grew stronger, and she swiped at the tears leaking from her eyes.

He nearly crumbled.

"I can't decide if you miss playing with other women, or you're plain mean. Don't flatter yourself, Jared. I'm not the type of woman to lust after someone who doesn't want me. I've been down this road before. I see all the signs. You want to break things off with me? Well, that's just fine."

"What do you mean, you've been down this road before?" His anger had him speaking without thinking.

"I allowed myself to fall for someone, and it didn't end well. He kicked me to the curb, and I suffered the consequences.

His hands fisted and a huge knot formed in his gut. "What consequences?"

She continued as if he had not spoken. "Matter of fact, I believe I will be better off without you."

"I did not kick you to the curb, he said, finally reaching for her."

She spun out of reach, spitting out a string of vile expletives. "To think I actually believed you cared for me."

He sucked air into his lungs. Her words stung. Dammit, he just wanted her to be safe. "If you want me to apologize—I won't," he said.

Her mouth hung open, then she snapped it closed.

He was running out of steam. This shit wasn't fair to her. He had to get out of here now. He took a step and halted when he saw her step backwards. Whether she feared him or hated him, it was clear she didn't want him to touch her.

Wasn't that what he wanted?

He spoke slowly and distinctly, forcing every word past his lips. "This is goodbye."

He marched to the door and walked out. Walked away from the best thing that had ever happened to him.

Suddenly, he wanted to do the very thing he told her he would not. Not only did he want to apologize, but beg her to forgive him. Make her promise to never leave him.

He shook his head. The idea of going back in and calming her down was ludicrous. The damage was done.

He had to keep her safe.

Chapter 25

Chuck couldn't let it go. This sort of thing didn't happen in their county. The woman, Alicia, had gotten under his skin. There had to be some sign of what happened to her. He shouldn't be mad at the team who'd searched all night. Neither should he expect to find anything new this morning, but his gut told him he had to try.

He drove back to the cabin hoping he would find some clue. The midday sun shined bright, making the chilly day more bearable. At least the wind had calmed down.

He entered the cabin with heightened senses. Careful to check behind the door, then he quickly scanned the room. He remembered seeing the pretty nurse there on his leather couch. How terrified she had been. He'd done his best to calm her. He hadn't imagined the heat that passed between them when he'd covered her hand.

Where could she be? Did they take her?

He didn't know what in the hell was going on, or who this perp was, but he was damn well going to connect the dots.

He pulled his gun out of his holster, and walked through the cabin, clearing every room. Nada. As he stood in the larger area of the living space, he tried to piece together what might have happened. The kitchen table had been moved. Whether shoved out of the way or knocked by a chasing perp, it had been moved.

If there had been a scuffle, there wasn't much evidence, other than the food on the floor. He checked the windows to be sure they were locked. His father always said a lock was only to keep an honest man out. A criminal would break in. The bathroom window was open—why hadn't he noticed it before? Guess he was too busy getting Jared and Jessica the hell out of there.

The window was small, but big enough for a slender person to get through.

Like Alicia?

Could she have escaped?

For the first time, Chuck had a sense of hope. Maybe she had gotten away.

Assuming there was more than one, the bastards that were after her could be lurking nearby. He holstered his gun, but left the snap open. Quicker to slide his weapon out when he needed it.

He closed and locked the window, and stared at the forest a hundred feet away, making a mental note to search in that direction. He couldn't detect a thing. Not even a critter stirring about.

He walked around the outside of the cabin then scanned the woods in all directions. With all the commotion last night, he hoped the stalkers were scared off. Or at least assumed the police had Alicia in custody.

Before he took the direction he'd mapped out in his mind, he walked to the back of the cabin, studying the ground, looking for footprints. He found several sets. Between the criminals and the police, he'd never be able to detect the ones he needed, so he strolled a wider perimeter until he reached the edge of the thick woods.

He stopped and looked back. The field was open from the cabin to the wooded area, about a hundred yards from the cabin. Any pursuer would have seen her, and if they had guns, a clear shot at their target.

Damn. He didn't even know if she got away. Or if they grabbed her and she never got to run at all. Still—he was a cop. He had to look.

Alicia seemed so sweet. When he'd spoken with her, she was scared, but the woman was intelligent. He'd gotten the idea she cared for people. Look at the way she wanted to protect Jessica. And the way she thanked him for his help at the same time not wanting to be a burden. He shook his head. Alicia was brave, he had to give her that.

The sun was in full brightness now. No rain or cloud in sight. Good. If there was anything to find, he would see it.

He checked the holster holding his gun. Most likely the thugs had long gone. Still, he considered his options. He turned back to his original direction. Staying close to the trees, he plodded slowly through the brush. Dissecting every branch, every bush, all the while listening for sounds of movement.

Quiet. For the forest, everything was eerily quiet. He kept his ears tuned for any sound. He looked for anything that would suggest someone had traveled this path recently. Human or beast, he would deal with either when he met them. He stepped over tree limbs, the smaller branches crunching under his boots. He almost stepped over an object, then froze.

Pink.

Chuck eased down on his haunches, to get a closer look. A shoe was wedged in a broken branch of a tree limb. The pink he'd seen was an emblem on the side of a black shoe.

His pulse sped up, then his training kicked in. Didn't mean it was her shoe. Still, it might be a clue. He scanned his immediate surroundings as if he was using a fine-tooth comb.

Nothing. No movement. Nothing out of the ordinary.

No sign of Alicia.

He reached for the shoe. It was stuck. He worked it out and recognized it as a female's running shoe. Not new. Not too old. If Alicia had gotten this far, there was hope.

Hot on the tail end of that thought was another. These galoots that were after her wanted her bad enough they wouldn't stop.

Damn.

He hoped he would find another clue.

He searched for another ten minutes and maybe a hundred feet, when he saw a strange shape balanced on a tree branch. Anyone else might easily miss it, but he'd been in these woods so many times, he knew when something was out of place.

Conscious of his steps, he crept toward the tree, toward the sound of ... shaking beads? What the hell? He moved quietly, trying not to give away his presence. But the quivering hum should cover any sound he might make. His eyes penetrated through the blurring branches.

Holy hell! It was a person. And the sound was clearly coming from her.

Alicia?

Her blonde hair shimmered in the golden sun. She was shivering so hard, the branch shook, obviously making the sound he had heard.

He rushed forward.

"Alicia? Is that you?" he spoke slowly and clearly. "Do you remember me? It's Chuck. I'm Jared's friend with the police department. Can you hear me?" He gave her time to answer. "Are you okay?"

The shaking continued.

"Alicia. It's Chuck. I'm here to help you. The men are gone." He scanned the area to make sure. "I'm here, Alicia. It's me. Do you remember me?"

"Help." Although it was faint, he heard her.

"That's what I'm here for. To help you. You're safe now. Can you get down?"

She finally turned her face to him. His gut clenched at her pale complexion. Damn, how long had she been out here?

"Alicia. I'm coming to get you. Are you able to move?"

"Chuck?"

"Yes. I'm right here." He stood still as a stone. His neck at a forty-five-degree angle, afraid to take his eyes off her.

"It's really you?"

"Yes. I'm here. You're safe. Are you okay."

"I think so. Are those men gone?"

He took another look around. "Yes. They're gone." Thank Christ, he'd found her. "Are you able to move?"

"I'm not sure."

"Don't fall." He braced himself, just in case. "How long have you been up there?"

"Uh ... all night. I'm scared."

"I know. You're safe now."

"I ran. He chased me. I climbed this tree. They didn't find me."

Thank God.

"That's great. You are very brave, Alicia."

"I've been crying. I tried to keep quiet. I was terrified."

His heart ripped a little. "You did good. Now I'm here. We're the only two people in the woods." He prayed he was right. He kept one eye on her and the other continuously scanning their surroundings.

"We are? I was afraid they would find me."

"They're gone. It's only you and me. Can you move?"

"I think so. My arms are kind of numb."

"I can help you. First let's see if you can move your arms."

"Ow! They're cramping."

"Okay. Shake one a little to loosen it up." He watched as she tried. "That's good. Now the other one."

She moved them both, and he breathed a sigh of relief.

"Okay. How about your legs? You're up there kind of high. Do you need me to come get you?"

"I didn't pay attention when I was climbing up here. Hang on. I think I can manage."

He watched her fumble around, and then work her way down to the next branch.

"I think you've got it, Alicia. That's it. Keep coming. One step at a time."

When she reached the bottom branch, he noticed her torn skirt. It better have been from the exertion used in climbing that tree. He'd kill the mother fuckers if either one of them had touched her.

Finally, she was on the ground, a twig in her long blonde hair.

Alive.

Unharmed.

Unbearably beautiful.

He held out his arms. She slammed into his chest and clung to him like a drowning victim would cling to a life raft. The floodgates opened.

"Hey," he said cooingly. "I've got you." He stroked her back while she cried with gut-wrenching sobs. He tried to let her know with his body, as well as his words, that she was safe. He had no idea of the time that passed as he held her. She smelled nice, even through the birch scent that clung to her clothes. She had a distinct aroma of her own. Tingles he should not be feeling were dancing in his gut. Soft words automatically drifted from his lips. Words of comfort, routinely said when trying to calm a hysterical person. Subconsciously. But he was more focused on her body and his reaction to it.

Of course, Alicia was scared. Now was not the time to forget she was a victim. He couldn't allow his emotions to interfere. He pulled back. "We've got to get you out of here."

She clung to him. "Don't let me go."

"I won't." The thought crossed his mind how good she felt, and how much he would like to hold her forever. But reality quickly approached.

"Look. I'm not going to let anything happen to you. Are you all right?"

Her head brushed against his.

"Okay." What else could he do but hold on. If she squeezed him any tighter, he'd pop. He continued to be aware of the woods around them. He prayed they were alone.

"Alicia? You're safe. Do you think you can let go? Maybe a little?"

"Oh, uh ..." She slowly released him, but never broke her hold completely. She swiped at her tears. "I'm sorry—"

"No need to be sorry." Holding up the shoe he'd found, he smiled. "I think this belongs to you." He tore off his jacket, wrapped it carefully around her, then helped her put on her shoe. "Hey. I need you to understand me."

She clutched the front of his shirt, so he tucked her into his side. "As soon as you pull yourself together, we can leave here."

She nodded her head, then darted her gaze about.

"Do you know where you are?" he asked.

"In the woods."

Well, she *was* right.

"We're alone. But I need to get you out of here."

In case they come back.

"Can you walk?"

She continued to nod. "I'm cold."

He placed an arm around her. "Come on."

When she stumbled, he tightened his grip, and then he practically carried her. He would toss her over his shoulder if he thought she would let him. At the edge of the tree line, he hesitated, scanning the opening between them and his Land Cruiser. He strode quickly across the clearing, and she kept up with him. When they reached the vehicle, he fastened her seat belt and then patted her hands. "Hold on."

He slammed his own door, cranked the engine and spun the tires. Now that the car was in motion, he could breathe a sigh of relief.

Damn, he found her.

There would be two people glad to hear his news.

As soon as his car turned onto the paved road, his cell phone dinged. Back in service. He pushed the number with a smile in his mind.

"Jared here."

"Hey, buddy. I have some news. But understand I want to keep it low key."

"You got it. Spill."

"I've got Alicia."

CHAPTER 26

Everything was in order and every item had its place. The guys might be slobs at home, but at the station, they kept the place spotless. Today happened to be a beautiful day with lots of sunshine. Perfect for a little cleaning up in the bay.

Also a good time for breaking in a new trainee.

The buzzer rang and Jared's pager went off like clockwork. All the guys stopped what they were doing and jumped into call action. The new guy was glued to Mike's hip, just like he was supposed to be.

His name was Barry, same age as Jared. Recently divorced and looking to live his dream as a firefighter. They had gotten a lot of those. Dreams were short-lived when the guy realized his life was actually on the line.

Barry seemed to be an okay guy. He paid attention to Mike, which was a definite plus. Cooper rode squad to make room in the quint for Barry. Laredo maneuvered the truck through the intersections and sharp curves like he was painting the path. The ladder truck was his baby.

The call was a bit suspicious; Shep didn't explain other than the truck was needed. When they pulled into a residential area,

Jared was surprised. A police squad was already there. A guy in uniform directed them to the curb.

"Around the back," Mike called out.

Jared wasn't sure what gear to take, but he followed Mike, thinking he'd soon find out.

Almost in a row, the team prodded forward. As he came around the end of the house, he spotted a tall tree. He froze. Then squinted his eyes, trying to focus on if what he saw was real.

"Laredo, bring the truck."

That's when Jared noticed he wasn't the only one who had stopped dead in his tracks. Barry looked like he'd been struck by lightning. Jared knew how the guy felt. It was the first time he'd seen a man hanging in a tree with a rope around his neck.

The team got it in gear and went to work getting the body down. Most of the suicides that the team responded to were drug related. This was just plain eerie. How had the guy gotten up there?

Laredo angled the truck; Jared went to the rope end that was tied to the tree. The knot was tight, so he used a knife. Mike and Cooper lifted the body down and carried the deceased man to the back of the truck.

Poor soul must have thought there was no way out.

The men didn't say much on the way back to the station. In fact, the inside of the cab was so quiet, Jared knew everyone was thinking of what they had seen. He'd heard of things like that. Barry must have known it existed. There were a lot of messed up people in the world. But to actually see it up close... the person who ended his own life.

What would make a man think death was the only way out?

Barry's first day on the job, and the 911 call had been a man hanging in a tree in his back yard. Barry had been shell-shocked. My God, who wouldn't be? Barry didn't quit. Hell of a first day.

Jared thought of the creep stalking the firefighters of Station Eight. The SOB was out there causing destruction, and there was a man who had been so depressed that he took his own life. The world balance was completely off its kelter.

One thing was for sure. Jared was a fighter. He would find the motherfucker and win Jessica back before he'd sink so low as suicide.

***

For days, Jessica had been existing between dreams and reality. She'd forced herself out of bed each morning when she despaired to face another day. She nibbled on snacks if she missed a couple of meals. She didn't care if she ate or her body wasted away.

He'd broken her heart, just like she knew he would.

She'd lost herself, ignored the promise she had made so many years ago. She'd allowed Jared into her life, her heart, her very soul.

She worked extra shifts, hoping the workload would take her mind off Jared. It didn't. She stayed awake most of each night. Her mind wouldn't turn off. She didn't sleep, her nerves were rattled, and in two weeks, she'd lost ten pounds.

Her sister noticed, her coworkers looked at her with sympathy, and she didn't care enough to change her habits.

If she could go back, undo the last few months, would she do things differently?

In all honesty, she would not.

She'd fallen hopelessly in love.

She'd shattered when Jared ended things. Whether he knew it or not, Jared loved her. He'd showed her with every touch, every sigh. She knew in her bones he cared for her.

She'd wasted precious time in denying herself for so long. Afraid to live. Afraid to take a chance.

And when she finally took that step, she'd found what she'd been missing. The very thing—the very person—who filled her soul. Who made her complete.

No matter how hard she tried, she hadn't been able to convince Jared to stay with her.

She knew he was thinking of her safety when he'd made his stupid decision. Okay, so he wanted her safe. She got that. The fact that he thought she would be safer without him is what she objected to. How could he not see that they should be together?

Yes, his job was dangerous, but that was not a problem. It was the larger threat that someone had a vendetta against firemen, and Jared was afraid she would get caught in the crossfire.

If that were the case, then it was too late. She'd already been mistaken for her co-worker. Alicia was possibly her connection to the same maniac, who was threatening firefighters. Staying away from Jared would not keep her safe from that situation. Oh, why wouldn't he listen?

Her heart was breaking. She'd fallen in love. Fallen hard.

She ached for him. Yearned for him. Wanted a life with him. She realized now that her foolish misconception in college was nothing. What they said about hindsight was clearly true.

What was she to do? There was no getting through to Jared. Stubborn man was determined to keep her at a distance. When he'd ended things, she thought she'd die from the pain. Even now, she struggled through each empty day.

However, there was a glimmer of light. Some comfort in knowing that what they had shared had been real. A sliver of hope that kept her going. No, if she had to live that part of her life over, she wouldn't change a thing. She now knew love like that didn't come easy, or happen every day.

Raven had tried. She knew what she'd been talking about because she had that with Chad. Jessica saw it every day. Even after years of marriage, three kids, and him being gone so much, they had a special bond. Jessica wanted that.

Be careful what you wish for.

She swayed and grabbed onto the counter.

"Hey, Jessica. Are you all right?"

"Uh, yeah. I got dizzy for a moment."

"You've been working too hard. Come over here and sit down." Sylvia took Jessica's arm and led her to the small room behind the nurse's station. Sylvia was so kind, she liked mothering all the nurses.

With only two years until retirement, Jessica hated to see the sweet woman go.

Sylvia grabbed a cloth and turned on the water faucet. "Are you pregnant?"

"What? No."

She pressed the wet cloth over Jessica's face. "Are you sure?"

Jessica thought back and counted her cycle. *Yeah. Pretty sure.* "I'm not pregnant."

"You look awful. We're worried about you."

"Who's we?"

"Josie, Carolyn ...

"I haven't been eating."

"You're a nurse. You know better." Sylvia wet the cloth again. This time she placed it on the back of Jessica's neck.

"You don't need to mother me."

"You've lost weight."

"I've noticed that too," Jessica said sarcastically, and immediately regretted her outburst.

"Okay. Tell me to mind my own business, but you need to take care of yourself."

"I'm sorry." Jessica closed her eyes. Jared's image assailed her. For as long as she lived, she would never regret loving him. Daydreaming about him would only make her realize how lonely her life was now.

"Here."

Jessica opened her eyes and saw a container of orange juice and a pack of Nabs. "I'm not hungry."

"You are not moving until you drink this." Sylvia shoved the OJ at her.

"Bossy. All right," Jessica muttered.

"What are you guys doing back here?" Carolyn asked, walking to the back. "Jessica, are you sick?"

"Just a dizzy spell."

"Oh my God. Are you pregnant?"

"No! Why does everyone think I'm pregnant?"

"You might want to lower your voice. There's a hot firefighter here to see you."

Jessica wished the floor would open up and swallow her. Her heart pounded so hard she thought it might break a rib. Damn, what he must be thinking if he heard her outburst.

Well, shit.

She might as well face the music.

Dread turned to surprise when she saw Mike. By the look on his face, she knew he'd heard her outburst.

"I am not pregnant. And I'd appreciate it if you keep what you heard to yourself."

He frowned, his expression one of disapproval. "Are you sure?"

"Very sure." She didn't have to answer to anyone. She crossed her arms. "Now. What can I do for you?"

"Do you have a minute?"

She thought of a sharp reply, but hesitated. Mike didn't deserve her being rude.

"We can go down here," she said motioning with her hand. She led him to a small room where supplies were stored.

"I, uh, brought in a patient and thought I'd stop and say hi."

"We needed a private room for that?" She figured he was there because of Jared. After what he heard, she could only imagine what he was thinking. Hopefully he wouldn't repeat his suspicions to Jared.

"When I heard—"

Jessica held up a hand, cutting him off. "You heard nothing. Anything you might have heard you must promise to forget." All she needed was gossip of speculation and not an inkling of truth spreading about. If such a suspicion got back to Jared …

"Mike, I've had a rough few weeks. That's all."

"You sure?"

What would it take to convince him? Once a seed of doubt had been planted, it grew like a weed. She knew better than anyone. The sensitive subject was hard enough for her to talk about. Even more grueling since, this time, there was no truth to the suspicion.

"Look. I like you. I don't mean to be short with you. There is nothing to tell. I need to get back to work."

His hand on her arm halted her movement.

"Jessica. I'm an EMT. Right now, I don't like what I see."

She glared at him. She knew she looked dreadful. She owned a mirror.

"You look tired. And thinner. You're not taking care of your-self."

He was right. *Give the guy a break.* She sighed with exhaustion. "Jump on the band wagon. There's a line in front of you instructing me on my health."

"Are you listening to them?"

She shrugged. "I guess I have to. I can't afford to lose any more weight."

"Are you ...?" Mike hesitated. She knew what he was asking.

"I'm sure my dizzy spell is due to lack of sleep and not eating."

"Dizzy spell?"

She was digging her own grave. "I have no appetite. I'm tired. My body is rebelling."

"Why don't I take you to lunch?"

"Yes," a chorus of voices sounded from just outside the door.

Jessica stepped into the corridor and found her co-workers. "You were listening?"

One rolled her eyes while the other nodded dynamically.

"I give up," Jessica said, lifting her hands up and bringing them down with a sharp snap. She turned to Mike. "If you can stand hospital food, you can buy me lunch.

"No!"

"No!" came the double reply. Jessica stared at the pair of traitors.

Carolyn guided her to the nurses' station while Josie shoved her purse at her.

"You need fresh air."

"Go."

Jessica knew what they thought. The hospital grapevine was alive and well. Word had already spread that she'd dated a fire-fighter. Apparently, Carolyn and Josie thought Mike was Jared. She didn't have the heart to tell them he was the wrong one.

***

Applebee's was around the corner and maybe they could get a booth in the back, so Jessica suggested they go there. The waitress gave them menus and left.

"I, uh, couldn't help overhearing ..."

"No, I am not pregnant."

"You can tell me if you are."

"Honestly, Mike, I know you're trying to make me feel better, but I'm not." She learned that lesson a long time ago.

"If you were, it would be cool, you know? I think Jared would—"

"Please do not mention anything to Jared. I'm telling you the truth. I haven't been eating."

"Why not?"

Right to the point. No fooling around here.

"I'm just not hungry."

"I can't imagine anyone not being hungry. Take a deep breath." He demonstrated what he wanted her to do. "Smell that? Food."

"I can certainly see where you have a healthy appetite."

"I'm a big guy. I like food."

"I like food, too. Sometimes."

He stared at her.

"At least I used to."

Mike folded his menu and placed it face down. "Look, Jared doesn't look much better than you do."

"Is he pregnant?" She was being flippant. Mike frowned as he stared at her. "Not funny, I know."

"I don't know if he is eating, and I don't care. He's a guy and he's a firefighter. He'll come around. On the other hand, you are—"

"A gal?"

"You're delicate. You need to eat."

She shook her head. "I am not delicate. I'm strong."

"Most stubborn people are."

It was her turn to stare at him.

"I didn't mean ... never mind. I know you're strong. You've been through a lot, with your friend and all. I think you like Jared, and he likes you. He's stubborn. He's a guy."

"You mentioned that."

"Well, guys do stupid things."

"What did Jared do?"

"I don't know. I figure he did something stupid and that's why you two broke up."

"I do like Jared, but he sees things differently."

"Jessica, I'm not here to play *he said, she said*. I'm not trying to interfere, or get you guys back together. It's your business. I'm here to be your friend. You look pale. Maybe scared. I don't think you're taking care of yourself. I want you to eat."

"Isn't that why we're here?"

"Yes, ma'am." He picked up his menu. "Let's see what we got. Steak is okay for lunch. Not a skimpy salad, unless it's a side. I like sweet potatoes. You like sweet potatoes?"

"Mike."

He put his menu down. "Yeah?"

"Please don't mention anything to Jared."

"I won't. I'm here to see you eat."

"I'll have a salad."

"As a side. What else do you want?"

The waitress took their order. Mike put in an order for cheese sticks, then made her eat some when they came. He didn't ask her any personal questions. Actually, they talked about cars. An hour had gone by before she knew it, and they had to cut their lunch short.

"You'll like Cassie. I'll bring her over tonight. That way I can check to see if you eat supper."

"You don't need to check on me."

"Are you telling me that Cassie and I aren't welcome at your place?"

Jessica gasped. "I never said anything of the kind." He didn't crack a smile. She wasn't sure if he was teasing or not. He had to be.

Their food arrived and he looked at the plates of food as if he was starving.

She smiled, thinking of how this nice man had taken time out of his day to cheer her up. She knew that had been his intention.

***

Mike was a hoot. Jessica couldn't get over how comfortable he and Cassie made her feel. He knew exactly what Jessica had needed. Jared had some pretty cool friends.

"Did Mike tell you how much he loves ice cream?" Cassie asked while she rolled her eyes at him.

"It looks like you bought every flavor in the store."

"He wasn't sure what flavor you preferred," Cassie said. "I brought chocolate syrup, caramel, whipped cream—"

"Where's the can for me, babe?" Mike asked, leaning over Cassie's shoulder, staring into the grocery bag.

"In that bag over there."

"Did you pick up some of those sprinkle things?"

"Yes. And M&Ms."

Mike found what he was looking for. A can of whipped cream. He shook the can and popped the top. "Hey, Jess, check this out." He tilted his head back and sprayed. Cassie just shook her head.

"I would tell him to act his age, but apparently, tonight he thinks he's ten."

Jessica laughed. "All that sugar will turn to fat."

"Not the way he works out. He uses the weight room at the station. Have you seen it?"

"No, I haven't."

"Nice equipment. Some rich guy with a check. He wanted the firefighters to get the money. There are fundraisers for the fire stations, for equipment, new trucks, etc. Sometimes, money allotted to the fire department gets delegated to other areas. This particular man wanted to give money that was to be used solely for the men."

"Shep arranged for a weight room to keep us guys in shape. Now, he's our hero."

A flash of melancholy came over Jessica. The guys were like a family at Station Eight. She wanted to belong.

"Mike has always been a fanatic with weights."

Jessica could tell. He was a big guy, with muscles to spare.

"Tell her how I use you for a dumbbell.

"Excuse me?" Jessica gaped.

Mike froze with his hand full of M&Ms halfway to his mouth. "Wait. That didn't sound right. I meant weights. You know."

When he raised his arms above his head, Jessica had no idea what Mike was talking about.

"Come 'mere." He grabbed Cassie around the waist and sat down on one of the kitchen chairs. Cassie squealed as he held her above his head.

"No, Mike. Not now. Put me down."

He ignored her. "Like this, Jessica." With one hand on her torso and the other at her hips, he lifted Cassie over his head and pumped up and down, as though she was a bar with weights."

Cassie gave up struggling. She plastered a goofy look on her face as she propped her head on her hand and rolled her eyes.

Jessica couldn't help it. She pulled a stitch in her side from laughing. "This is a Kodak moment."

"Are you done, Mike?"

He carefully lowered Cassie, then gave her a hot kiss.

Wow.

Jessica spoke quickly to cover her awe. "You have got to stay for Sundaes since you brought all this stuff."

Mike cocked a brow and gave her a look that she wanted to shrink from. "Did you eat dinner?"

She propped a hand on her hip before answering. "I learned my lesson today, thank you very much. I didn't eat a whole bunch, but I did eat."

"What?" Mike asked, giving her another glare.

Cassie poked him in the ribs. "Don't scare her."

"Ow, baby," Mike crooned.

The two acted like cooing love birds. It warmed Jessica's heart just watching them.

"You can bet I'm going to eat as much of this ice cream as I can stuff into my mouth," Jessica told Mike.

"Now you're singing my tune."

CHAPTER 27

"We're throwing back a few at The Pitt Stop. You coming?"

"When?"

"One hour. Later."

Cooper was always ready to hit their favorite watering hole, The Pitt Stop. Trucks, cars, and Harleys filled the parking lot most nights, while neon beer signs lit up with Bud, Coors, and Corona, filled the space above the windows. He'd more or less been Jared's wingman for the past year. When he wasn't with Jared, he hung out with Laredo. Maybe they weren't the best role models for a young man, but they were honest.

Cooper thought Jared was a sex god. He didn't mind being the kid's idol, but since meeting Jessica, Jared's thinking was a lot different. He'd never been much of a drinker. When he did go to bars, most nights he nursed one beer, sneaking in a glass of water now and then. The other guys were involved in themselves, or too busy checking out the ladies, and never noticed.

Jared reached into his closet and chose a blue button-up shirt. A drink sounded just the thing. Going out was better than sitting at home raking his ass over the coals. He was missing Jessica something fierce.

I've been down this road before.

Wondering what she had meant was driving him mad with jealousy. He might drink more than one beer tonight.

Memories always crept up when he didn't want them. He had died on the inside when he'd found those legal documents. James had said, fuck the papers, they were still brothers. It'd taken two years for him to stop feeling numb. Two years to get his head screwed on straight.

Look at him now. He wasn't in much better shape.

His condo wasn't the Ritz, but it was private. Compared to the hovels some people lived in, it was damn nice. He lived on the second floor of a huge two-story house that had been divided, and had his own garage—which he hardly ever used. A leather couch, sixty-five-inch TV, and lots of space for what he needed. Which wasn't much. Mostly gym bags and fire gear.

Not as large as the mansion he grew up in. Yeah, he'd been raised with the best things, name brand clothes, but his ... father brought him back down to Earth really quick if he acted like he was better than anyone else. He'd always been a sharp dresser. Maybe he couldn't afford the expensive stuff anymore, but he believed in looking good.

His father. His father could afford the best of everything.

But he couldn't buy his son's love.

Jared shook off the old memories before they could take hold. He held up the shirt as he stepped in front of the mirror, and saw it was the same teal-blue as his eyes. The ladies loved to compliment him on the color of his eyes.

Jessica's image flashed into the mirror. She'd never mentioned his eyes. God, he was lonely without her. Since leaving his father's house, he'd felt like he'd been missing something. Someone. He'd thought he was missing his brother, the home he grew up in. He'd been empty and lost. Jessica had filled the void and made him feel whole.

He remembered the first time he met her. How they had shot sparks off each other. Even then, he'd been captivated.

His cell phone vibrated in his pocket.

"Cooper, you said an hour," he said out loud. He glanced at his phone and saw it wasn't Cooper.

"Hey, Chuck. What's up?"

***

Fifteen minutes later, Jared knocked on Chuck's door.

The door opened and Chuck motioned Jared inside. "Hey, man, thanks for coming over."

"Sure thing. I'm glad you called. I've been wondering about Alicia."

"She didn't want to go to a hospital, and to be honest, I didn't want her to. The fewer people she comes in contact with, the better. I took her to a doctor to get checked out. Then I brought her home."

"She's here?"

"She, uh, won't let me out of her sight."

Jared shook his head. "You can't blame her."

"How about a drink?"

"I was headed to The Pitt Stop," Jared replied.

"Since I'm holding you up, how about a beer?"

"Sure."

Chuck went to the kitchen and came back with two long necks.

"That's what I'm talking about." Jared took the cold bottle and turned it up. "Man, that's good."

"You know, Jared, you might think no one's noticed, but I'm a cop. I notice things."

Jared narrowed his eyes, wondering what Chuck was getting at. "I don't doubt that."

"You usually nurse your beer. That's the first time I've seen you actually enjoy one."

"You got me. I like being in control. Never cared for a drunk, but this does taste exceptionally good."

The sound of a door latch echoed from down the hallway. Alicia slowly drifted to the living room.

Jared hid his surprise. She looked haggard. She moved slow and reluctantly met his eyes.

"Hi, Jared."

He stood. "Hi, Alicia. How are you doing?"

"Okay. I'm staying with Chuck. I just wanted to get something to drink."

"Will you join us?"

She crossed her arms over her chest. "Uh, no. I think I'll go back to my room. You guys can talk. Will you do something for me, Jared?"

"Anything."

"Tell Jessica I'm okay."

At that moment, Jared realized he never told Jessica that Chuck had found Alicia. Jared figured someone else must have told Jessica. He hadn't seen her. That was no excuse. "Of course. She'll be glad to hear."

"Thanks." She lowered her head and went to the refrigerator. He didn't say anything else, and neither did Chuck.

Her bedroom door closed, before Chuck spoke. "I'd rather you didn't tell Jessica that Alicia is here. The less people—"

"I get it." Jared took a swig of his beer. Then sat down. "She looks so … lost."

"Yeah. If you knew someone was out to kill you, I guess you would too."

Jared gave Chuck a dumb look. "Uh, right. I guess you are sort of in that situation. Alicia is fragile, right now."

"I understand."

"I called you because you and Jessica were with her. I knew you'd want to know she's safe."

"I wondered where she was. Jessica will want to know."

"You can tell her Alicia is safe, but we're not letting out her location. You won't be lying to her."

Who knew when he would see her. "Jessica isn't very happy with me right now."

Chuck leaned back in his chair. "What happened?"

"Shit, Chuck. It's this mess with the perp who's out to get firefighters."

"Jessica can't handle it?"

"I don't want her in harm's way."

"Don't you think she already is? The more I think about this situation, the more I think there could be a connection. What if the guy after Alicia is the same one targeting firefighters?"

"Laredo had the same idea.'

"Think about it. The strange incidents all happening in the last few months. Alicia's car set on fire. There has to be a connection, and I'm going to find it."

"Damn. That would mean the perp could get to Jessica in another way. Not through me."

"The police are on alert. The fire department is on alert. Just keep an eye on your girl."

Jared hung his head. "She's not my girl."

"Didn't look that way to me." Chuck took a pull of his beer.

"I broke things off. I'm afraid she'll be in danger if she continues to see me. That's one reason I wanted to talk to you, Chuck. I want you to take care of Jessica. Keep her safe."

Chuck's expression turned to puzzlement before he answered. "You're putting a pretty tall order on me, Jared. I'll try my best to keep everyone safe. But don't push Jessica away thinking that will protect her. Remember, the guy that grabbed her was looking for Alicia."

"What about the asshat targeting firefighters?"

"I know you've probably heard this, but anyone can get hurt or killed at any time. It doesn't have to be criminal. Anybody can have an accident." He held up a hand. "Crossing the street, getting choked on a peanut. And I'm not patronizing you."

"Hell, I know that, Chuck. But there's no sense in tempting fate."

"Do you care for Jessica?"

Care. Love. Need.

"Of course, I care for her. That's why I broke things off."

"Big mistake."

"So you say."

"Yes, I say." The tone of Chuck's voice had Jared paying closer attention.

Chuck sat his bottle on the low table. "Listen to me, Jared. We don't know what's going to happen tomorrow. But we can't live our lives hiding in the shadows, waiting for what *might* happen. You can miss out on everything that's important to you if you hold back. Being afraid of everything is not living."

Jared gave Chuck a side look of skepticism. "Do you know what I do for a living?"

"Same here, Jared. I'm a cop. That's why I know what you're going through. You aren't afraid for yourself. Most people think firefighters are crazy. Any man running into a building that's on fire when everyone else is running out has got to have a few screws loose, right?"

"I've heard that too many times."

"What about Jessica? How does she feel about your profession? Don't you think she worries every time she hears the fire alarm. Don't you think she wonders if you'll get hurt or even die in a fire?"

"What the hell, Chuck?" That only strengthened Jared's position. He didn't want her to worry about him.

"Jessica is a strong woman. She has to be to date a firefighter. I'm sure she worries, but the woman I saw cares for you. She didn't bail on you, so don't bail on her."

"You want her in the line of fire?"

Chuck shook his head as he answered, "Not what I said."

"Then what are you saying, Chuck?"

"If you love her, don't push her away."

"I ..." Jared shoved a hand through his cropped hair. "Christ, Chuck. I feel like I'm losing my mind. I don't know when it happened, but ... yes, I love her."

"Then don't take a chance of never seeing her again. Tell her you love her. Tell her now."

Never seeing her again?

Chuck sounded like his engine was about to run off the rails. He was dead serious. "Hey, man. Are we talking about me and Jessica?"

Chuck set his bottle on the center table and stood. He paced to the window and back. "I'm speaking from experience. I fell in love with a girl. Waited an entire year before I asked her out. Man, she was the best."

Oh shit. Jared didn't like where this was going.

"We dated a few months, and I knew. I knew she was the one for me. I knew I wanted to marry her." Chuck dropped into his chair. By the look on his face, he was reliving painful memories.

Jared kept quiet.

"My partner was shot and killed. I could barely handle the loss. How could I put her in that position? What if I was shot? She was everything to me. I broke things off."

Chuck looked at if he had been shot.

"Then you should understand where I'm coming from. I can't take a chance of Jessica getting hurt. It's not the job. It the motherfucker who's targeting the firefighters."

Chuck stood up and strode to the window again. He stared out, and Jared had the feeling Chuck wasn't seeing anything. He must have been remembering the breakup.

"Jared, I still think you're making a mistake."

"Putting Jessica in danger is a bigger mistake."

Chuck stared out the window for several more minutes before he spoke again, "On shift one day, a call came in ... a bad accident on interstate. Fucking I-81."

Oh, hell. Fatalities happened on I-81 every damn day.

"When I got to the scene, I saw her car." Chuck was quiet for a long while. "I never told her I loved her. Don't you think she would have liked to know?"

What was he supposed to say to that? "Damn, man. I'm sorry."

"Don't tell me you're sorry. You don't want to live through what I did." Chuck came back and stopped in front of Jared, staring down at him. "Every night I question why I sent her away. Sure, my job was dangerous. But accidents happen. You can't prevent something if it is meant to happen."

"I'm damn sure going to try. I don't want that nutjob coming after me and have her end up being collateral damage."

"Wouldn't you rather spend time with her while you can? Tomorrow is not promised. We can protect her as much as we can, Jared. But we can't put her in a cage and throw away the key. Besides, this shithead went after her friend. He doesn't need to go through you to get to her."

"Well, doesn't that make me feel better. Christ, Chuck."

"I know I'm messing this up, but regret is hell. Don't deny yourself love. At least give her a choice."

"I'm really sorry you had to relive— Shit. How long ago did it happen?"

"Five years. I poured myself into my work. Tell her, Jared. Tell her everything you want to say, now. Don't wait."

Damn. Chuck had really opened up. And he'd said some pretty heavy stuff. "You've given me a lot to think about."

"I'm going to catch this guy, Jared. I promise you that."

Jared stood and clasped Chuck's shoulder. "I know you will, man."

"I'll tell you something else." Chuck glanced down the hallway with a wistful expression. "Alicia is the first woman in five years who has stirred something inside of me. I'm not going to waste a moment with her."

Waste? Was that what he was doing? He'd been pretty stupid. Jessica had called his bluff. Called bullshit. She was smart. And stunning, and wonderful.

Chuck's story hit him right in the gut. If a man needed a good woman, it was Chuck. "That's good to hear, Chuck. I wish you luck."

"Don't ignore what I said. Life is too short. Talk to her."
Talk. Beg. Whatever it took.

"If we manage to get this perp off our back, who's to say she'll want to stay with me?"

"There's only one way to find out."

Jared didn't want Jessica caught up in the fire department trouble. But if the incident with Alicia was connected to the creeper, she was already on the guy's radar.

God, he missed her.

CHAPTER 28

Jared finished with his weights and just sat on the end of the bench; a towel flung around his neck. He used the thing to wipe the sweat running into his eyes. His hands were shaking and his heart was breaking.

He couldn't get the image of Jessica out of his mind. Her stricken face grabbed him by the balls, but he'd had to do it. He had to do his part to protect her. And the best way to do that was keep her away from him. Keep her away from this nightmare that the firefighters found themselves living in.

He missed her. He wanted her back. Never in his imagination had he thought a woman could affect him this way. But then, she wasn't the one who had ended things.

He thought he was satisfied. He'd thought he'd been happy rolling along without commitment, using one woman after another, and he hadn't cared if they used him. As long as they were in agreement and no one got hurt, what was the problem? He got what he wanted and so did the ladies.

He'd been a fool.

He'd been lonely. Empty.

He'd thought passion was the drive he and his partner needed to reach completion.

He'd thought caring was in the way he made sure to give a woman pleasure.

Desire? You had an itch that needed to be scratched.

He'd thought his father had loved his mother.

He'd thought his father's wife was his mother.

Christ. He scrubbed a hand over his face.

He had believed he and James were brothers. Guess that was all in the definition. Yes, he'd even believed in love—until then.

After finding out his father's secret, Jared had figured love must be a lie. His father hadn't loved his mother, so how could his father love him? Love was a word used when two people reached ecstasy.

So, he left. The home he'd grown up in belonged to James.

Jared had made a good life for himself in Staunton. The Blue Ridge Mountains had called him to Virginia. At the time, he thought he couldn't run much farther than the east coast. Still, he'd met people and made new friends. And he wouldn't trade his firefighter job for any other job in the world.

He liked working with his hands. There was no feeling comparable to saving a life or going up against a towering inferno.

Heavy footsteps came in the training room, and he knew it was Mike. "You working out or just passing time?"

"I finished a set."

"Without a spotter?"

Jared wasn't interested in talking, about a spotter or anything else. He sure as hell wasn't ready to deal with the fact, he'd brought this shit with Jessica on himself.

"Why are you beating the shit out of yourself this morning?" Mike grumbled.

"Skip it."

"She's starving herself, and you're trying to kill yourself."

Jared jerked his head to Mike. "What the hell are you talking about?"

"Jessica," Mike replied as he tossed a towel on a bench. "I saw her at the hospital. She looks as bad as you."

Jared's curiosity flared. He wanted to ask about Jessica, but he gritted his teeth, determined to remain silent.

"She's lost weight. She looks ill. She's not, in case you're interested."

Ill? Dammit. Mike was goading him.

"Last night, Cassie and I took ice cream to Jessica's apartment. We made sundaes."

Jared frowned. "Since when did you become besties with Jessica?"

"Since you kicked her to the curb."

Anger bit his insides. "Dick."

Mike stepped directly in front of him. "Talk to me, Jared."

"Don't want to." He flipped his towel to the floor and laid back down.

"Why'd you do it?"

He reached for the bar. "Leave it, Mike." He lifted the weights and struggled with the extra pounds he'd added to punish himself.

"No. I will not," Mike growled. "If you're going to keep pumping iron like that, I will not."

"Like you have room to point the finger," Jared grunted.

"You might as well make up your mind. We might not want to talk about our problems with women, but we damn sure have them. So fess up. What's doin?"

Aww shit.

Passion. He had that with Jessica.

Desire? Even after he'd found his release, he'd still wanted her.

Love. The burning sensation that made him feel like a man. A feeling like no other. Unexplainable. Undefinable. But more powerful than anything he'd ever known.

Jessica.

"Shit." Jared clanged the bar in its holder and sat up, sweat pouring from his temples. "The asshat that's targeted Station Eight for one."

"Thought we were talking about women."

Jared reached down and grabbed the towel. "I can't have a relationship with Jessica until the bastard is caught."

"That's bologna."

"Mike, you know about her co-worker. The bomb in her car. Jessica works at the same hospital."

"That's exactly why distancing yourself from her is not going to help. The bastard has targeted us, and it could be he's targeting nurses."

Jared cursed under his breath. "I can't stand this ... This not knowing. When he's going to strike. How? Who will get hurt?"

"I know, man. It sucks. But we're here to do a job."

"The job part I can handle."

Mike caught his gaze. "Are you sure about that?"

Jared held the stare. "Completely sure. Being a firefighter is my life. I'll do my job, no excuses."

Mike gave a snort. "Didn't expect any."

Jared stared at the wall in front of his bench. "I'd like to catch that piece of rubbish and put an end to all of this."

"That's what we all want." Mike walked to the back of the bench to adjust his weights.

"How do you keep from worrying about Cassie?"

Mike paused to glare at Jared. "I know you don't mean that."

Hell. He hadn't meant to offend the big guy. "I mean, well, I'm sure you worry."

"All the time. But we can't let this fucker dictate how we live our lives. Cassie has her routine. I make her promise to be careful and watchful. She can't live in a damned bottle." Mike found his desired weight, and then flicked the lock-pin into place.

Jared asked, "She tell you that?"

Mike stood up straight, placing his hands on his hips. "That and more. We'll get this guy. Don't cut Jessica off because some sucker is trying to scare us. He's going to slip up. When he does, we or Chuck, or someone will be ready."

Jared absorbed Mike's words. He wanted them to be true. He wanted Jessica with a fury that grew more every day. He'd fallen in love. She was the woman for him. If he didn't make this right, he could lose her forever.

God he was a mess.

Mike reached for the handles and pressed. "You're pathetic."

"I know."

Mike released the weight slowly so the weights didn't slam. "You want her. Go get her."

"Advice from the dating king?"

Mike pressed again, the veins in his arms protruding as his muscles bunched. He pressed more than anyone else in the department, and didn't even break a sweat. His biceps were already the size of hams you got at the butcher shop.

"Are you trying out for Mr. Universe?"

"Don't change the subject." He lowered the weights. "Cassie and I are good. You and Jessica would be too, if you weren't too busy being a jackass."

Jared felt like the hind end of a donkey, but what else could he have done?

Ah, hell. Who was he kidding? He would give her the world if she would give him a chance. Another chance, that is. Jessica had spirit; he'd give her that. She was brave, courageous, downright forceful when she had to be. He'd seen the tears in her eyes, but she wouldn't let them fall. Then she'd gotten mad. Called him stupid, and a few other things he'd been surprised were in her vocabulary.

Just thinking of her caused a heat in his lower region. Heat, protectiveness, and something more. Something he had avoided in the past. Emotions were creeping up on him, possessiveness churning through him.

Jared wanted her. She had given him back his soul. With her in his life, he felt like a new man. An honorable man. A man with a purpose.

He recalled the way Jessica had trembled when he'd held her in his arms. The fear in her eyes, the trust when he promised he wouldn't let anything happen to her. He kept his promises. He would protect Jessica with his life. And that wasn't going to change.

He wanted to protect her. Cherish her.

Love her.

He wanted her naked in his bed, her head on his pillow, her hair spread out waiting for his fingers to feel the silkiness. He wanted to make slow, sweet love to her from her head to the tips of her toes, caressing every inch, loving every indentation, inhaling every sigh.

He knew he wanted Jessica.

It amazed him how much.

***

Jessica drove into the parking lot of her apartment building. She was worn out. Not eating didn't help. She promised Mike she would do better, and she was. She grabbed her purse and the pizza she ordered, and then got out of the car.

She slipped the key from her pocket and headed to the front door. She couldn't wait to get inside. The pizza smelled delish. She was following Mike's instructions and told herself she would be okay. If Jared came back, or if he stayed gone, she would be okay.

Her phone rang right before the elevator doors opened. She looked at the caller ID.

Mike.

Knowing she'd lose the signal in the elevator, she stepped to the side and answered.

"Hey, Jessica. You at the hospital?"

"No. I just got home."

"Oh."

"Why?"

"Dropped off a patient from the squad tonight. Thought I'd say hi."

"Check up on me, you mean. Well, I'll have you know I picked up a pizza on the way home."

"Good girl. With all the trimmings?"

Jessica rolled her eyes, even though Mike couldn't see her. "Pepperoni."

"Make sure you eat it."

And she'd thought her father was bossy. "A whole pizza?"

"It can't be very big. You can do it."

"You sound like a cheerleader."

"Team Jessica."

She laughed.

Mike checking up on her showed the kind of man he was. She'd never had a male friend. Not one she could be free and comfortable with, and be friends. Cassie was a lucky woman.

"Have I mentioned how much I appreciate your little check-ins? I do, you know."

"Glad to do it." Mike spoke in short sentences, but he got his point across. She ended the call wondering if Jared knew about Mike checking up on her.

The bell of the elevator dinged just before the doors opened. She stepped inside and hit the button for her floor.

Within minutes, she walked up to her apartment door, trying to balance the pizza and her keys. A hand came around her face and cut off her air. A band of steel gripped her middle and crushed her against a hard chest, causing her to drop the pizza.

She knew it wasn't Jared. He would never scare her like that.

"Stay calm, little lady. You're not the one I'm after. Tell me where your friend is, and I'll let you go?"

A million things raced through her mind. Who was this? Did he have a weapon? Would he hurt her? Would he kill her? Was he a burglar?

Friend? What friend?

"That's more like it. You follow directions better than that snotty friend of yours? Now, where is she?"

Ice filled her veins. He meant Alicia. He must be the guy after her. Dear God, what was he going to do?

Jessica mumbled. His hand was over her mouth, how was she supposed to answer?

"Do not scream or it will be the last sound you make. Now, nod your head if you understand."

She wanted to faint. She'd never been so scared. Could she believe him? Did she have a choice. She tried to nod.

The man loosened his hold just a bit. She sucked in air.

"Well?"

"I … don't know."

He clamped his hand tight over her mouth. "Wrong answer."

"Please, I don't know," she mumbled against his fingers. Of course, it came out sounding like mush.

"You are going to tell me one way or the other. Where is she?" He slowly moved his hand.

"We to-took her to a ca-cabin. Later, we went back, and she was gone. I swear."

"Open the door."

No. What would he do once he got her inside of her apartment?

Jessica fumbled with her keys, her hands shaking so bad she had trouble inserting the right one into the lock.

Click.

The mechanism in the door sounded like thunder to her ears. Was there no one else around to see him? To see them?

She turned the knob and— He shoved her inside so fast she fell to her knees. He slammed the door. She tried to swallow her fear, praying he would not kill her.

Silence.

She didn't move. Waiting for him to tell her what to do, she wrapped her arms about herself and kept her eyes closed.

And waited.

Silence.

She slowly turned and saw the door to her apartment closed. No one in sight. Her head darted from side to side, and she quickly searched the room for her attacker. He must have shoved her to the floor so she couldn't get a look at his face.

Thank you, God.

Jessica pulled herself together and immediately bolted her door. This could have gone so many different ways.

She was alive. The scary man hadn't hurt her. Still, she couldn't stop shaking. A nagging thought entered her brain. They don't have her. Alicia must have escaped.

What to do now?

Jessica stumbled to the couch and fell onto it.

My God. Who was that man?

She wasn't sure how long she sat there before her brain started working again. Her first thought was to call Jared. Should she? Or her sister? Raven would panic.

Jessica stood up, found her legs were working, and went straight to the liquor cabinet. Never mind the wine. This called for the hard stuff. She had a bottle of Crown Royal a coworker had given her. She grabbed the bottle and ripped the plastic from the cap. Then she snatched a shot glass and poured the thing half full. She'd never done this before, so a full glass would probably choke her. She tossed back her head and downed the liquid.

Oh. My. God.

It burned all the way down. Her throat was on fire. But it tasted pretty good.

She shook off the aftereffects and decided to bite the bullet.

Jared.

She had to call Jared.

Before she could pick up the phone, the image of their last reunion flashed into her mind. His haggard face when he told her she could not be in his life. She'd broken down. Jared was her life.

At least, she'd thought so then.

He told her they couldn't be together. At first, she felt betrayed. The playboy had gotten what he wanted. Just like the boy in college.

But Jared wasn't anything like that jerk. Jared had truly been hurting when he broke off with her. No matter what he'd said, his eyes told her otherwise. She'd tried to reason with him, but he wouldn't listen. Then her stubborn side had kicked in and she practically threw him out.

Time had a way of healing. Did he regret his decision?

Nothing was accomplished if she didn't take a chance.

He would come. She knew it in her heart.

Jared would come.

CHAPTER 29

Jared slammed the petal to the floor and pealed down Route 250. Every nerve in his body was jumping. His heart had done a dive when he heard Jessica's voice. The bastard had dared to put his hands on her—again. The SOB knew where she lived.

Using his Bluetooth, Jared punched in the saved number for Chuck. The ring echoed through the cab of his truck.

"Come on, man. Pick up."

"Detective Winston."

"Chuck. This is Jared. The bastard waylaid Jessica!"

"Woah, buddy. Slow down."

"That asshat. The one who's after Alicia."

"Where are you?"

"In my truck, headed to Jessica's now."

"I'll meet you there."

Jared ended the call, then pounded his fist on the steering wheel. "Son of a bitch." What if— Hell. It was too late to play *what ifs*. "Get out of the way!"

He was driving like a maniac, and he knew it. He'd even turned on the flashing light he used when responding to a fire call. He took the next curve, sliding sideways, and didn't give a shit. He had to get to Jessica to make sure she was all right.

When her building came into sight, he pulled onto the grass and slammed the shifter into park. Tough shit if no one liked the way he parked.

He took the stairs two at a time. Fuck the elevator. He rushed to her door, and found a pizza box on the floor. Ignoring it, he pounded the door with his fist.

"Jessica. It's me, Jared." The lock slid and then the door cracked open. As soon as she saw him, she leaped into his arms.

"Jared!"

"I've got you." He half carried, half dragged her inside, then closed the door behind them. "Are you all right?" One hand roamed her back while the other crushed her to his chest. He had to know she was all right.

"Thank you ... for ..."

"Shhhh. I'm here. I'll always be here." He lifted her and carried her to the couch, then sat with her on his lap. "I've got you."

"Oh, Jared. He was here."

"I know, baby. I know. But he's gone now." All the while, he kept his hands on her body, hugging her, letting her know she was safe.

She raised her head from his shoulder. "God, I was so scared."

"Did he hurt you?"

"No," she answered, shaking her head. "He wanted to know where Alicia was."

"What?"

"Jared, don't you see? That means they don't have her. Where could she be?"

"Umm, Jessica. About that." Guilt rose to choke him. Jessica was going to kick his ass. "I didn't have a chance to tell you. Actually, Chuck thought you'd be safer if you didn't know."

"Know what?"

"Alicia is with Chuck. He's keeping it a secret." *Oh shit.* Her face froze. Then turned red with anger.

"What? How did you know?"

"Well, he told me..."

"I can see that."

"Don't get mad. We, uh, broke up ... sort of."

"Did Chuck think I wouldn't want to know Alicia was safe?" she screeched. "I've been worried sick."

"Don't you see, Jess. If you would have known, you'd act different. The guys after her would suspect and maybe come after you."

She gave him a cold look that said that reasoning was stupid.

"Yeah, I see your point, but the guy let you go. He didn't harm you. If you'd known about Alicia, he might have taken you. Used you to trade or something. I don't want to think about what he might have done to you." To his surprise, Jessica snuggled back into his side.

"I understand, Jared. I'm glad you care."

He instinctively drew her close. "I told you. Always. I'm here for you."

"I just want this over with."

"You and the whole fire department." He savored the feel of this woman in his arms.

"I knew you would come." Her lips vibrated against his neck, making him tighten his hold.

"I couldn't get here fast enough. I care, Jessica."

"You really mean that don't you?"

Everything in him willed her to believe him. "I'll always be here for you, sweetheart."

She raised her head and met his gaze. "What does that mean, Jared? From a distance? Like tonight?"

"God, no. I can't stand being away from you."

"I think I'm beginning to really see you." She met his gaze. "Jared, what do you want?"

"The same thing I've wanted every day since laying eyes on you. I can't eat, I can't sleep, I can't do anything without thinking of you. Something has changed in me. I can't fight it. So, I may as well surrender to it."

He laid his finger against her cheek. Her skin was so smooth. "We're in this together, babe. Haven't you figured it out yet? Jessica, I love you."

Yeah. Just put it out there.

She jerked up as if the fire alarm had gone off.

Damn. He knew he should have kept his mouth shut.

She stared at him for what seemed like an hour. Heat rushed up his neck. His heart was jumping ahead of his brain and his emotions were all over the place. He'd be damned if he would take it back.

Then she started to cry.

Oh, hell.

"I ... I can't believe you said that."

Neither could he, at the moment.

"The one thing I wanted to hear from you ..." *Sniff.* "...and I didn't think ... Oh, Jared. I love you, too." She sniffed again. And before he could get out of his shock, she cupped his face and leaned in, placing her lips on his.

The kiss was delicious, lingering, and soothing. And oh, so stirring. He squeezed her. "I don't ever want to let you go. I want to hold you forever."

"I'll not complain. Although, your lap might go numb after a while."

His lips curled up into a wicked grin. "Then I guess we better move to the bedroom."

"You say the nicest things."

He growled, loving the smile on her face. Then her doorbell rang, and she damn near leaped off his lap. "I've got you." He pulled her close. "That's probably Chuck. I called him."

An hour later, Chuck left with a promise of meeting Jessica at the ACPD in the morning to give a full statement. Jared locked the door and swept her off her feet. She loved his playfulness. She'd missed him so. He carried her to the bedroom, then lowered her feet to the floor.

"Do you want to change into pajamas or something?"

Pajamas?

"Wow. That's romantic."

"You're exhausted. You had a bad scare. Only an asshole would take advantage."

Yeah, she was drained. The shock had worn off, and now she felt like a limp noodle. His consideration warmed her. "I want you to stay."

"I'm not leaving. I'm going to take care of you. While I put the glasses in the dishwasher, you can have some privacy. Okay?"

He gave her a quick kiss on the lips. Too quick.

She wasn't that tired.

Jared paused in the doorway. "Of course, if you'd rather put on a sexy negligee ..." He winked.

He was joking, and he had no idea how sexy he looked.

She went to the master bathroom and freshened up. Then she chose a long silky nightgown—not pajamas, and not a negligee.

He stepped into the room just as she turned off the bathroom light.

His eyes devoured her, and she knew she'd chosen well.

She stood there, waiting. Hoping.

He cleared his throat. "Feeling better?"

"Yes. Thank you for coming."

He quickly strode to her and placed his hands on her shoulders. His heat bled through the fine silk.

"You knew I would, or you wouldn't have called."

"I was scared."

"I know," he whispered as he drew her against him. "I'm here. His hands roamed her back, but there was nothing sexual in his touch. "Do you want anything? A drink? Or—"

"You, Jared. Just you."

Was that him trembling? Or her?

He led her to the bed and turned back the covers. "In you go."

She hesitated. "Only if you join me."

His jaw tensed, making his face draw tight. "I'll lay on top of the covers."

"What difference does it make? If we want to do anything, covers won't stand in our way."

He leaned his forehead against hers. "Honey, I just want to protect you."

"I'm not going to fall apart, Jared. I want you to hold me. Shed those jeans."

"Yes, ma'am." There was that devilish grin she loved so much. He left his boxer briefs on, then crawled in next to her. His skin was hot. So hot.

She placed her head in the crook of his shoulder and placed her hand over his heart. Her fingers toyed with his fine chest hair. His arm cradled her, making her feel loved. She was happier than she ever thought she could be.

"Jared, I love you."

"I love you too, babe." His fingers stroked up and down her arm.

"Jared?

"Hmmm?"

"This is perfect."

Just Perfect.

EPILOGUE

"I didn't tell you to go after that woman."

"I thought—"

"No more thinking, and no more doing anything without my orders. Got that?"

"Got it."

Seth stepped to the window, wondering where Carl had gotten the idea to take things into his own hands. Carl was a follower. Seth gave the orders. Now he had to deal with the fall out.

He didn't need added heat. The cops would be watching the hospital and that other nurse. How the hell was he supposed to find the snotty nurse after Carl's bullshit?

"Seth, I'm sorry."

"Shut up, Carl. Just remember who's the brains of this operation. I have a plan. Any missteps, and the plan is useless."

"What do we do now?"

Patience.

Putting his anger to the side, he spoke in a calm voice, "Wait."

"Wait?"

Seth turned to face Carl, meeting him eye to eye. "Yes. Wait. No more sudden decisions from your ass."

"How are we going to find that nurse?"

"Your spontaneous encounter made her more important. I don't need the police connecting the dots. We lay low."

"I know you don't like loose ends, boss."

"I don't like anyone interfering with my plans, either." He glared at Carl, clearly letting him know that *he* was pissed off. Carl wasn't a total failure. He had tried to help. But Seth was the one in charge, and Carl needed to remember that.

Seth turned back to the window. The clouds outside fit his mood. He stared at nothing, completely aware that Carl was watching him.

"You can breathe, now. I'll focus on our main problem."

"We just gonna wait?"

Not much else he could do at the moment. Besides, playing cat and mouse was a game he'd come to enjoy.

"Good things come to those who wait. I've been planning this a long time. We'll watch. Monitor their patterns, the way we have been. And then we'll give them a big hello when that nurse shows herself."

Seth couldn't let this deter him from his main goal.

One brother for another.

The End of Book 3: Jared.
Be sure to read on for a sneak peek of Book 4: Laredo!

Sofia freaks out when a car runs a stoplight and broadsides her. Her terror turns to amazement when the fireman who rescues her is the guy she has been in love with for years. Despite the icy barrier he keeps between them, she is determined to melt his resistance with her flames of passion.

***Keep Reading for an Excerpt from
Laredo: The Firefighters of Station #8 – Book 4***

LAREDO

Chapter 1

Despite his enjoying the quiet time, Laredo got a rush hanging out at Station Eight. When the pager went off, his blood spiked and he mentally shot into gear. Not knowing what to expect or how bad the fire might be, it didn't matter, he loved his job. He couldn't imagine doing anything else.

He grew up in a family of five, counting his *Madre*. Being the baby, he'd been spoiled by his siblings, and of course, he was the last one to leave the nest. But he never did, so to speak. His *Madre* still spoiled him. His brothers and sister came home often. Besides, they were close. All was well in his world. There was no place he'd rather be.

Being a firefighter was in his blood. Right before Laredo graduated, his uncle's store had caught fire. Not only did the incident make a huge impression on him, he saw how quickly a member of his family could be hurt, or worse. But the biggest impact had been the firefighters. Their courage, tackling a fire without fear. The speed with which they moved, as though every second counted, and it had. The courtesy they showed his uncle. The assistance and encouragement. It blew his young mind. He knew right then and there the direction he wanted his life to go.

With little money, each of his siblings had to make their own way, supporting themselves. His mother had taught him right from wrong, and he didn't dare cross his *Madre*. She supported his decision when he told her he wanted to join the fire department. For him, showing up at the firehouse everyday had paid off. Some guys volunteered ten or fifteen years before they got hired on at a fire station. He'd been given the job at the age of twenty. He could still remember the celebration at his house when the family found out.

Four years later, he'd been promoted to be the driver of the quint. You'd think he'd been given the moon. The roar of the engine shot a rush of adrenaline cannonballing through his veins like nothing else could. It didn't get any better than that.

Mike was the medic of the team. Each firefighter had a certain amount of training, but Mike was EMT certified. He had taken the morning off, probably to spend with his new honey. So Laredo climbed into the back of the ambulance to restock supplies.

"Laredo!"

"In here, Cooper."

His co-worker's face popped around the ambulance door. "Cap is looking for you."

As far as captains go, Shep had to be the best. He ran a tight crew, kept every man in line, but he was there if you needed him. Shep was a good man. Laredo couldn't ask for a better captain.

"As in, this is good? Or this is bad?" he asked.

"You have a phone call," Cooper answered.

Laredo frowned. He pulled his cell from his pocket to see if he'd missed any calls. None. Who would be calling him at the station?

"It's your mom."

Mierda.

Blood hammered through his veins. Something terrible has happened. Why wouldn't she call him on his cell phone?

He jumped from the back of the ambulance and raced up the steps to Shep's office. Cap stood as soon as Laredo stepped inside.

"You looking for me, Cap?"

"You can use my office, Laredo. I'll be down in the bay."

Joder.

He grabbed the phone and pushed the blinking button. He spoke in Spanish.

"Madre? This is Laredo."

"My baby," she cried.

Since his family was known for drama, he didn't panic—yet. Either something good had happened, or something very bad.

"I'm here. What has happened?"

"Tia Maria."

His Aunt?

Mierde.

"Madre, please do not cry. You know it breaks my heart."

She wailed on the other end.

"Are you all right?" He shouted. She was moaning so loud he wondered if she heard him.

"Tia Maria. She is gone. Oh, poor Sofia."

Gone?

"What do mean, gone? What has happened?"

"Maria. What shall I do. My *hermana* is ..."

Oh no.

Maria was not related to *Madre* by blood, but their friendship was as close a relationship as two sisters could be. If something happened to Maria, his mother would be devastated. "Madre. I will be right there. Can you hear me? I'm coming home."

"What?" She stopped crying. "No, no need to come home."

"But, Tia Maria. You need me."

"I don't need you. Maria needs to apologize." His *madre* was now angry.

Apologize?

"She has done the unthinkable. Poor Sofia. Sofia had to call to tell me." She started wailing again.

What the hell? Laredo held the phone from his ear as his *madre* went on a tirade.

Evidently her close friend, that he called aunt, had not died.

"*Madre*." He practically shouted so she would hear him. "Is Tia Maria all right? Is she at home?"

"No she is not all right." Her voice turned bitter again. "I told you. She is loco. No, she is not at home. She has run off with her lover." That was all he heard before she let loose another spray of outrage.

Lover? Yes, she definitely said lover. Tia Maria?

"*Madre*. You're not making any sense."

"Do you no listen to me. Maria has run off to elope. She got married. Without telling her sister."

So that was it. *Madre* was mad because she'd been left out. Maria's husband had died two years ago. Guess she found someone else. Just because his mother never remarried, didn't mean Maria had to live the rest of her life alone.

Sofia. Now, there was someone he hadn't thought of in a long time. The little sister of his teenage best friend. Alejandro and Laredo went everywhere together. And Sofia followed them every chance she got.

"*Madre.* Sofia called you?"

"Yes. I had to hear it from her baby daughter."

Sofia was no baby. As a matter of fact, she was married.

"Is Sofia upset?"

"Of course she's upset. That no account husband of hers. And now her mama has left, too." As his mother went into another wailing of Spanish, Laredo tried to make sense of what she'd just said. Did Sofia think the man Tia Maria married was no good? Is that why she ran off?

Whatever had happened, it was not the end of the world. His family had a tendency to overstress everything. Especially, his mother.

"*Madre.* Do you think you can console yourself until I get home? You can tell me all about it then."

"My son, the *importante* firefighter. I am so proud of you. Yes, you go put out the fire. I will call your sister. She will want to know that Tia Maria has gone loco. Sofia will come to live with us."

His *madre* hung up before her words registered. Sofia would come to live with them? What the hell did that mean? As he hung up the phone, he shook his head. He could breathe easier now. For *Madre* to call the firehouse, he had expected a catastrophe. *Madre* had her tail in a spin, but at least he now knew it wasn't an emergency. Why in the world would Sofia be coming here? There was more to the story. He'd learn it all when he got home.

Shep and Mike were at the bottom of the stairs when he came down.

"Everything all right?" Shep asked.

"My mother is having a panic attack. It sounds like her best friend eloped, and *Madre* is having a fit. I think she's more upset because Aunt Maria didn't tell her first."

"She sounded pretty upset."

"I'm sorry about that Cap." He would have to remind *Madre* not to call the station.

"Don't worry about it. I hope everything works out. Mike was just filling me in on Jared."

"Mike's here?" Laredo quickly shifted his mind to the business at hand. The entire fire department had been on alert. For some reason, a man had targeted firefighters, and accidents were suddenly happening without warning.

Only they weren't accidents. A crazy man had been sneaking in and out of firehouses. The latest incident—the *bastardo* had messed with firefighter equipment.

"What about Jared?"

"His mask was laced with Etomidate."

"What's that?"

Mike stuck his head around the ambulance door. "In short, Etomidate is an anesthetic agent. Mostly, it's administered only by intravenous route. Etomidate mixed with dimethethane, can knock out an adult or even kill a horse."

"That sounds dangerous," Laredo said.

"Very," Shep replied. "Jared is lucky."

"When I saw him fighting with Cooper, I thought he'd gone berserk."

"That wasn't like him. I read the signs. Jared knew something was wrong. He said he smelled something strange. Must have been one of the drugs. He kept pushing his mask away, so I called for a new one. Thought it would calm him down."

"Good thing, Cap. Did the hospital release him?"

Mike answered. "He left with a nurse. The one that handed him his ass."

Laredo grinned. "I knew those two would end up together."

***

Sofia scooped her clothes from the dresser and threw them into the suitcase. As soon as Dario found out her *madre* was gone, he would come. She tore out of the house and tossed her suitcase into the trunk of her 2005 Camery. The passenger door had a dent where Dario had backed into it. The car had two hundred thousand miles on the odometer, but she didn't care. As long as it cranked up and got her to work and then home, she was satisfied. Dario had to have a new truck, and big wheels, and shiny trinkets, so he could flash his importance about. She didn't have to put up with his bragging any more.

It was a miracle that she'd managed to get a divorce. Only because Dario's *madre* and her *madre* were close friends. She had left with the clothes on her back, and didn't care that he'd kept everything. She just wanted out. Out of a loveless marriage. Out of the brutal fighting.

It was her friend, Camila, who convinced her she didn't have to stay with a man just because they were married. She'd been faithful. She'd been a devoted wife and given everything to her husband. But she could no longer be a punching bag. If she'd stayed with Dario, he would have killed her spirit. Whether *madre* approved or not, Sofia had had enough.

She'd taken her first breath when she fled to her mother's house, not knowing if *madre* would accept her. No decent woman ever left her husband. Divorce was sacrilegious. You were married in the eyes of God and you stayed faithful and obedient to your husband.

Not anymore.

As it turned out, she didn't have anything to worry about. After her mother saw the bruises, she threatened to go after Dario with her rolling pin. For six months, Sofia tried to make a life for herself, with the threat of Dario hanging over her head like a cloud. So far, he'd left her alone. But he was always there, lurking. From a distance. He made sure she saw him parked down the street from the house. Or his truck out in front of the deli where she worked. She just knew he would try to come to the house as soon as he found out her mother was gone.

She turned onto I95, driving north, praying her beat-up old car would get her there. In six hours she should be in Virginia. When Tia Isabella demanded Sofia must come, it was like the world had been lifted off her shoulders. She saw it as a golden opportunity. Safety. The answer to her worry of being in the house alone.

After calling Tia Isabella and breaking the news of her mother eloping, Isabella demanded Sofia come to live with her. She thought Sofia couldn't take care of herself. If Tia Isabella only knew what all Sofia had been through.

Sophia had learned to protect herself, and not be afraid of Dario. She learned to fight back. But she wasn't stupid. No sense hanging around, thinking he would leave her alone, when she knew he was a mean *bastardo*.

Isabella had unknowingly saved her. This was her chance. No one would suspect her going to Isabella's. Dario would never find her there. And after a reasonable time, or when *Madre* came home, Sofia would return. Not only would *Madre* be back from her honeymoon, there would be a man in the house.

It was only a matter of time. Dario wouldn't miss this opportunity. Rather than wait for the fight she knew would happen, she'd get out of here. Tia Isabella's offer was perfect.

No. There was no need to tempt fate. If she was gone, Dario could do nothing. And, a vacation would do her good. Being with Tia Isabella and her cousins promised to be fun.

Yep. She felt better already.

Sofia put on her sunglasses, turned up the radio, and settled in for a long drive.

Her fingers tapped to the lively music as she saw the sign for Richmond, Virgina. This was a good time to stop for food and gas before she took the connecting interstate. Anxious to be back on the road, she quickly filled the tank, and got fast food and snacks to eat on the way. She hopped back in the car and took I64 west. In two hours, she would see her family.

Well, they were just like family. *Madre* and Isabella were the best of friends before Isabella moved from Florida. Actually they were more like sisters. Even with the distance, they remained close.

Laredo. Her brother's best friend.

Her pulse sped up as she thought of her childhood sweetheart. Her brother's best friend who saw her only as a child. She remembered her childish behavior at the age of ten. She idolized Laredo. Every time he came over to see Alejandro, Sofia would follow them around. Sometimes her brother had been patient with her—and sometimes he would tell *Madre* she was a nuisance.

What a dumb kid. She had stars in her eyes back then. Was he as deliciously handsome as he used to be? Probably more so. Just the thought of him had her blood pumping. He couldn't use the excuse that she was a child anymore.

Raindrops struck the windshield.

"Oh, great. It's raining."

Sofia quickly turned on the wipers, and just in time. The heavens opened up and poured. She eased off the gas and squinted through the windshield looking for the next sign. Man, it was really putting it down. She turned on her headlights, because a trucker told her once—'the minute it starts to rain, turn on your headlights. Whether you can see or not, us truckers need to see you.' Sounded good to her, and she never forgot.

She had to be getting close.

Ah, there. Staunton.

She put on her turn signal, giving plenty of time to alert the traffic behind her. When she saw the turning lane, she eased over. She slowed for the circle that seemed to go on forever, then pulled into the lane going north. All of a sudden, lights blinded her. She threw up a hand to shield her eyes, and at the same time she stomped on the brakes. In that split second everything moved in slow motion, and she knew the vehicle headed straight for her was going to crash. Her stomach plunged to her toes as her heart lodged in her throat. A sickening crunch of metal and a bone jarring impact—and it was lights out.

Laredo: The Firefighters of Station #8 – Book 4
Coming late 2024!

ABOUT THE AUTHOR

Samanthya Wyatt writes sizzling hot romance with suspense. Intensely emotional characters with a deep passionate love for friends, family, and most importantly—between the hero and heroine. Although her first love is historical romance, this award-winning author also writes contemporary romance under the pen name S. R. Wyatt. Additionally, she has written a book of one family's struggle based on true life events.

Samanthya left her accounting career and married a military man traveling and making her home in the United States and abroad. She now lives in the Shenandoah Valley. On a sunny day, you can find her and her husband driving on the Blue Ridge Parkway or going to car shows in their 1969 Mustang convertible. She loves long walks, and a book to read on a sandy beach. Starbucks is her favorite drink and she likes hearing from her fans.

She invites you to lay the worries of the world off your shoulders and get lost in the pages of a romance, where you embark on a journey with the hero and heroine, become involved in a dream, plunge into a world of fantasy, and live an adventure your heart can share.

To find out more about Samanthya Wyatt and her books, please visit her website: https://samanthyawyattauthor.com/